Lethal Investments

Also by K. O. Dahl

Lethal Investments

K. O. DAHL

Translated by Don Bartlett

*Minotaur Book*s
A Thomas Dunne Book
New York

This is a work of fiction. All of the characters, organizations, and events portrayed in this novel are either products of the author's imagination or are used fictitiously.

A THOMAS DUNNE BOOK FOR MINOTAUR BOOKS.
An imprint of St. Martin's Publishing Group.

www.thomasdunnebooks.com
www.minotaurbooks.com

Library of Congress Cataloging-in-Publication Data

Dahl, Kjell Ola, 1958–
   [Dødens investeringer. English]
   Lethal investments / K. O. Dahl ; translated by Don Bartlett. — 1st U.S.
ed.
      p. cm.
   ISBN 978-0-312-37572-0 (hardcover)
   ISBN 978-1-250-01793-2 (e-book)
   I. Title.
   PT8951.14.A443A2 2012
   839.82'38—dc23

                                                      2012032919

First published in Great Britain by Faber and Faber Ltd

First U.S. Edition: December 2012

10   9   8   7   6   5   4   3   2   1

Lethal Investments

1

As he opened his eyes they felt like sandpaper. He stared up at a greyish-white ceiling and knew it was day, knew he was sleeping in an unfamiliar bed, just didn't know where. Until he felt her arm against his chest.

The dawn outside brought soft shadows to the room. It was morning and he had to get up. Go to work.

They couldn't have been asleep long. Her body was silhouetted in the half-light from the window. Her skin glistened dimly in the gloom, only her legs and feet were covered by the duvet, which lay crumpled at the bottom of the bed.

Slowly he levered himself up. Leaned against the wall to clear his head. Tired. Wanted to lie down. To pull the duvet over himself, sleep some more. But for a shit of a foreman deducting pay from the first half an hour, he would have.

It was half past five. No hurry.

He fumbled for his underpants and the rest of his clothes. Gathered up everything in one big pile under his arms, went to the bathroom. The old-fashioned tap took ages to run warm. Gave him time to study his reflection in the mirror. A pale, unshaven face beneath long, black hair. Realized he needed a wash. He stared at all the bottles and jars on the bathroom shelf. Tiny, creased panties and long tights hung quietly in the white light. Sleepily, he put on his clothes; his hands splashed water in his face.

Best to creep out, best not to wake her. Ring later, perhaps in the afternoon, or the evening. But first have to go back in to search for socks. Couldn't see them anywhere. Weren't under the bed, either.

Knees cracked as he stood up. She lay as if dreaming, sleeping soundlessly with her knees drawn up in front of her breasts. White skin and full lips. Short, blonde hair that fell over her eyes.

There they were. His socks were in a ball under the bookshelves.

Bang. Hit his head on a shelf as he straightened up. He grabbed his head and mouthed a curse. At the same time he heard the duvet rustle. She was awake.

'Are you going?'

Her voice was husky, sleepy, her skin warm.

'I'd been hoping you wouldn't wake.'

He trembled as his mouth met her wonderfully soft lips.

'I'd been hoping we'd wake up together,' she whispered. He gently nuzzled her cheek and caressed one nipple with the palm of his hand. He said: 'I'll ring you,' and reluctantly sat on the spindleback chair by the small desk. Pulled on his socks as her hands fondled his hair.

Then the telephone on the table rang.

The *brring-brring* cut through the room's grey light and made him peer up at her. Her eyes were fixed on the telephone.

He kissed her stomach. Cute navel, he thought as she hesitantly moved her arm towards the telephone that was still emitting its jarring tones. 'Is it for you, do you think?' she whispered in a tremulous voice.

'Me?'

Her face was no more than a dark shadow against the dawning light from the window.

'No one knows I'm here.'

She was still hesitating.

'Pull out the plug then. If you don't want to speak to anyone now.'

She lifted the receiver in one swift movement. 'Yes, Reidun here!' Decisive voice.

Silence on the line.

'Hello, Reidun here.'

She smiled down at him. Held the phone between her head and shoulder and tousled his hair again, with both hands.

Still no sound.

He felt her stroking his hair backwards, gathering it.

'Like this,' she smiled. Her hand wagged the pony tail she had formed with his hair.

Why not? he thought. A pony tail would be all right. Especially if she liked it.

He bent down and tied his laces while she stated her name for the third time. No answer.

Her breasts rippled as she shrugged her shoulders and stared at the receiver. At that moment they both heard it. A dry click.

Whoever it was had rung off.

She slowly put down the receiver.

'Do you often get calls like that?'

She turned and looked out of the window.

'No,' she said at length. 'No, in fact, I don't.'

Something had happened. They weren't whispering any longer.

'Why have you got to go?'

Her voice had acquired a slightly different timbre.

'I have to go to work soon. Got to go home and change first. Bye,' he whispered by the door. Again he felt his knees give way as he tasted her lips. Waited until she had locked the door before jogging down the stairs, tearing open the front door and taking a deep breath as it slammed shut behind him.

The backyard was a tarmac area with bike stands. The gate in the dark archway was closed. No handle on the lock.

Nonplussed, he ambled back, stood still in the middle of the yard. He was locked in! The impregnable block of flats towered up on two sides. The door to the staircase was locked, the gate was locked. However, to the right there was a wooden fence, not a brick wall. There was probably a demolition site on the other side. Impossible to know for sure. The fence blocked any view. But he ought to be able to clamber over. A shade under three metres. Were it not for the barbed wire on top. It was rusty, but still aggressively coiled in rolls.

Should be OK, he thought, pulling the refuse container into position. *Shit! What a racket!* On to the lid. The crate started rocking. *Never mind. Bend your knees, launch yourself! Right!*

Fuck!

He lay on the ground staring up at a blue sky and dark windows with white bars against pink brickwork. A gull circled above. Screaming. He held his head. Fingers bleeding. Another go. The container had to be stood upright again.

Now. The fence creaked and swayed under him. But it held. He managed to position a leg and heave himself up. Threw himself over and heard rather than felt the barbed wire tearing the seat of his trousers.

Correct. Demolition site. Greyish-brown tufts of grass between the remains of red bricks on the ground. Another wooden fence facing the street. But this one was lower. He ran up and jumped. The barbed wire snagged on his jacket. He was out. Silence. Just the sound of a car could be heard a long way off as he brushed himself. His shirt had ridden up from his trousers and he was bleeding more than he had at first thought.

A taxi came to a sudden halt beside him. Two people alighted, took very long paces to the gate and let themselves in as the taxi drove off. Typical! If he had waited a few minutes he could have strolled out.

Strange start to the day, he thought, wandering the few metres over to the gate which had been left unlocked and ajar by the taxi's passengers. The gate creaked as he pushed it open to its fullest extent and walked back into the yard. Then he saw the bells by the door. Idiot! A quick press on the button and she would have come down with a key and let him out. A slip of paper with her name written next to the bell. Smudged writing in blue biro. The sight of the paper reminded him of the touch of her skin.

He could go back up. Get into bed with her and sleep a bit more. Until twelve or one. Wake up with her.

He pushed the door. Unlocked. All he had to do was run up.

Further away, a tram rattled down a side street. He remembered her hands fondling his hair. Caught in two minds, he stood looking at his wristwatch. A car door slammed somewhere. Sound of footsteps. Someone turned into the gateway. Coming towards him.

He took a decision. Work was waiting. He stepped off, but first nodded politely to the newcomer.

2

Once home, he changed into fresh work clothes. Time was on his side. So he rested on the bed. *Just have a little doze, fifteen minutes.* But went out like a light. Overslept his shift. Had forgotten to set the alarm clock. Slept until two in the afternoon. Thought of her as soon as his eyes opened. Thought of the night before, of her body. Of her wriggling beneath him. Of them lying side by side afterwards, of him holding her face in his hands, chatting, stray fingers on bare skin.

He had left her and skipped work afterwards, though unintentionally. Had lost six hours of a hundred per cent overtime and annoyed the fat-bellied firebrand of a foreman into the bargain. But he didn't ring in. That would have been asking for an earful. So he sat up in bed, found her telephone number with a yawn and dialled.

Televerket automatically broke the connection. He put down the receiver and then picked it up again. Dialled the same number and let it ring, but without success. Until Televerket cut him off again.

* * *

The sound of a phone doesn't carry. But if the flat is small and the door is open and banging, then it does. If the phone stops ringing, you know someone is at home. If it doesn't, no one is at home. A problem emerges when all the indications tell you someone is at home, but the phone carries on ringing. The continuous ring is a signal, a warning that something is not right.

If you are washing the stairs, you don't listen. But three-year-olds have not learned what you should or shouldn't do.

Three-year-old Joachim had a little cloth in a bucket and of course the bucket tipped over at the bottom of the stairs between the second and third floor. Joachim smiled. 'Wet', he shouted and laughed, then started washing like mad. Until it was dry and Mummy had to go down with her bucket and give him a top-up. While she was there she noticed that Reidun Rosendal's door was open. The door was banging. The lock kept knocking against the door-frame in the light draught there always was on this staircase. What was strange was the silence inside. Reidun had a small flat, so she ought to have been heard from inside the door. Mia Bjerke didn't know Reidun that well, they just said hello, the way that neighbours do as they pass on the stairs.

But then, when she was halfway through the cleaning, the telephone rang inside the flat. For a long time, and when it finally stopped, it started up again. From the bottom of the steps, tiny Joachim said:

'Ringing, Mummy!' Twice he said that and twice she answered it was probably because Reidun, who lived there, wasn't at home.

But then she opened the window on the landing between

8

the floors to let air in and Joachim said that Reidun was at home. 'You're fibbing, Mummy!' Joachim said.

For by opening the window Mia had created a kind of through-draught. Possibly because of a sudden gust of wind. At any rate, the draught was so strong that the door to Reidun's bed-sit banged wide open.

'Come here, Joachim!' she called sharply. And Joachim listened to her. Perhaps because of the sound of his mother's voice or perhaps because he was affected by the atmosphere that had developed on the staircase.

A naked foot on the floor of the bed-sit told Mia Bjerke that someone had been at home the whole time.

3

Inspector Gunnarstranda was taken aback by the sight of the figure opening the door. But not by her reaction, neither the look she gave him nor the one she cast afterwards at his ID. He knew this look, and was inured to it. For no natural authority emanated from his short, thin body. He was one metre sixty in his stockinged feet. All of his fifty-seven years had left their marks. His face was wrinkled and his pate shiny, almost bald. There was just a dishevelled clump of hair clinging on. He combed a few frugal wisps into position every morning, over from one ear to the other.

Gunnarstranda was conscious of his sad outward appearance. For this reason he was tolerant of her askance look, from top to bottom, as if he were an insect she had espied under the mat.

He unleashed his whitest smile by way of a response. Watched her confusion grow. Few people expected such a toothpaste-white row of teeth from such a short-arse in a threadbare coat, with nicotine-stained fingers and scorch marks on his shirt. Then there was all the dental work. A kind of porcelain. The finery that Edel had once paid for with her lottery winnings. 'Finally we're going to get your ugly mouth sorted out,' she had said with her glasses well trained on the list of prizes. She must have been heartily sick of the cactus landscape in his cake-hole. He didn't know. If that was why, she would never have said. So he had never asked. Edel always got her own way whatever happened. And now it was too late to ask. Four years too late.

The smile helped him on this occasion, as indeed it always did. The smile that obliterated the impression of scruffiness. The smile that caused people to fumble rather than punch him in the face. The rascally smile.

The woman returned his smile, and they were friends. She blinked, and consciousness returned. Moved to the side and held the door open, told him to make himself comfortable while she saw to her child in the kitchen.

He stood at his ease looking around the large, airy living room. A newly decorated flat. White jute wallpaper. Varnished parquet flooring without cracks or flaws. Curtains in light pastels hanging lightly over large windows. Simple expensive furniture, linen and dyed leather. On the floor some children's games, even though a coffee table in thick, tinted glass and a glass display case suggested disciplined behaviour indoors.

On the walls were three originals by a modernist painter Gunnarstranda neither knew nor could name. But his seasoned eye soon detected the touch of class in a genuine signed oil canvas.

He found himself in a flat that distinguished itself by its youthful affluence.

Surprising.

In itself it was no strange thing to be in a pleasantly furnished flat in an apartment building in upper Grüner-

løkka. It was the elegance that caught his eye. Oil paint-
ings and the style of the dignified woman he had made up
his mind to like. She seemed dependable, despite her Oslo
West-accented Norwegian. 'Would you mind waiting in the
living room,' she had said. *In the living room!* Her pronunci-
ation of the words made him pay attention to her choice of
clothes. The jewellery around her neck. The manner with
which she tackled the conflict between the child in the kitchen and his unspoken demands from the door.

On the sly, Gunnarstranda had studied her languorous
gait from the hallway to the kitchen. The natural rotation of
her hips. A lithe and well-proportioned woman of around
thirty. Finished with her studies, he imagined. So, the sensible type. Job first, then children.

He stood by the window, looking down on to the street.
Thought about the old days, skating in Dælenenga, the
brewery horses, the sub-zero outside privies and the utility
sink in the kitchen where you pissed at night.

And nowadays high society put down genuine parquet
flooring over the old boards. Bizarre, he thought, posh folk
tripping around in slippers so as not to scratch the floor.
Here, in this old block.

A few years ago, it had been acceptable for snobs to live
in lower Grünerløkka too, in Markveien and Thorvald Meyers gate. But most had shipped out now. Shipped up. Now
he could confirm that the upper reaches of Grünerløkka
were holding their own. And this was rather surprising. Because the woman in the flat shoes in the kitchen was, so-
cially speaking, different compared with the Pakistani next

door, who walked around in seventies clothing. His flat was furnished with flimsy, wobbly furniture from the Salvation Army shop. An unusually polite, plump man with fleshy cheeks and a toothbrush moustache. The type that shooed his wife straight into the kitchen the moment she shuffled in through the door. The man had been like a wind-up doll. Hands against his back and a rictus smile on his face. Hadn't heard or seen a thing. Never did, and definitely not last weekend. Nevertheless the man did fit in here. Him and the two dilettantes on the floor above. Two tall, skinny hippies dressed in garish clothes, who were trying to grow marijuana on the window sill. The man fortyish and un-employed. The woman, barefoot in flares embroidered with flowers. Two living fossils from the sixties wading through piles of newspapers and half-empty wine bottles. Both were far too concerned to point out how little they knew of the world outside, above all on a Sunday morning when they were on their way back from a party.

It was different here, in this flat. What did she think about, this wealthy woman? A girl murdered downstairs. Did she think that this wickedness would implicate them, her and her family? And if they wanted to move, where would they move to? Lots of money had been invested in this flat. These were people who undoubtedly had the means to take the final step. To move to Bærum, or to Nord-strand. Without stopping a few hundred metres further up, in Valdresgata, where the blocks were newer and there were still enough journalists and union bosses for high society not to feel comfortable.

He leaned his forehead against the window pane and stared down on to the street, patiently waiting until she was finished and had returned from the kitchen.

'You've been lucky with this flat,' he exclaimed with his back to her. 'And you've done the place up nicely. Imagine, when I was growing up, there wasn't even a toilet in the corridor. And at that time it was as cold inside the block as it was outside.'

He turned and pointed to the sun beaming down through the pane. 'You've got the sun here, too. Not many people have that here in Grünerløkka.'

She nodded politely, a bit apprehensive.

'I grew up here, I did,' he said, pointing out of the window. 'In Seilduksgata, down from Dælenenga, so I wouldn't be at all surprised if I haven't hung out in this place at one time or another.'

The latter accompanied with a broad smile.

He strode across the floor and took a seat on the curved pink leather sofa.

The little boy clung to his mother's trouser legs. Staring at Gunnarstranda with large eyes. Her bright blue eyes glinted nervously above a small strained smile that told him he should not reminisce about old times any more than was necessary. He squinted at her across the table, ignoring the boy. Children did not particularly interest him.

'Are you a policeman?' the boy wanted to know.

'My father worked at Freia, the chocolate factory,' Gunnarstranda continued, rapt in thought. 'Got a good pension as well. He was famous for it, company director Throne-

Holst was! Gave his workers a pension before the idea had even occurred to anyone else. Yes, you've heard of Throne-Holst, I suppose?'

The woman shook her head, wary.

He leaned over to her in confidence. 'Please excuse me,' he broke off, bursting with curiosity. 'But for someone like me who grew up in these parts I have to say an incredible amount of work has been lavished on this flat. It can't have been cheap.'

Her smile changed at the compliment and Gunnarstranda inferred she had played an active role in the re-decoration. But the smile vanished. She was serious again.

'Well, that is the issue, isn't it?' she answered. 'Now that she has been killed downstairs. Joachim and I are worried the prices are going to plummet, and then we would lose loads of money on this.'

'Are you going to move already then?'

Gunnarstranda essayed a little smile with the boy as well. 'So, you've started work as an estate agent, have you?'

She smiled. 'Joachim is my husband. This is Joachim Junior.'

She patted the boy on the head.

Joachim Junior, Gunnarstranda repeated to himself. Took a deep breath. 'The murdered . . .'

Met her eyes. 'How well did you know each other?'

She hesitated for a moment, considering the question.

'Depends what you call well.' She took her time. 'I said hello to her quite a few times, of course. She seemed . . . well . . . quite nice. Seemed the easy-going type to me . . . and to

Joachim.' She hesitated again. 'I don't think he knew her any better than I did. That's my opinion and I'm sticking to it,' she laughed with a slight undertone.

Gunnarstranda wasted no time. 'How do you mean?'

She looked down. 'It was a joke,' she said with a strained smile. 'As you know, she was a very attractive woman.'

The words were spoken with a face that said she was the kind to keep an eye on her husband.

'So he did talk to her once in a while?'

Gunnarstranda detected some irritation at his question.

'We were neighbours in a way, weren't we, and yes . . . no!' She threw out her arms.

'You didn't have much to do with her then, you didn't have mutual friends?'

'No.'

'Do you know if she hung around with a particular group? Was there anyone who visited her a lot?'

'I'm afraid I can't help you there,' she said firmly. But continued when the inspector said nothing.

'Yes, she lived below us, and the times I met her she was on her own by and large. I suppose I must have seen her with other people, men and women, as you would expect. She was just a normal girl living alone and we, well, we've hardly been here six months, not even that.'

'Are you at home all day?'

'Half of it, yes.'

The boy grew restless hanging from his mother's arm, and she was being distracted.

'Would you recognize any of these people, from a photograph?'

'Which people? Stop it now, Joachim!'

She grabbed the wriggling boy's hand to restrain him.

Gunnarstranda stared at her patiently. 'The ones you've seen her with.'

'Excuse me,' she said, and got up. Bent down to the boy and talked softly to him while looking him in the eye.

'Mummy has to talk to the man. Now you go and find something to do. Play with your bricks.'

'No!'

The child was not in a co-operative mood. In a huff, he eyed the policeman, who took out his tobacco pouch and started to roll a cigarette. The lad was intrigued by the roller and turned to watch Gunnarstranda making a stockpile of filter roll-ups on the glass table.

Mummy had time to think. 'To be honest, I don't believe I noticed any of them she was with, don't think so anyway.'

The inspector didn't glance up. 'But you've been living here six months! And there hasn't exactly been a stampede on the staircase, has there.'

She didn't answer.

'And she was quite a good-looking woman,' he continued. 'The sort your husband would have cast an appreciative eye over!'

He met her eyes and noted the confusion there. But he didn't give more than a glimmer of a smile. He could see she was of a mind to interpret the question in the best spirit. 'To be honest, I don't think I would recognize anyone in a

17

photo after a brief encounter on the stairs. No, I don't think I would.'

Gunnarstranda gathered all the roll-ups together. Got to his feet. At that moment they heard someone come through the front door. The boy ran towards it with his mother behind him. He lit a cigarette. Went over to the window and opened it a crack while she welcomed her husband. He could hear the father indulging in horseplay with his child and the couple whispering.

So as not to offend anyone, he tried to blow as much of the smoke as he could through the window.

Soon they were in the living room. 'Feel free to smoke,' she assured him, flustered. 'I'll find you an ashtray. This is the gentleman from the police.'

The latter was said to her husband, who trooped in behind her.

They greeted each other.

The man was getting on for forty, but had stopped somewhere along the way. Clammy hands, maybe as a result of wearing gloves. His hair was thick and bristly and fell in front of his eyes as he made a very formal bow. At the back of his head his hair had been cut in a straight line around his neck. His frenetic eyes emphasized a repellent energy in his nature.

'We're investigating the murder of a young woman on the lower floor,' Gunnarstranda said gently.

'Yes, well, it's about time!'

Gunnarstranda looked the man in the eye as he flicked

the ash from his cigarette into the ashtray the child's mother had provided.

Sensitive mouth. Suggestion of a grimace around the lips.

The police officer elected the direct approach. 'Have you ever been in her flat?'

A hesitant silence cast a shadow over the other man's self-assurance for a second. It was a shadow of cold calculation. For Gunnarstranda this was enough.

'Yes.'

Gunnarstranda felt the woman's eyes burning into his right shoulder.

'How many times?'

This time the silence was longer. 'I gave her a hand, didn't I, Mia? . . . Helped her start her car with jump leads in the winter, there was also . . . well, after all, she was one of our neighbours.'

The man spread his hands as if to crave understanding.

Gunnarstranda gave a pensive nod. 'Her flat is much smaller than this one. Would you mind if I had a little look around?'

'I most certainly would!'

Joachim Senior's top lip was visibly curled. Gunnarstranda took another drag of his cigarette. He looked the other man straight in the eye. 'You are interested in having this murder cleared up, are you?'

The man glared back and snarled. 'First of all, you kept yourselves to yourselves all yesterday morning, banging around, people and cars everywhere. Then we waited all afternoon for you. I cancelled two important appointments.

At that speed you'll have the murder cleared up some time in the next century!'

'What's your job?' the policeman asked.

'Financial consultant, auditor.'

Gunnarstranda nodded. 'Private?'

'Yes.'

'Do you have a business card?'

With a resigned expression, the man took out his wallet and passed over a card with the stamp of his company and a colour photo. Gunnarstranda flicked it backwards and forwards between his fingers. 'Well, herr Bjerke,' he said, focusing on the other man's eyes. 'Since this flat is so private, perhaps you could tell me which of these rooms is closest to Reidun Rosendal's?'

'The bedroom.'

This answer came from Mia, still holding the child on her arm, with a nervous glance at her husband. 'Our bedroom's right above her flat, more or less,' she continued, with a strained smile. 'The bedroom is where you realize the walls are very thin in these old blocks.'

Gunnarstranda turned to her. 'Saturday night, did you hear anything in particular then?'

'No, we went to bed early, we generally do, Joachim Junior wakes up at an unearthly hour, you know, and we like to go walking on Sundays, and . . .'

'Her flat was in a terrible mess, as you probably noticed,' Gunnarstranda interrupted. 'Perhaps it was a burglary. That kind of burglary does not necessarily make a lot of noise;

on the other hand, a scuffle between the intruder and her would have made quite a racket.'

Her husband stirred with impatience. He burst out:

'No one breaks into a house early on a Sunday morning when people are sleeping!'

Gunnarstranda turned to him. 'It's happened before,' he answered, ice-cold. 'It's also happened that single women have been attacked and molested in their own homes, while asleep, on Sunday mornings.'

He had intended to say more. It was on the tip of his tongue, but he kept his mouth shut. Instead he addressed her. 'And neither of you heard her coming in on Saturday night?'

'No, it was all the same as usual.'

She spread her hands outwards.

'And on Sunday morning?'

'I got up at eight,' she answered, contemplative. 'And by then Joachim was in the shower, because you'd been out jogging, hadn't you.' She smiled at her husband. 'We had breakfast and did normal things, you know what Sunday mornings are like, and . . . yes, we went for a walk by the river, just a little morning stroll.'

'You said the door to the crime scene was open and banging before you found the body. Did you notice if it was banging when you went out for a walk?'

Joachim shook his head. Mia sat thinking. 'I'm simply not sure,' she concluded at length. 'What I do remember is that I noticed it at once when I was washing the stairs afterwards, but perhaps that's because Junior was standing there and it stuck in my mind for that reason, but I'm not sure.'

'And you, herr Bjerke?'

Gunnarstranda addressed her husband. Stressed the formal tone. 'You came back from your jog before eight?'

The man nodded, but his expression was surly.

'How long had you been jogging?'

He shrugged his shoulders. 'I usually go before breakfast. After waking up. It's a health thing.'

He cast a sidelong glance at Gunnarstranda's ashtray on the table. 'In contrast to certain other habits people have.'

The policeman ignored the barbed remark. 'Did you see anyone?'

'If I did, I don't remember who.'

'Was the front door locked when you left in the morning?'

'No.'

'Sure?'

'Yes, quite sure.'

'Is that normal?'

The man shrugged again. 'Sometimes it's locked, sometimes it isn't. I suppose it depends on who comes in.'

'The gate outside, was that locked?'

'No, it wasn't.'

'Is that usual or not?'

'Both. That depends, too.'

Gunnarstranda rested his chin in his hands and stared at him in silence. Since that failed to have any effect, he concentrated on Mia. 'You didn't hear Joachim leave the flat or return?'

She glanced uncertainly from her husband to the policeman and back again. This question was uncomfortable for her.

He addressed the husband again. 'Did you observe anyone outside the block or in the vicinity as you left the entrance?'

'No.'

'Or when you returned?'

'There might have been a taxi, or a car in the street, a tram, who knows. I didn't notice anything in particular. I was out for a run.'

'And the door to the crime scene, was it open and banging?'

'I've already answered that question.'

'But you passed close by the door on three separate occasions in the course of the morning.'

'Yes, that is correct.'

'Did you go into her flat on Sunday morning?'

'No, of course not!'

'And did either of you hear any sounds coming from her flat Saturday night or Sunday morning?' Gunnarstranda looked at both of them, but it was Mia who answered.

'No.'

'Have you ever been in her flat?' He spoke directly to her.

Joachim answered for her. 'No, she hasn't.'

Gunnarstranda looked up at him from the corner of his eye. Knew instinctively his reaction was too abrupt, he could feel the anger burning in his cheeks. 'Your wife is over eighteen years old and legally responsible for her actions.

She can either speak for herself, without your help, in her own home, or in the more formal surroundings of my office where she will not be interrupted by you!'

Joachim Senior fell silent. Gunnarstranda turned back to Mia. Took a deep breath and treated her to a white smile. 'Have you ever been in her flat?'

Even before he had finished the question she had shaken her head several times.

The inspector got to his feet and took the notebook from the table. 'That'll be all at this time,' he concluded. 'The methods employed in this case will be no different from those of others. We spread a wide net at the start of a case. For that reason we will return and focus on detailed statements later in the investigation. We are therefore dependent on the goodwill of all witnesses. It's one of the premises of our procedure.'

He didn't need to say any more. Neither was interested. He left. Neither of them accompanied him to the door.

4

Down on the street, he had to wait exactly four minutes before Frank Frølich came along in the patrol car, slowed and drew up in front of him.

Gunnarstranda got in without putting on the seat belt. 'What have you found out?' he wheezed while adjusting his coat so that it wouldn't be creased to death.

'I rang her workplace.'

Frølich stretched behind to grab a worn, dark brown leather case from the back seat. And removed a pile of papers. 'She worked in what's called customer service, in other words, she was a saleswoman. Responded to an ad and was taken on six months ago.'

He faced forward again. 'I spoke to a woman in the office there, Sonja Hager. Must have been a small firm – I got that impression anyway. Set great store by staff flexibility, the woman said. So Reidun must have done other things as well.'

It was cramped at the front when Frølich was the driver. The big man's knees were almost banging against the steering wheel even though the seat had been pushed back as far as it was possible. When he lifted the papers from his lap Gunnarstranda had to squeeze up against the window to give him room for his arms.

'She took her school-leaving exams in her home town, somewhere up in the north-west, Møre and Romsdal.'

The driver scratched his beard. A full black beard with streaks of grey, just like his hair. His hair and beard were as bristly as a broom. Gunnarstranda was jealous. The sole crumb of comfort was the hint of grey, even though the young man had not yet turned thirty.

'Then she moved to Oslo.'

Frølich spoke with a slightly nasal tone whenever he made reference to documents. The man breathed through his nose and used his mouth to speak. 'We've turned up a couple of casual jobs from two temping agencies. That covers a few months,' he began to summarize. 'Otherwise it's all a bit vague, but I did manage to find confirmation that she had worked at the Post Office for a year. Finished the PO job eighteen months ago because she wanted to study. Enrolled at Oslo University on 13th January last year. Didn't sit for any exams. Signed on at the Job Centre on 4th May. Started with A/S Software Partners, as the company is called, at the beginning of October last year. Did a few weeks on the till for a co-op store now and then.'

Gunnarstranda nodded. His colleague flicked through the papers on his lap, said the flat where she lived belonged to a teacher who was working in Finnmark pro tem to reduce his study loan. Been there for two years.

'This teacher fella has rung twice and nagged us to find him a new tenant.' Frank Frølich sighed, working his way through the pile. 'Dry old stick, the teacher.'

'Go on.'

Gunnarstranda was still facing the street. He stared at the two hippies from before, who came trudging through the archway. Two lean crow-like figures wearing large flapping clothes swaggered up towards Sannergata while Frølich informed him that the woman's father was dead, but that her mother was alive and that the sister, who was two years older, was married to an offshore worker and had settled down in Flekkefjord. Both the mother and the sister had received visits from her, and the mother was wondering now about practical details regarding the burial.

'Finances?'

'Unclear for the time being.'

'Her letter box is empty, too,' Gunnarstranda was able to add after a moment's silence.

Frølich leafed through the papers. 'Neither the sister nor the mother remember any names apart from Software Partners, the company where she was working. Neither of them has seen her for a good while and neither has met her or noticed a new tone in her letters. Overall, the murder came as a total shock to them.'

'Money in the bank?'

'Zero. As I said, this is a bit unclear, but we have located the account her wages were paid into, and it's empty.'

'Good,' mumbled Gunnarstranda under his breath. Frølich had managed to dig up a fair bit. Placed the woman in a sort of frame, so that now she appeared as more than a dead body. But the picture was blurred, lacked detail. 'No one has seen or heard a thing,' Gunnarstranda added. 'Not even objects falling, or fighting.'

He lit a cigarette. Frølich slowly rolled down the window.

'We have the couple that came home from the party on Sunday morning.'

Gunnarstranda nodded towards the hippie couple up the street. 'Those two. They claimed that there was a bloke with a blood-stained face and a pony tail hanging round the gate when they arrived. And neither can remember if they had locked the gate or the door after them.'

Frølich nodded. 'We could put them together with an artist and ask them to give a description.'

'They're a waste of space,' Gunnarstranda opined. 'They were so doped up it took them a quarter of an hour to re-member the bloke had a pony tail. No, that wouldn't be any use.'

He sat smoking for a while in silence. 'She was covered with stab wounds. That suggests a fury at the moment of death.'

The cigarette was burning unevenly. Gunnarstranda blew on the glow to try to redress the imbalance. 'But then there's the terrible mess, which makes me wonder. Drawers turned upside down and all the junk on the floor. That suggests someone wanted to relieve the young lady of her valuables.'

'Nothing stolen though,' Frølich parried in a neutral tone. He read from the report, 'Stereo untouched, TV and money intact.'

'She might just have put up a fight,' Gunnarstranda muttered. 'But I don't like the fact that the door isn't dam-aged. On the other hand, it wasn't locked when Mia Bjerke found the body.'

'Bolt lock,' Frølich said with his nose in the stack of papers again. 'Which does not click shut.'

He stroked his beard, leaned back against the head rest. 'She might have forgotten to lock the door at night or she may have opened up for the perp and let him in.'

Gunnarstranda looked into the street. 'No one climbed in through the window,' he declared. Eyeballed his partner. 'Think this is a rape case? I mean, she was only wearing a dressing gown.'

Frølich's dark eyes seemed to turn inwards. 'Of course we don't know when at night this happened,' he mumbled. 'But if she was sleeping and a guy rang . . .'

He paused, searching for words. Gunnarstranda leaned forward and stubbed out the glow of cigarette in the ashtray. Held on to the butt.

'If she flung on a dressing gown,' Frølich continued, 'and opened the door to a guy, who raped her, someone must have heard something.'

Gunnarstranda thought of the Bjerke family. The bedroom that was above the deceased girl's bed-sit. 'No one heard a thing,' he repeated grimly. 'In fact, none of the neighbours has told us anything, except that she was a good-looking girl. But we already knew that. None of them knew her and it seems no one had any kind of contact with her.'

Frølich nodded. 'That's how it is. I've lived in my flat for four years. But I've got no bloody idea how many people live on the same floor.'

'Not everyone's as dopey as you!'

29

'The point is that people don't know one another even though they live side by side.'

'No, they don't know one another, but they do keep their eyes open! They're inquisitive!'

They said nothing.

'What if she had a boyfriend?' Frølich asked after a while.

Gunnarstranda slowly rolled down the window. Flicked the crumpled cigarette on to the road. 'Jealousy? A row?'

He angled his head. 'That might square with the loose dressing gown around her body. But I still don't like the door being open. The boyfriend would have locked up after him.'

'Maybe he fled in panic?' Frølich suggested. 'Or he didn't have a key?'

'Mmm.'

Gunnarstranda recalled the sight of the dead woman's chest. 'You saw the way she looked, didn't you?'

'Indeed I did.'

Gunnarstranda fumbled with the door. 'Could a boyfriend do that?' he wondered aloud. Didn't bother to wait for an answer. Opened the door. 'Come on, Frankie,' he mumbled. 'To work!'

5

Frank Frølich was left sitting with his lips twisted into a small ironic smile. It sounded odd to hear his boss calling him Frankie. It was what most people called him, though. Boys in the street had soon realized that Frankie was cooler than Frank and sounded best when apple scrumping or at football training. The nickname had followed him ever since. But Gunnarstranda was slow to pick up on things like that. 'Right, Frølich?' was more the tone. 'What do you reckon, Frølich?'

With a feigned cough and fidgety fingers. It almost sounded a bit comical. Hearing this aloof old hothead with the gimlet eyes call him Frankie.

He packed away the papers and followed Gunnarstranda, who had stridden off across the road, stopped and was gazing upwards. Then he turned and crossed the street quickly again. Studying the façade of the building.

Frank squinted up as well. Was taken by surprise, as always, at the beauty of the cornices and sculptures on these old apartment buildings. One was newer than the others. Square window panes with no ornamentation.

'There,' Gunnarstranda pointed. 'That block has the right view. Let's go to the top floor.'

Upon reaching the top floor at last, they were both

panting. On the landing outside the front doors the light had gone, so the name plates were barely legible. Two flats, but only one was occupied. The second door was partially concealed by cardboard boxes and rubbish piled up against the wall. Frank stooped and read the name engraved in the blackened brass:

'Arvid Johansen.'

'Cops?' mumbled the old man who opened up. 'Thought it wouldn't be long before you lot were on my back!'

They entered a cramped and poorly ventilated flat. A heavy stench of smoke, dust and something reminiscent of stale fish offal met their nostrils. Large dust balls had collected in the corner of the hallway. A variety of stains adorned the lino floor, which was unwashed and sticky underfoot.

The well-built old grunter, once a hulk of a man, had an erect bearing, but his legs were stiff and his breathing crackled with asthma. His hair was grey, short and thick. Beneath his eyes and chin hung deep bags of wrinkled skin. His reddened right eye gleamed at them; a blood vessel must have burst.

He shuffled ahead into the little sitting room and sat down on a worn, grey wing chair by the window. At the other end of the room there was a small TV and a video recorder.

The TV picture showed a woman sucking dick while emitting moaning noises. It took Frank a while for his brain to cut in and inform him what was going on.

By then Johansen had already raised the remote control and frozen the picture on the screen, put down the remote and grabbed a roll-up from the ashtray on the table. The cigarette had not gone out, so he puffed it into life and took a drag, which was followed by a lengthy bout of coughing. His throat gurgled. After the fit had finally subsided he spat into a handkerchief and stared up expectantly at Gunnarstranda, who had ensconced himself by the window. Frank looked around the room. Bare walls. Floor heaving with porn magazines. Glossy paper strewn with nude women. Faces of tarts with their tongues sticking out. Such as there, on the sitting room table, a large centrefold of a naked girl with a Father Christmas cap on her head and a yellow banana up her crotch. Two strong masculine hands forcing her legs apart.

'That'd be something to keep out the winter cold!'

Johansen had followed Frank's gaze. His mouth laughed behind a clenched fist. The laughter degenerated into coughing.

Gunnarstranda stared out of the window until the man was breathing normally again. 'Come here, Johansen,' he ordered without turning. The man in the chair obeyed. Gunnarstranda's little head reached up to the middle of his chest.

'The flat down there, at an angle to us, in the pink block with the curtains drawn.'

'That's where she lived, that is.'

Johansen had sat down again. 'Our young filly.' He winked at Frank. 'Pert pear-shaped tits, the type that bounce around!'

He illustrated with his hands. 'High buttocks. Rounded, and ginger pussy hair.'

The hand with the cigarette shook. The man wheezed, got up and, standing next to Gunnarstranda, pointed. 'That's where she lived,' he pointed with rasping breath. 'That's the very one.'

The grunter started to pace to and fro, stiff-legged, across the floor.

Frank tried to avoid looking at the bloodshot eye. It flashed like a brake light every time the old man turned on his heel.

'You've got to find a young bloke,' the man gasped, 'mid-twenties, no special characteristics, but long, black hair which he keeps in a pony tail. They like that, girls do.'

He stared up at the ceiling before sitting back down. His cigarette was out, but he lit it with an ancient, peeling lighter. It wouldn't light at first. The two policemen watched him struggling to retain control of his fingers with every flick. At last it caught. He blew out smoke and went on:

'I watched 'em all night. The nitty-gritty.'

Frank looked up. Met Gunnarstranda's eyes.

'She was a little rose, you know, she knew what we old boys like.'

He gave a moist grin. Winked at Gunnarstranda.

'What did you see?' Gunnarstranda asked.

'What did I see?'

The old boy's breathing crackled. 'What d'you think I saw?'

He raised his right hand and made a circle with his thumb

34

and forefinger. Then he began to poke his left forefinger in and out of the hole. An amusing sight. The old man laughed, got into difficulties and had to hold his fist in front of his mouth to curb the asthmatic fit of laughter that exploded into the room.

Frank drifted over to the window as well, and opened it an inch or two. Put his face in the current of air that entered. For a moment all was quiet. The noise of traffic outside mixed with the sounds of Johansen's asthmatic rattle.

'They had all the lights on,' the crackling voice continued. 'Curtains were open, so I just sat here enjoying myself while she lay on her back down there waggling her tits!'

It went quiet again. All that could be heard was the old man in the chair leaning forward and stubbing out his cigarette.

'Gratis and for nothing.'

A dark expression had formed between the man's wrinkles. 'Buggered if I can understand why he . . .' came a new tone from the chair.

Frank stared at him. The muggy offal smell was not so strong now and a pained air was visible on the man's drawn face. He was searching for words. Hidden behind his hands. 'I can't get my head round why he had to croak her afterwards!'

The skin on his hands was coarse and lined.

'How did he kill her?'

Gunnarstranda's voice cut through the silence even though the intonation was friendly, no more than curious.

Johansen twitched. 'How? I don't care so long as you get 'im.'

The little pain there had been in his voice was gone. His eyes were cold, like when he opened his front door.

'You haven't answered my question! How did he kill her?'

'He stabbed her, for fuck's sake!'

The silence in the room became palpable.

'Who did this crazy thing, me or him?'

Gunnarstranda went up close. 'How?' he repeated in a low voice.

Johansen didn't answer. He just glared back at the gimlet eyes of the short, balding detective in front of him.

Frank tried to read the expression on Johansen's face. Was it fear or just defiance?

Then Gunnarstranda went round the table, apparently having backed down. Sat on the sofa and began to study the magazines without another word. 'What taste you have, Johansen!'

The derision in his intonation was unmistakable.

The old man didn't turn, hadn't even stirred in his chair. His eyes looked straight ahead, were fixed on a point on the wall.

'Look here!'

Gunnarstranda held up a magazine. 'Look here, you,' he mumbled. 'You, Johansen!'

He turned. The inspector laid the magazine on the table in front of him. Frank peered over his shoulder, curious to see. It was a magazine with no text. The photographs were in black and white, a series of pictures, amateur judging by the quality, peculiar angles, bad lighting, blurred. Gunnarstranda thumbed through, slowly, page by page. The series illustrated the fate of a blonde woman. Bound to a chair at first, tied with rope and chains that dug into her skin. Helpless, undressed, with a cloth forced into her mouth. Frightened eyes, round as plates, swollen blood vessels down her neck, *as if something was hurting a lot*, Frank thought. He caught himself wondering what it was that could hurt so much. In the next picture she was hanging upside down, still chained, still undressed and still with this silent scream of pain etched into her face and neck. Then one man's rough hand held her hair while another held a dagger against the skin of her throat stretched to the limit. Frank wondered if the black stain on the blade was the woman's blood. Probably, he concluded.

Gunnarstranda peered up from the magazine. 'Was this how it happened perhaps?'

Johansen didn't answer.

Gunnarstranda turned over the page. Another woman. More rope. Black rope taut across her breasts, rope holding up her legs in an unnatural position. Two hands this time. Two hands trying to choke the woman with a rope tied tightly around her neck.

'You like seeing women with rope around their necks, you do, don't you, Johansen,' Gunnarstranda whispered. 'Perhaps you dream about pulling the rope yourself, perhaps that was what you were dreaming when you sat up here with your dick in your hand that night, about going down to the nice little girl and slowly putting the rope around her neck and pulling and pulling and feeling her tremble helplessly in your arms?'

Johansen's eyes were dulled. Passive and expressionless. They stared at the little man, who had got up and gone back around the table.

'You know better than that, you evil bastard,' the old man spat with hatred at the vulpine head now only five centimetres from his own.

'If it's so damned obvious, Johansen, tell me, at your leisure, how the hell you saw anything at all in the flat if the curtains were drawn?'

'She drew them afterwards. She drew them after he'd gone. She let me see everything until he left, then she drew them. She waved to me and drew the curtains!'

This last piece of information came in the same pained voice as before.

Frank frowned. Waved, did she indeed, he wondered.

Gunnarstranda had straightened up. The distance between him and the old man was about half a metre. 'So he left, did he? Without killing anyone?'

'He waited, waited until she had drawn the curtains, then he croaked her.'

'You're making this up as you go along!'

'It's obvious to anyone with any nous.'

Johansen's normal complexion was back. The threatening tone was gone. His hand clutched at the pouch of tobacco.

Gunnarstranda walked over to the window and leaned back against the glass. 'I want to know what you saw in precise detail,' he explained calmly and he, too, lit a cigarette.

'Nothing else, not what you imagine, not what you believe, simply what you could see.'

Johansen got to his feet. 'I'll give it to you straight then,' he said suddenly. Upright, he towered over the policeman, even though he was resting his palms against the window sill and had not drawn himself up to his full height.

'I'll tell you,' he mumbled with a haughty cackle and a triumphant smile around tight lips. Frank straightened up with excitement.

Johansen pointed downwards. 'Can you see the wooden fence by the demolition site?'

The man pointed to a gaping hole at the front beside the murder victim's block of flats. A tall wooden fence blocked off the demolition site.

'That's where he got out,' Johansen said in a hoarse whisper. 'After he'd killed my little rose.'

The old boy's eyes were dimmed and turned inwards. For the most part he was speaking to someone who wasn't there, to himself.

'He couldn't fool me because I saw 'im. I suppose he didn't want to be seen, so he kept away from the gate and the main door, he sneaked out, over the fence. I saw 'im climbing over the fence. With blood all over his face! And when he got there at least a quarter of an hour had passed since she'd drawn the curtains!'

Gunnarstranda stared out of the window, lost in thought. Johansen gave a faint chuckle and his asthmatic coughing started again.

'A quarter of an hour,' he coughed behind his fist and sat down with the same triumphant expression on his face.

Gunnarstranda, doubtful, frowned. 'You think first of all he went into the yard, climbed from there into the demolition site, then jumped over the wooden fence when he could have strolled through the gate into the street, do you?'

'Christ knows how he got into the demo site, but I saw 'im climb over the fence!'

'It didn't occur to you that this was a hell of a lot of hassle to get to the street?'

Johansen sneered. 'He'd have to expect a bit of hassle if he was going to kill 'er!'

Gunnarstranda stood mulling this over, then spun round. 'What time was it when they arrived that night?'

Johansen shrugged.

'What was it that attracted your attention? Noise in the street or what?'

'No,' mumbled Johansen, getting up again. 'I just saw there was a light in her window. She had switched on the light. Must have been about one at night. I'd just been to the loo, saw there was a light down there, and well, since she had this guy with 'er then . . .'

In the ensuing eloquent pause he smiled that wet smile of his. 'Now we're gonna see something, gramps!'

Johansen's laughter once again erupted into a fit of coughing. His hands shook as he tried to flick the lighter into life.

'Did anyone go into the block after the young man had left in the morning?'

The man gave this some thought.

'Did you see anyone go through the gate,' the policeman calmly rephrased his question.

The man didn't speak.

'Did you see anyone go in?'

'No,' the man said at length, without meeting Gunnarstranda's gaze.

'Are you sure?'

'Yes!'

'When did he leave her?'

'Five, maybe six.'

'I know there were people coming and going between five and six, Johansen.'

Johansen didn't answer.

'Perhaps you just weren't following very well, Johansen, eh?'

'I've told you what I saw!'

'Just not all of it?'

'I've told you what I saw, for fuck's sake!'

'What did the guy do after he'd climbed over the fence?'

'Do?'

'Yes, did he run off or what?'

'Yes, he legged it.'

'The man with the pony tail?'

'Yes.'

'If I say I have two witnesses who swear they saw the man with the pony tail outside the gate between five and six . . . ?'

'So?'

The inspector moved closer. 'Are you sure about this fence business, Johansen?'

'I've told you what I saw!'

'But why didn't you see the other two there?'

Johansen stared intently at Gunnarstranda. 'Now I remember!' he said coldly. 'They arrived in a taxi. That's right. Two of 'em. About the same time as he was climbing over the fence.'

Frank studied the old man's closed face. It was impossible to say what was going on inside. His breathing gurgled, faint and rhythmical, as before.

'Did you see anything else?' Gunnarstranda fired at him.

'I've told you what I saw.'

'You didn't see anyone else?'

The man shook his head, a closed expression on his face.

'This is absolutely crucial, Johansen! Did you see anyone else go in the gate?'

'I've told you what I saw!' Johansen glared at Gunnarstranda. 'He jumped down from the fence a quarter of an hour after she'd drawn the curtains!'

Gunnarstranda seemed not to hear, instead with his teeth bared in a smile he asked: 'Did you see her shagging with anyone else?'

Johansen subjected him to a stare. A lingering stare.

'But she waved to you before she drew the curtains, did she?'

Silence.

'Why do you think she waved?'

The man smoked. Studied the ceiling.

'You said she had a ginger pussy. You must have studied her pretty closely, mustn't you?'

Johansen stubbed out the cigarette in the ashtray. Also had to extinguish some old tobacco that had started to glow.

'How did she like it?'

The man's breathing grew heavier.

'On top or underneath?'

'How long did they keep at it as a rule?'

He was breathing heavily. His breath crackled quietly.

Frank caught himself looking at his watch. Received a little nod from Gunnarstranda, then concentrated on the old man again.

'So, you sat up here the whole of Saturday night, did you?'

'I slept here.'

Johansen stirred in his chair. 'I slept in the chair as I usually do. It's so much bloody hassle making a bed on the sofa every night.

Frank followed his gaze towards the sofa and a pile of dirty clothes. Eventually he managed to identify the classic chequered pattern of a flannelette sheet.

6

Frank Frølich's interest in salmon fishing had not had an easy birth. Born and bred in Oslo as he was, he had never rowed boats for rich folk with enough money to hire fishing rights on the river Namsen. The fishing adventures of his childhood were ice fishing in Østmarka and the odd pike in the nutrient-rich puddles nearest to the capital. But since fishing was his all-consuming hobby, it was not long before there was a fly-tying vice under the Christmas tree, a tool which at that time was kept stowed away in a cupboard. Until the event that was to change his attitude to fishing for ever.

A few years before, he and two pals in the Oslo Hunting and Fishing Association had gone on holiday in Frank's old Taunus 17M, which that year was as yet free of big end trouble. They stopped at the Jazz Camp in Molde because Albert King was performing. From there they made their way up north, and one night they were fishing illegally on a quiet river bank where large silent pools lay gleaming beside a slow current. It had been damp and cold and their hands holding the rods itched from mosquito bites. The river had exuded the cool night atmosphere that bore within it the scent of water and nectar and summer, all at the same time. He had swung out a home-made telescopic rod and savoured the sight of the line lying on the skin-like surface of the stream. The large red moon hung in the night sky, with its magnified reflection on the crystal-clear water, casting a magical column of light from bank to bank.

Then it happened.

A tug on his arm. A line that tightened like a tent guy. The first moves in a struggle of which he would recall very little. Only the anxious paralysis of his thighs, the sensation in his legs vanishing in the icy river as he let the line run and shouted to his pals. Their white faces as they walked along the bank searching wildly for the fishing gaff and shouting advice. The strong rod that jerked and dipped towards the water. The powerful pull of the fish, the strain on his upper arm. The panic-stricken fear that the fly was not fastened securely enough to the line. The feeling of triumph for every metre reeled in. Until the moment when the black spine of the salmon slithered submissively towards his boot and allowed itself to be caught.

It took no more than a tug. And he was in thrall to a disease that would never relinquish its grip. Fly-fishing had become his great passion.

It was early morning now. While waiting to be received at the Institute of Forensic Medicine, he had been to Tanum bookshop and bought a weighty tome about insects. About the development from egg, larva, pupa to fully fledged flier of the majority of the insects known to flap their wings through a Norwegian summer. It was Gunnarstranda who had planted the idea. Frølich had mentioned he needed real models. And had ended up buying this book.

Afterwards he drove home with it, his stomach aching with hunger as he turned off the motorway, took the short cut past Manglerud Church and twisted his way down to Havreveien.

The street was littered with the spring's No Parking signs as a yellow road-sweeper vehicle attempted to brush away the gravel strewn across the pavement. So he reversed up the entrance to the block and parked. Took the lift to the ninth floor. Let himself in.

As soon as he opened the door he could hear Eva-Britt humming in a loud, unconstrained voice, the way people do when they wear headphones and think they are alone. A smile broadened in his beard. He had not expected to see her back for a while. So, he put down the book and tiptoed in. Stopped in the doorway. She was reclining naked on the lounger. Her ample breasts spilled to each side and she was lying with her legs crossed. The room was lit up by the sun beaming in through the large panoramic windows. A large yellow square stretched across the white carpet covered with long blonde hairs and dust; dust that danced in the sunlight. Her toes splayed out to the rhythm of the music as if someone were tickling them with string. The movement caused her breasts, with the dark pink nipples, to wobble. But the face under the headphones was ugly and unreal. It looked like a sculpted plaster-of-Paris figure. A balloon with papier-mâché stuck on.

She sensed his presence from his stare, opened her eyes. They shone like two black stains in the porridge-like surface.

'What the hell have you done to your face?' he gasped as she removed the headphones.

'Yoghurt,' Porridge-face said. 'Face mask.'

'Sheesh!'

He went in and sat beside her. He couldn't restrain his hand. Stroked the faint crease on her neck. 'I thought you were at university.'

His hand followed his urge, down the taut abdomen.

'Couldn't be fagged.'

'Your daughter?'

'With her father.'

The eyes in the facial porridge had turned blacker. Her hand caressed his forearm, up and down. 'Your fingers are a bit cold.'

Her voice sounded as if she didn't have enough breath to say everything. He nodded and ran them lightly across her breasts. Bent down and licked off a bit of the face.

'Good,' he said, smacking his lips.

She giggled at the tickle of his tongue; he held her neck with one hand as he licked upwards and filled his mouth with yoghurt. Swallowed.

'It's only half past ten,' he heard her say as his fingers strayed across her stomach, downwards. Licked. Swallowed. Licked. Ate the yoghurt. Soon her chin and one eye were clear. He stooped over her in the lounger. Trying to get un-dressed at the same time. Got one arm stuck in his sweater so that both arms were trapped behind his back.

Almost all the yoghurt daub was gone. Her red lips shone through the muck. He hopped on one leg with both arms behind his back. Fell to the floor, struggled up on to one knee. She grinned and helped him. Until he was as naked as she was.

'My God, you're so fat!' she exclaimed with delight and escaped from his arms. He ran after her. His erect penis stirring and banging against his stomach. Into the bedroom, Frank launched himself, airborne. Gotcha. She screamed.

They hit the bed in the middle. The mattress sank to the floor as the bed gave way with an ear-deafening crack.

'Are you alive?' he asked solicitously.

She sniggered. 'Think so.'

* * *

Afterwards they lay beside each other. The sun blazed a sharp whiteness on to her rump. She was asleep. The telephone rang. He tried to wriggle his thigh out without waking her. The bed frame towered like an abandoned theatre set above them. He had his hand around the receiver as she sighed softly in her sleep and rolled over and away. His pecker drooped and wilted as he got up.

'Yes,' he said, knowing who it was. 'Yes,' he repeated.

'I'm on my way.'

She lay on her back in the sunshine. Rested her head on her arms and languidly kicked at the foot of the bed.

'Who was it?' she asked sleepily.

'Gunnarstranda.'

'You'd better go then.'

'Yup.'

'Your willy doesn't seem to want to go.'

He grinned.

'In all the novels I've read all the boys have limp willies after a bonk,' she said, pointing an accusatory finger at the thing stubbornly pointing back at her.

'In all the books I read the boys have three or four bonks in a row.'

'That's because you read such bad books.'

He peered out. Blue sky and the top of the neighbouring block of flats. Windows.

'Anyway, you've broken the bed,' she added as he left for a shower.

He and Eva-Britt had once been in the same class at school. They had then lost contact until they met again three years ago. On the number twenty-three bus. A woman with an hour-glass figure and a pram struggling to man-oeuvre it on to the bus; he had recognized her as he jumped out to help.

Two hours later they were in bed together in his student room recalling the old days, while sixteen-month Julie was asleep in the turbo-pram in the communal kitchen. They lived in their own flat, Julie and her mother did; Eva-Britt had had bad experiences with close relationships.

'Will you get a bottle of red?' she shouted from the kitchen when he switched off the water.

He came out. Her breasts were screaming to be fondled as she threw a dressing gown over herself. She could read his thoughts, and grinned.

'Fine,' he mumbled, enjoying the slight gasp that escaped her lips before she slipped into the bathroom. 'I'll get a bottle of red.'

7

He stopped at Manglerud and did his booze shopping at the vinmonopol there. His head still buzzing with nosy neighbours. *Did Reidun Rosendal know what kind of neighbours she had,* he mused in the queue, trying to imagine her type. *OK, the old pig could be as mad as a hatter and actually believe that the woman was letting him see what he wanted that night. But could that really be the truth? That number was mostly for married couples in a mid-life crisis, spicing up their sex lives with the excitement of being seen by others, wasn't it?*

The thought would not let him rest. After all, there had been two of them that night. The boy and the girl. Under normal circumstances, with eyes only for each other. Perhaps so madly in love that curtains on the windows were of secondary importance. But that was the point. The woman had been killed. Was the man she had invited into her flat in love? Did that type exist, someone so crazy he would stab a woman to death after making love to her all night?

Frank picked up Gunnarstranda in the Grønland district of Oslo and headed for the Institute of Forensic Medicine, where they were met by Professor Schwenke who then powered ahead of them. The man's white coat fluttering behind him. His thin legs making his office trousers look like flares.

The professor led them into his office. Here he proceeded to hold an illustrated lecture with photographs of the dead girl. The man's combed-back greyish-white hair had such a will of its own that a strand at the back refused to stay in position and rebounded forward over his forehead. His square glasses were gold-rimmed, and his complexion was dry and yellowy. The professor put the top photograph on the desk, bent forward eagerly and analysed the sequence of events.

'The angles of the various cuts reveal that the murderer stabbed her in the chest even when she was down on the floor,' he explained with professional dispassion. 'No fewer than three times in fact. Incredibly, the knife didn't strike a bone and didn't get lodged until the final blow.'

Schwenke's voice was thick; he seemed to be speaking with toffees in his mouth.

Frank Frølich let the other two converse. He observed Gunnarstranda, whose arms were resting against the back of his hips with his fingers interlaced. His piscine eyes fixed on Schwenke's face, the police inspector looked like a hooked fish: his bent-back arms raised his shoulders a smidgeon, his head hung slightly and his eyes were focused upwards on the professor's face.

'She died in a relatively short time,' Schwenke said, pointing to the picture. 'In fact, she was stabbed nine times. This,' he indicated to clarify the point, pulling out another photograph in which the woman's lacerated chest was magnified. 'This stab on its own would have been enough to kill her. The incision has not only punctured the lung but brushed the heart.'

He paused and stroked his chin with two long, bony fingers, the yellowing nails untrimmed. 'There was clear evidence of sperm in the vagina, so she must have been sexually active before she was killed, hard to say exactly how long before. The results of our tests may tell us more.'

Schwenke passed the stack of photographs to Frølich. Gunnarstranda did not move.

'Was she on drugs?' he barked.

'Definitely not,' Schwenke established with total assurance.

'Rape?'

Schwenke wavered. 'From a physiological point of view there is no damage to the central organs,' he concluded at length. 'But she had clearly had sexual contact at some point before the murder. What is rape though? Hypothetically speaking, a rapist may have forced her . . .'

'So you can't rule out rape?'

Schwenke stroked his chin again, ruminating. Made a decision.

'Rape cannot be ruled out,' he stated in an official tone. 'But I assume it has to be regarded as a legal question, dependent on the circumstances surrounding the sexual act.'

He smacked his lips thoughtfully and added:

'If you can find out what happened leading up to the murder.'

They left the office and went to the lab. Inside, the walls were covered with shelves of glass tubes, flasks and sundry varieties of small boxes. A strong aroma of formalin filled the whole room and Frank prepared himself mentally to snatch any cigarettes from his boss's hands, for fear of an explosion. In the background, fans whirred vainly trying to dispel the thick chemical atmosphere that enveloped them. In the middle of the floor there was a steel table on castors, enshrouded in a sheet. Beneath which you could clearly see the outline of a body. The cover seemed to have been cast over the body in a hurry and there were bloodstains in the corner. A couple of stained plastic gloves lay on the lid of a sinister-looking plastic bucket beside the table.

'No, no, that's not her!'

Professor Schwenke followed Frank's gaze. A sudden thoughtful expression crossed his face. 'Suicide,' he sighed, mostly to the corpse. 'Two bottles of sleeping tablets, all in one go.'

All three of them stared at the table in silence.

'What time of the day did she die?'

Schwenke regarded the policeman with bewilderment. 'Did who die?'

'The girl with the stab wounds!'

'We're checking her stomach contents right now. All the tests are being done routinely, as I have made clear. In general, there is quite a bit I am unable to say as of yet.'

He nodded towards the table and added a couple of toffees to his voice. 'I know the fluctuations, the state of the market, you might say. And now it's the peak season for this kind of . . .'

'Would she have screamed?'

There was an irritated expression in Schwenke's eyes as

he turned back to Gunnarstranda. 'Would who have screamed?'

'How likely is it that the knife wounds would have made her scream?'

'She might have screamed, but she could also have been paralysed. The stab that punctured her lung might well have been the first.'

He drew a deep breath and addressed Frank. 'It's the way it's always been. I remember when I was the Regional Medical Officer in Troms. If someone had hanged themselves from a beam in the barn you could bet your life it happened on the night of a full moon.'

'The stabber, did he get a lot of blood over him?'

Schwenke smiled unperturbed and winked at Frank before turning round again. He produced a photograph, which he passed to Gunnarstranda. 'As you can see, the handle of the knife is drenched with blood. So the hands holding the knife would definitely have been soiled.'

He paused. 'In fact, here it's difficult to be precise,' he concluded. 'The murderer would have been covered with a fair amount of blood, but it's impossible to say how much. As you saw, there wasn't much blood on the floor. And from what I could glean there were very few signs of blood being sprayed around.'

The professor turned to address Frank again, but was prevented from continuing. A grey telephone on one of the work benches interrupted him.

'It's for you!' he shouted to Gunnarstranda, who grabbed the receiver with a hurried 'Yes!'

Frank and Schwenke hardly managed to exchange a word before the police inspector had banged down the receiver. 'Frølich! We've got the man with the pony tail.'

8

'So you're quite sure she locked the door after you?'

'Yes.'

'Did you check?'

'No, I heard it.'

'You're sure it was that? Not a window banging or something?'

'I'm sure. It was the lock.'

'Hm.'

Detective Inspector Gunnarstranda supported his head on one hand. In the other, he held a cigarette which he tapped on the ashtray to remove the end. Frank watched in amazement as the thick, blue smoke wafted up to the man's eyes, without it seeming to affect him.

A young man sat in the chair on the other side of the desk. He was in his mid-twenties and had long, black hair tied up in a pony tail. Frank observed him from the side. A small, child-like nose protruded from a cheek partially covered by a new, dark, downy beard. On his temple there was a plaster which was not large enough to cover a brownish-red scab. His clothes, which were all dark, hung off his slim figure. He was a well-formed young man who seemed neither muscular nor particularly fit.

Frank realized he would have trouble writing down

everything that was said. For that reason he switched on the tape recorder and swivelled his chair back to his computer screen. Ready to write down whatever he succeeded in catching.

'How long were you down in the yard?' he heard Gunnarstranda ask.

'I don't know.' The man cleared his throat nervously. 'Ten minutes tops.'

Frank Frølich wrote down the answer. For a second the muffled tapping on the keyboard was the only sound in the room.

'Did anyone see you?'

'I don't know.'

'You don't know? You must have made a hell of a racket if you were fiddling around down there for ten minutes, just imagine!'

The young man cleared his throat and gulped again. 'I honestly don't know.'

Frank gave up writing. Heard his chair creak as he swivelled round towards them. Watched Gunnarstranda stub out his cigarette, get up and walk around the table. He squatted down and supported himself on his thighs. 'You're frightened,' he confirmed and continued in a soft voice. 'You're trembling.'

The young man looked away.

The thick, blue smoke wreathed in the light of the desk lamp.

'Why did you climb over the fence?'

'I've told you. I wanted to go home!'

'Why didn't you ring her so that she could open the door for you?'

'Because . . .'

'Why?'

'I don't know.'

Gunnarstranda turned abruptly. Sat back down.

'Why did you come to the station?'

'Why?'

'Yes, how did you find out about the murder?'

'I read about it.'

'There were no names or addresses in the papers.'

'I had a feeling.'

'Feeling?'

'She didn't answer the phone. I rang and rang, and she didn't pick up. I had to know if it was her.'

'And so you didn't know her before?'

'No.'

'You got to know her on Saturday then?'

The young man's breathing was laboured. He didn't answer.

'Please answer the question.'

'She's dead.'

'Thank you, I am aware of that.'

Silence descended once again. A faint buzz in the room, that was all, the buzz of Frank's PC.

'How many times did you make love?'

No answer.

'Answer the question. How many times did you make love?'

'Twice.'

'Any form of protection?'

'No.'

'Not even a condom?'

'No, I assumed she had ... she had a coil or something like that.'

'In these times of AIDS?'

'Yes, but I didn't have a condom.'

'So you go out on the pull and leave the practical details to women?'

'I wasn't on the pull.'

'But you screwed her!'

Silence.

'Answer for Christ's sake.'

The man in black drew a large breath.

'OK, you weren't on the pull that night. What happened?'

'We met, as I said, we chatted, drank wine ... and ... well ... we decided to go to her place.'

'Where did you meet?'

'At a restaurant called Scarlet.' He hesitated. 'Yes, it's called Scarlet. I'd never been there before, I didn't know her, had never seen her before, she was sitting on her own ... we danced ... and ... well ... so I sat with her ... and ...'

'Was she alone there?'

'Think so.'

'What do you mean *think*?'

'It seemed so.'

'She was sitting alone and waiting to be picked up?'

'No.'

'What do you mean *no*? She was alone, wasn't she.'

'Yes.'

'But she wasn't alone after all?'

'She was alone, but it wasn't like that.'

'What was it like then?'

'She didn't dance with anyone in particular.'

'Ah! So she danced with several men?'

'Yes.'

'And you kept your eye on her?'

'Yes.'

'And you danced with her?'

'Yes.'

'And now you sit here and claim you weren't on the pull! You're lying!'

Gunnarstranda had pushed the swivel chair away from the desk. Moved back and forth, impatient.

The young man sat impassive, looking ahead with a fixed gaze.

'Why did you go there on Saturday?'

'Don't know. It was a Saturday. I could have gone anywhere. I was walking through town.'

'And what happened afterwards?'

'Well, we started talking, getting to know each other, like.'

'OK. What happened at her place?'

'Mm . . . we slept together.'

'How was it?'

Silence.

'I'm asking you how it was. What did you do?'

'We . . .'

'Did she offer herself?'

'Offer herself?'

'Did she get undressed and lie on the bed with her legs apart?'

'No . . . we . . . '

'Come on, tell me what happened!'

'You're talking about a dead person!'

'As I told you, I am well aware of how dead she is!'

Gunnarstranda pushed off with his feet and rolled into the desk with a bang. Leaned forwards: 'For Christ's sake tell me what happened after you came in the door!'

'I put my arms around her.'

'Where?'

'We kissed.'

'Where did you hold her?'

'I stroked her buttocks.'

'And then?'

'Then we lay down.'

'Dressed?'

'I undressed her.'

'And she screamed!'

'Screamed?'

'Yes, she screamed and said no. Isn't that right?'

'No, it is not!'

Gunnarstranda banged his fist on the desk. 'It's not right? She didn't scream? She screamed and screamed until you had to shut her screaming bloody gob, didn't you!'

'No!'

'Have a look at this then!'

Gunnarstranda got up and slung the photograph of Reidun Rosendal's mutilated body on the desk.

The young man took the photograph and shot a quick glimpse. Frank was unable to interpret the man's reaction. Dead bodies are not attractive, he thought. Not this version, either. All the blood with the stained knife handle between her breasts.

'Can you see the tie?' Gunnarstranda asked in a hushed voice.

The man shook his head in disbelief.

'It's sticking out under the edge of the shower cap.'

The man nodded, but didn't give the photograph a second look. He turned it over.

'That's your tie, isn't it?'

'I didn't kill her!'

'Is it your tie?'

'I didn't do it!'

'Is it your tie?'

'You lot can't accuse me of something I didn't do!'

'Answer my question! Is this your tie or not?'

'Yes, it bloody is. It is my sodding tie!'

All of a sudden the man stood up. And threw the photograph down on the table.

Not a sound. Gunnarstranda had moved his chair back from the desk again. A circumspect cigarette bounced up and down between his lips. He stared. Put the roll-up aside and inched the chair forward. 'Do you often lose your temper, Sigurd?'

The aggressive posture was gone immediately. His thin

legs trembled. He groped behind him to find his chair. Sat down.

'I haven't lost my temper.'

The young figure stared ahead, silent and confused.

'I asked if you often lost your temper.'

The young man looked away.

'On the rare occasions you lose your temper, Sigurd, you get very angry, don't you?'

He shrugged.

'Did you eat anything that night?'

'Yes . . . we had a few slices of bread . . . and fried eggs.'

'When was that?'

'I didn't keep an eye on my watch.'

'Was it after the first screw?'

The man nodded.

'What was she like as a screw?'

The man hesitated.

'Active?'

Silence.

'Or did she lie there like a sack of potatoes and allow herself to be despoiled?'

The man didn't answer.

'You like girls to offer a bit of resistance, do you, Sigurd?'

No reaction.

'Answer me when I'm talking to you, lad!'

'You're ridiculing a person who is no longer with us!'

'OK.'

Frank watched Gunnarstranda get up and throw his

hands in the air. Pace round the room for a while. 'So you ate bread,' he recapped. 'And you fried eggs.'

Gunnarstranda deliberated. 'Who cut the bread?' he asked at length.

'Me.'

Gunnarstranda walked back to the desk. Plunged a hand into the desk drawer and pulled out a knife. Frank watched him intentionally allow the light from the Anglepoise to glint on the polished steel. The steel blade was curved in such a way it had a kind of abdomen.

The room went quiet as Gunnarstranda carefully placed the knife on the table. The blade scraped the edge of the table making a dry rasp.

Frank heard Sigurd swallow.

Gunnarstranda slowly took a seat. 'Pick up the knife, Sigurd,' he demanded in a gentle voice.

The man swallowed again. His legs stirred with unease.

Gunnarstranda leaned on the desk with both elbows. 'Pick up the knife,' he repeated.

Sigurd stared up at the ceiling. For a long time.

'Pick up the knife!'

The policeman's voice resounded between the walls like a whiplash.

'No!' came the whispered reply. The young man took a deep breath. Swallowed. Tried to collect himself to say something.

'Why?' he tried, but had to snort hard to clear the congestion in his nose. 'Why?' he began again. Then had to stop once more. 'Why can't you leave her in peace?'

Gunnarstranda took the knife and started playing with it. Cleaned his nails with the point. 'Have you ever had any dealings with a solicitor, Sigurd?'

Frank observed Sigurd's head sink and come to rest against the edge of the desk.

'Did you jab her with the knife, Sigurd?'

The latter didn't answer.

Frank met Gunnarstranda's resigned eyes. Nodded and switched off the tape recorder.

'Frølich,' Gunnarstranda said in a harsh voice. 'Chuck the man back in his cell.'

9

Eva-Britt had got out at Ullevål Stadium. It was early morning. The worst of the traffic was over and Frank Frølich was in a good mood. The drive through Smestad had been pretty smooth and it was barely nine when he parked in front of a relatively new office block in Drammensveien by Lysaker. He just took a notepad and a few pencils with him.

The building stood out. A piece of commercial architecture inspired by Eskimo igloo architecture and pre-Christian temple styles. The name of the creative force behind the whole thing adorned parts of the façade.

The automatic doors slid open and he entered a hallway. The floor was tiled with honed and polished natural stone in a variety of hues. This arrangement had doubtless cost serious money, but it was also intended to give an impression of unity from a distance. The walls were painted white. At chest level, a varnished golden dado rail ran around the whole room.

Opposite the entrance was a large reception area. With huge ceiling-to-floor glass panes reminiscent of the Oslo Underground. In the middle of the opening, between the large panes, stood a receptionist, a woman who attracted everyone's attention. She was probably around thirty years old. Dressed as an office clerk in a kind of uniform, a skirt and jacket in a greyish-blue woollen material. Her hair was thick and brown with a red sheen that made him think of a car bonnet. As he approached, his gaze focused on a distinct black birthmark in the hollow between her chin and her broad mouth.

She nodded to him and spoke into the telephone receiver on her shoulder while her hands busied themselves with other things. They were strong. Nails were short, no varnish.

He leaned over to the counter as she pressed a few buttons and finished speaking.

'Software Partners are here, aren't they?'

'Third floor.'

She seemed uncomfortable in her office clothes. They clung too tight. The result was a physical ungainliness that was not at all necessary. She hesitated and was about to pick up the telephone again.

'Don't bother!'

He motioned towards the telephone.

'I'll find my own way there.'

As the lift doors opened, he walked straight into a large open-plan office where he was instantly met. So the woman with the birthmark had rung after all.

'You are the police officer, I presume?'

'Mhm.' Frank shook his hand.

'Øyvind Bregård,' the man bowed. 'I'm Head of Finance in this outfit.'

He was a tall, well-built fellow of around forty. The outstretched hand was not markedly large, but his chest, arms and thighs had undoubtedly been built up with weight-training. His head seemed strangely small in comparison with the robust body. Formidable bristles under his nose. Moustache. Shaped into two arcs, one on each side and blond like his short hair. Behind him sat a blonde, somewhat plump, lady in front of a screen.

'And this is . . . ?'

Frank took a step towards her with his arm held out. She stood up so quickly her chair was sent flying. Curtsied in a flurry of confusion. Her hand was as limp as a rubber glove and hung in mid-air when he released it.

'Lisa Stenersen.'

The name was delivered at second attempt after a nervous cough. Broad, flat shoes made her seem tubby, short. But her beautiful blonde hair was a perfect frame for round cheeks and a double chin.

Frank Frølich turned back and noticed a tiny ring in the weightlifter's left ear.

Silence.

'Well?'

Bregård rocked on his feet to and fro, not at ease.

'Perhaps we should find somewhere to talk,' Frank obligingly suggested.

The Finance Manager nodded and led the way to a door at the other end of the room.

The man's office was sparsely furnished. A desk, and not much more. But the chair that accompanied it was a classic. Velour material, head rest and an inbuilt tilting mechanism. A chair that was ideal for planning the year's fly-fishing, for tipping back and putting your feet on the desk. Otherwise there was nothing apart from a wobbly stool which the policeman placed by the wall to have something to lean against. Pink walls. Decorated with advertisements for computer equipment. Pretty glossy stuff. A babe, full-length, pulling on fishnet stockings and supporting her legs on a computer. Unusually attractive legs. And unusually thick hair on her head.

Bregård sat down in the swivel chair. Now wearing narrow, rectangular rimless glasses.

Frank tore his eyes away from the fishnet thighs. 'This is about, as I'm sure you know . . .'

'Reidun,' Bregård interrupted with several nods. 'I've understood as much.'

Frank smiled. Jotted down 'ASSHOLE' in capital letters on his notepad and went on to draw Kilroy behind a wooden fence.

'Reidun Rosendal was employed as a saleswoman?'

Bregård nodded.

'From what I've been told, you sell computer technology?'

'Administrative systems, office solutions.'

The man pulled a drawer out of his desk and rummaged in it. 'We're about to embark on a fairly large expansion programme.'

The words tumbled out staccato as he searched through the drawer. Finally he lifted out a pile of brochures, passed it to the police officer and slammed the drawer shut. 'Reidun was part of that, too. Finding distributors and interested parties for the expansion. And of course selling standard services,' he added, folded his hands in a business-like fashion on the table in front of him.

Frank flicked aimlessly through the brochures. Colour bar graphs and fine words about profitability. The moustachioed face of the man before him smiled up at him from the glossy middle-page spread. Nice pic. The policeman compared the photograph with the man on the other side of the table. The ring in his ear was not visible in the photograph. And he was more formally dressed than in real life. The picture revealed a classic office worker in a white shirt, tie and grey jacket. The same glasses as now. The Finance Manager was giving a thumbs-up the way Allied pilots did during the Second World War. 'Trust me' the speech bubble above his head said.

'Did anyone else work in the sales department other than Reidun?'

'Svennebye, our Head of Marketing. And me.'

He opened his palms wide. 'We're a small enterprise, lots of overlapping. Engelsviken, the manager here, also does sales work if he has time.'

'How many employees are there?'

'In all, five; sorry, four. There were five of us with Reidun.'

The policeman picked up the brochures. 'So the company is planning to grow?'

'It will become very big,' Bregård corrected immodestly. 'We're in the process of acquiring new distributors all over the country in fact.'

'Anything home-grown?'

'No, we have a foreign agency.'

He tilted back in the chair. Spread his fingers and lightly tapped tips against each other. 'It's all in the name. Software Partners. The company has been built on that concept and will grow by linking up with joint venture collaborators.'

Frank nodded. 'With regard to Reidun . . .'

Bregård waited, composed.

'Do you know a restaurant called Scarlet?'

Bregård's eyes went walkabout. He leaned forwards and rested his elbows on the desk. Stroked his moustache.

'Scarlet?' Ran the name over his tongue. 'Yes . . . indeed . . . in fact I've been there.'

'Long time ago?'

'Probably a few weeks back.'

'You weren't there last Saturday?'

'No.'

'Where were you on Saturday?'

'At home.'

The detective allowed the silence to linger, then said:

'Can anyone confirm that?'

'In fact, I spent Saturday evening on my own!'

'Watching TV?'

'No.'

'There's just crap on the box, isn't there,' Frank posited, testing for a reaction. 'I never watch TV, either. I tie flies.'

The Finance Manager stared across the desk, without making a comment.

'When I tie flies I listen to the radio.' The detective scribbled on his pad. 'Lots of good music on a fair number

72

of stations. Much better than tired TV family entertainment. Don't you think?'

Indulgent smile from Bregård. 'Yes, I suppose you're right.'

'You weren't listening to the radio on Saturday by any chance, were you?'

The smile vanished. 'No, I wasn't.'

'Married?'

The man shook his head.

Frank stretched out his legs and slipped off his worn-out boots. A faint aroma of stale socks filled the room. Bregård's face went stiff. Frank followed the man's eyes and identified a hole in the toe of one sock. A bony little toe poked out, inhaling fresh air. He splayed his toes. Made a mental note that he ought to cut his toenails.

'Girlfriend?' he asked.

The man didn't understand.

Frank sighed. 'I asked if you had a girlfriend!'

'No,' he answered with irritation.

'What were you actually doing on Saturday, Bregård?'

'I was at home!'

Face of rebuttal. 'I didn't watch TV, didn't listen to the radio. I went to bed early.'

Frølich nodded.

'Went to bed early because I had to be up early on Sunday.'

The detective frowned, one raised eyebrow.

'For a long walk through the fields.'

'Isn't it too wet underfoot now?'

'It's wet, but I go anyway.'

'Alone?'

'Alone,' Bregård stated with a nod.

'Often?'

'Yes, often.'

Frank eyed him. *Tanned features. Muscles. Wouldn't be unusual to meet this guy in the forest. Not at all. Just a change of clothes. A thick jumper instead of the white cotton shirt, green walking trousers instead of fashionable jeans. Walking boots and thick socks. Yep, the guy probably was the outdoor type. Whether he had been hiking on the Sunday morning in question was quite another matter.* Frank decided to change the topic:

'Did you know her well? Reidun, that is.'

Bregård hummed and hawed.

'You worked together for six months,' Frølich pressed. 'Did you get to know her?'

'A bit.'

The guy was in two minds about something.

'I'm sorry,' he said, heaving a resigned sigh. Fidgeted uneasily and placed his hands on the desk. 'This is too awful!'

He got to his feet, walked over to the window and stared out. Broad shoulders, slim waist and unusually powerful thighs.

'On Friday she was here with us!'

He said something else that was drowned in an intense grimace. His facial expression was reminiscent of a character from a TV drama. Hands clenching and unclenching in an over-animated fashion. Emotional toss of his head at the same time. There was something over the top about all of this. Something feigned that was uncomfortable to watch.

'When did you see her last?'

'Friday afternoon. I invited her out, but there must have been a problem.'

The detective waited. But the man was keeping the rest to himself.

'So you two had been out together before?'

'On occasion.'

'Were you a couple?'

'A couple?'

The guy turned, scented something. Frank took a deep breath and returned a cold stare. 'Have you been with her?'

'What do you mean?'

'Have you been to bed with her, shall we say?'

The man returned to his chair and sat down. Surly now. 'Yes, I have slept with her.'

Dismissive expression.

'Did you often sleep with her?'

'You've got what you wanted now, for Christ's sake! Do you want to know how long we were at it as well?'

Love and Geography, Frank thought. The Bjørnstjerne Bjørnson play in which a man is forever fussing around and yelling about his maps while neglecting his family.

'Was it a relationship?' he asked in a friendly tone.

'No! We were not in a relationship.'

'So it's a while since you last slept together?'

Bregård didn't answer.

'Or could you just ring and order a quickie when it was convenient?'

Bregård slowly removed his glasses. His fingers were not trembling. But he looked daggers across the table. 'You can count yourself lucky you're here on official business. Otherwise I would . . .'

'Oh, right!'

Frank shrugged his comment aside and lifted his notepad to remind the man what they were doing. He went on: 'When you asked if she wanted to join you on Friday, and she turned you down, do you think she had another date?'

'You mean, was there someone else?'

He had calmed down. Swivelled round on the chair and stared thoughtfully at the wall where the woman with the hair was still trying to roll up her fishnet stockings. She was standing with her back half turned to the camera. And a silver tanga up her ass like a thread. The head with all that hair faced the photographer and she was pursing her lips into a kiss.

Bregård had fallen into a reverie. 'No,' he said at length. 'She didn't have another date.'

The detective held his gaze. 'In other words, she was keeping you at a distance?'

Bregård formed his mouth into a resigned smile. Didn't answer.

'What was she like?'

The smile dissolved. His eyes were two black dots.

'You mean, was she hot?'

The detective paused, waited. The idiot wasn't finished

yet. His face was agitated. He gripped the desk with white knuckles.

'She liked it from behind,' he hissed. 'Why don't you take a wander down to the red-light area and buy yourself a bit of skirt? That would be a lot better than taking notes on what others get up to!'

Frank felt his lips moving into a patient smile. 'When Reidun Rosendal was not being taken from behind, or the front, but was working here with you, what did she like? What was she like as a person?'

'Clothes,' the man suggested mechanically. The outburst was over. Bregård was caught in the same melancholy as a moment before. He stared dreamily into middle distance again. 'I think she loved clothes . . . and her dog. Of course she couldn't keep it in her bed-sit, so it was at her mother's place, in Vestland. By the way, she always talked about her home area, the south-west coast.'

'Wasn't she happy in Oslo?'

'I think she was happy enough. It was just the way she was.'

He snapped his fingers to find a suitable description. 'She was . . . herself!'

He was satisfied. 'She was herself,' he repeated with a nod.

'You said she loved clothes, what was her style?'

'No special style.'

He breathed in. 'All-rounder. If you get my drift. She could wear anything. One day she looked like a schoolgirl, the next she wiggled her hips like a jailbird's dream. She . . . I suppose that was what made her a bit special, maybe.'

Jailbird, he jotted that down and looked up. 'Yes?'

Bregård was gazing into space. No more putting on an act. 'She was . . . no,' he broke off. 'It just sounds so flat in retrospect.'

Frank Frølich waited, but the man had dried up. His profile was pale and somewhat featureless. One of the bristles in his moustache had dislodged itself and was wedged between his lips, which were thin and bloodless.

'Who did she have most contact with here?'

'Sonja.'

The man with the moustache swivelled back and gave a resigned sigh. 'Sonja Hager. She'll be here soon.'

Frank pulled his boots back on. Taking his time. Tying them up, tight. Stood up. Bregård was still seated and rocking his chair. His mind elsewhere. Frank left. Turned in the doorway. Bregård was absentmindedly rolling a biro between his fingers.

'If you should think of something that might be helpful,' the detective said in a friendly tone of voice, 'get in touch with us.'

He didn't wait for an answer, just about-faced and went back to the large room with the lift doors.

10

Lisa Stenersen's face was smooth and girlish. Nevertheless, now that she was wearing her outdoor clothes, her age came clearly to the fore. She had thrown a padded cloak over her shoulders. That, and two flat, slipper-like shoes, made her look like a revue act. All that was missing was a flower in her hat. She seemed shy now. Glanced nervously at her watch as soon as he appeared. An anxious smile on her face as she fidgeted with a piece of paper.

'Is this an inconvenient moment?' he asked, to be obliging.

She blushed. 'Not at all!'

Ran her eyes down her clothes, bewildered, down the cloak, and her face went even redder.

At that moment the telephone rang. She hurried over to one of the desks in the middle of the room. Grabbed the receiver while Frank sprawled on the sofa immediately behind her. Gazing at the window to study her reflection there.

'No, I'm afraid he hasn't been in today,' she said formally and was about to ring off. But she didn't get that far.

'What's that?' she exclaimed in a loud falsetto voice, suddenly engaged, pacing up and down, ill at ease as there wasn't a chair close by. 'Yes, I see, yes, of course.'

At the start of the conversation the well-rehearsed

phrases streamed out in a relatively sincere way. However, the sincerity waned as time passed. And the more she writhed, the clearer it became that she was having difficulty bringing the exchange to a close.

After finally cradling the receiver, still disconcerted, she stood biting a nail and convulsively clenching her other hand. It looked as if she had a problem.

'You're going to be late after all,' Frank remarked.

She released the nail, and chewed her lower lip instead. 'I suppose I will.'

'Who were you talking to?' he asked, feeling no shame at exhibiting his curiosity.

'Egil Svennebye's wife. He's the Marketing Manager here.'

She perched stiffly on the edge of the seat some way from him.

'She's worried. It seems he didn't go home last night. She claims he's gone missing.'

Eyes downcast, she smiled. Frank Frølich waited for her to look at him. 'Has she reported it to the police?'

Lisa shrugged her shoulders. 'I don't suppose she wants to get the police involved.'

'But she did sound pretty alarmed, didn't she?'

'She was alarmed, yes,' Lisa confirmed, lost in thought. 'Perhaps you could talk to her?'

Frank met her eyes. 'We can't do much unless she wants us to.'

'But it might calm her nerves,' Lisa countered with optimism. The paper she had been fidgeting with was crushed into a tiny ball in one hand. 'She seemed . . . frightened!'

Frank nodded. 'Of course we would very much like a chat with her husband as he works here,' he said reassuringly. 'So I can pop by his house, can't I.'

She brightened up a bit.

Frank hastened to change the topic. 'You used to work with Reidun Rosendal, didn't you?'

The woman threw a swift glance at her watch. 'Not so much. Reidun was out a lot, visiting customers. I deal mostly with correspondence and so on.'

'But you got to know her a little?'

'Yes, I did.'

She shuddered. Pinched her eyes shut. 'Was . . . was she tortured?' she asked, full of apprehension.

Frank looked her in the face. 'We don't know.'

Lisa Stenersen folded her hands in her lap, mumbled something with her eyes closed. A gold crucifix hung from a chain against her throat.

'She was great,' she said in the end.

'You mean attractive?'

'Mm, lovely hair, nice figure . . .'

Frank lifted a finger and tapped his temple.

'What about here?'

'Don't know.' Lisa Stenersen smiled. 'Doubt if she was lacking in that department either, but . . . she hid.'

The woman in the padded cloak stared at the floor. 'There are some people you can never quite fathom, or so it seems!'

With more emotion: 'Who look at you the way people on TV look at you. What they say is clear enough but you never know if it's you they are addressing.'

Frank nodded slowly. Lisa Stenersen could have been a member of his mother's sewing circle. So, it was easy to imagine how Reidun's words had fallen on stony ground whenever she spoke to her.

He observed her big hair, registered the roll of women's magazines beside the brown handbag on her desk. The wedding ring that had become buried in the flesh of her ruddy finger. Lisa Stenersen, a representative of the silent army that knows all about meringues, birthday cakes, England's dismal royal family and how to grow Christmas begonias from cuttings. An age gap of at least thirty years from Reidun Rosendal. A gap that did not necessarily mean much in some cases, but did bear some significance here.

Lisa Stenersen squirmed under his gaze and looked away.

'That would suggest she wasn't that stupid,' he ventured.

She paused.

'Did she have lots of suitors?'

'Don't know. There was no talk of a steady boyfriend at any rate. She and Bregård used to josh around. But that was the tone with her, if you see what I mean. Reidun was probably used to a bit of all sorts, flirting and so on.'

The latter was followed by bashful laughter. She added: 'There was always a frivolous atmosphere around her.'

'You two were not very close then?'

'No, we weren't.'

'Do you know who she was closest to here?'

'Kristin Sommerstedt.'

'She doesn't work with us,' she added with alacrity. 'But I'm sure you saw her in reception.'

He remembered the receptionist with the birthmark under her lip.

'I think they had a lot in common,' she said and peeped at her watch again. 'Do you think . . . ?'

'Yes, no problem at all,' he assured her amiably. 'That's fine. We'll be in contact if there is anything.'

'I'm happy to go to the police station,' she declared, grabbing the roll of magazines and her handbag from the desk. Glanced at her watch. 'It's just that I . . .'

'No problem at all,' Frank repeated patiently, accompanying her to the lift. 'Aren't you coming . . . ?' she asked, at sixes and sevens when he made no attempt to join her.

He didn't answer. Just gave a reassuring smile and let the doors close behind her.

11

Frank walked slowly around the room. A frugally furnished office. Desk and various items of office equipment. Just one niche for meetings, two sofas and a couple of good chairs assembled around a table, broke the impression of workplace. Quite a large archive partition closed off the meeting area.

He took his time. Studied the brochures in the wall-mounted displays. Read the titles of the literature on the various shelves. Went over to the filing cabinet and tried a drawer. It was locked. Frank frowned. Tried another. Locked. All the drawers were locked. He examined the lock. It was new. Along the cracks between the metal and the drawers he could see marks. The drawers had been forced and someone had changed the lock. *Why would anyone go to the trouble of locking up this filing cabinet? Five employees in a tiny company. Didn't they trust one another?*

The light from the windows fell on two other desks. On one there was a white strip of paper taped to the side of the telephone. Reidun Rosendal's. Her name in neat blue writing. Small flattened loops between the curves. Her place, he thought, and sat down. Opened the drawers. Examined them without finding anything of interest. They were empty. No engagement diary. No personal papers. Just loose pens, a coloured ribbon for a printer and some files. An empty

Coke bottle rolling around in the bottom drawer when he opened it. On top, under glass, a passport-size photograph. He lifted the sheet of glass, coaxed the picture out and studied it. Black and white photograph. Face in half-profile. A blonde leaning back, tossing her hair while looking in the mirror. Self-satisfied expression. A woman who liked what she saw in the mirror. But she was young.

He placed the photograph on the desktop. How old was it? It had been taken in a machine and he thought he detected a haze over her eyes. Bit tipsy perhaps. Permed curls and long hair. The girl he had seen dead on the floor had had spiky, relatively short hair. So the picture was not the latest.

She liked it from behind, Bregård had said. Frank discovered something he had not seen in that transparent dead face of hers. Something the photograph had succeeded in catching. Something special about the mouth, about the lips. It was this combination. The mouth, the eyes and teeth that made her face sensual.

Whoever adopted Bregård's approach did not know what they were missing, Frank thought, putting the photo in his inside pocket.

At that moment the lift hydraulics sounded. The lift stopped on his floor and a woman emerged.

12

A woman, also in her best years. Attractive full lips and discreet make-up. An elegant shoulder bag banged against her hip as she panted along, laden with her shopping, before she collapsed in an office chair and noticed the policeman, who got to his feet. Then she stood up and swayed over to him while removing a pair of black leather gloves. Hands: slim, elegant, not too much gold. The metal was limited to a row of thin bracelets that jangled as he shook her hand. It was dry and nice to hold.

'Morning,' she said. 'I'm Sonja Hager.'

With her she brought a breath of fresh air from outside. Stared him in the eye with a curious little smile as he introduced himself.

'Then we've already spoken to each other,' she exclaimed in recognition, and continued in a hushed tone:

'It was a terrible shock. It's one thing having a person you see so much of die and quite another to hear she has been killed in such an awful manner.'

She turned and hung up the furry animals she was wearing on a small hook behind the lift doors. Then she appeared in lady-like culottes and a flowery waistcoat over a loose blouse. Dark, thick hair in free fall over her shoulders.

An affluent lady. Someone who drove an expensive car and almost certainly collected Royal Danish porcelain.

'Some men should be castrated, that's my opinion,' she opined airily, adjusting her blouse.

Frank observed two chains around her neck. A short one in gold and a longer one with the pendant hidden, along with her breasts which rippled somewhere beneath her clothes.

'It has not yet been established whether she was sexually molested or not.'

'But it's patently obvious she was!'

She burrowed in a cabinet drawer and pulled out a packet of biscuits which she waved around. 'Would you like a cup of coffee?'

'Please.'

She was already by the telephone, dialling a short number and speaking.

'It's better like that,' she told him afterwards. 'I wouldn't like to be interrogated in the canteen.'

'This is not an interrogation.'

'Call it what you will.'

She took a seat on the sofa on the opposite side of the table. 'We owe it to Reidun to help so that you can apprehend whoever took her life.'

Frank lifted his notepad with an apologetic expression.

'How well did you know her?'

'Barely at all. She was new here, wasn't she. But very . . .'

She searched for the word. For a moment she seemed absent.

'Positive,' she concluded after a spell of gazing inward.

'We communicated well,' she added. 'An intelligent girl able to conduct herself would have friends everywhere. But there was nothing of any depth between us.'

Frank nodded. There was probably quite some distance between the bed-sit in Grünerløkka and the palace where this woman resided.

'Definitely a good sales person,' she stated.

They were interrupted by a middle-aged lady carrying two cups of coffee on a tray, which she placed on a box by the door. Sonja got up to bring the tray over. Flicked her curls into place before swaying back. Sat down, crossed one leg over the other and tore a little hole in a cardboard carton of cream.

Frank refused politely – he drank his coffee black – sipped warily at the cup and asked: 'A good sales person in what way?'

'In what way are people supposed to be good at sales?'

No flies on this lady. Answers questions with a question. 'Well . . .'

He dragged out his pause.

'Slick,' she suggested with the same unchanging smile. 'Sales staff are slick, slippery and it's never easy to know where you are with them.'

Was she telling him something? He couldn't quite get a handle on her smile. It was a bit too set. And at the back of her eyes there were two piercing arrows.

'Did Reidun Rosendal have such attributes?'

'Reidun was intelligent, attractive and . . . young.'

'Did she have any enemies here in the building?' he asked calmly.

'Far from it.'

'Was there anyone she was particularly fond of?'

Sonja swallowed a mouthful of coffee. 'No.'

Frank made a note before continuing: 'Bregård said he was in a relationship with her.'

'He said *what*?'

She stared down into her coffee cup.

'Well, that was the impression I was given.'

'Which impression?'

The reaction was a second too fast. The smile designed to take the edge off the question too rigid. Her lips quivered. Out of control.

Frank concentrated. Leaned forward and poured a bit of cream in his coffee as well, to gain time.

Thereafter he fixed his gaze on a point diagonally above her so as not to ruin whatever had caused the air to go electric. Forced an awkward smile. 'Nowadays a relationship can mean anything from an engagement to . . .'

That was as far as he got.

She interrupted him with distended lips. '. . . a bonk, as some are wont to call it.'

Intense eyes. Taut jaw muscles in two unbecoming knots. As though someone were standing behind her pulling wire fastened to the corners of her mouth.

His eyes met hers. She didn't appear to notice. Her voice carried towards him from afar, as though she were sitting in a boat on calm waters talking to someone he could not see:

'As is well-known, some women choose to allow them-selves to be used like rags.'

A bubble had burst. For a brief second she stared down into her cup. On raising her eyes again, she was as before. Controlled. Proper. Breasts camouflaged in a loose-fitting blouse. Long, slim legs under shapeless culottes, and her face made up in a cultivated manner to emphasize person-ality.

'It's been a few years since we burned pornographic magazines in the streets.'

Ironic smile.

Frank played along. Returned the smile. Led her off on a tangent, turned his head away, stared out of the window for a few seconds. She took the bait. He could feel her eyes on him, scrutinizing him. He looked back. 'I apologize if I've been clumsy, but I honestly didn't know that you and Bregård . . .'

'That's not how it is, though!'

She laughed, her mouth open wide. When she laughed she was good-looking. Good-looking and proper.

'Goodness me! Am I so easily misunderstood?'

Not at all, he had not misunderstood anything. But there was something here, something he hadn't grasped, but which he assumed was lying on the desk in front of him, gift-wrapped, he just couldn't see it.

'I run this business with my husband. He's the Managing Director here.'

Frank peeped down at his notes. 'I thought for a moment

I had been tactless,' he lied with a prepared smile for the exuberant woman who had taken up residence in her eyes.

She took the bait again. Billowing ripple under the blouse, slight flush of the cheeks.

'So Terje Engelsviken's your husband?'

She nodded tentatively. 'My point is merely that . . .'

She cut herself off in mid-flow. Wrinkled her nose in contempt and looked down in her cup. 'It makes me so angry! Things happen too easily! It's not right that everything should revolve around sex!'

'There is something called love,' he ventured gently.

She raised her head, cautious. 'Maybe', she assented. 'But what is it, love, I mean?'

Sticky question. 'Well, I'm not exactly a great philosopher.'

'But is it philosophy?'

Clearly, this was a matter that preoccupied her. Serious, carefully considered thought was engraved in her features. 'Human relationships,' she mused. 'If two people find each other and build up an existence together, what is it all based upon?'

Sticky one, thought Frank, toffee paper sticking to your fingers.

'Love,' he suggested to evade the issue.

Smile came back. Patronizing. From somewhere high up, on a pedestal. Staring down at him, faraway look. 'Love is a fickle term.'

Didactic tone. Her eyes said: make allowances for him. They were solicitous towards the idiot on the other side of the desk. She was weighing her words now, frightened that he wouldn't be able to follow, the dim-wit.

'Fickleness is unable to support anything at all. Certainly not anything as constant as two people's shared life.'

Frank sighed, stirred his coffee and tentatively cleared his throat.

'Shared life?'

'Has it never occurred to you that a vow for some people is serious,' she harangued. Her taut bloodless lips quivered in her face. Frank spilt coffee on himself. Snatched a serviette from the tray and wiped off the worst. But she was oblivious.

Bent forwards. Fingers as white and trembling as her top lip. 'For better, for worse, for richer, for poorer, in sickness and in health. What does it mean?'

'For ever,' he suggested.

The answer appeared to be correct. She composed herself. Not another word.

'So it has come as a surprise to you that Bregård and Reidun had contact outside working hours?'

She didn't answer. Just sat staring into the distance. Frank was unsure whether she had heard the question. He coughed.

'She was thinking only of herself,' she said all of a sudden.

Frank gawped.

'Please don't take that amiss! It's just that the word *relationship* does not make sense. I would guess they were drawn to each other, but ...'

He nodded. 'They were two ... good-looking, young people who found each other?'

She breathed in. Her voice a touch frosty. 'I assume it can be expressed in that way.'

There it was again. I suppose they should have got married first, should they, he thought sarcastically, and made so bold: 'You mean they coupled?'

Calm hands. Vacant, dead eyes. The hand put down the cup without a clink.

Game over.

He leaned back in his chair. Absorbed her. Her beautiful face, closed and impregnable, professional, behind an invisible glass wall.

Frank Frølich was in no hurry. He flicked through his notes without urgency. 'I've spoken to Lisa Stenersen and Bregård.'

Cool nod.

'What sort of loss will Reidun Rosendal be for the company?'

'Marginal.'

He inclined his head. 'Marginal?'

'As soon as we heard about it we had a meeting. Terje has already found a solution.'

Terje, husband, Managing Director. 'I haven't seen Terje yet.'

Another cool nod. 'I'm afraid he isn't here today.'

'We'll have to save him for later.'

Nod.

'We have to trace Reidun Rosendal's last known movements. Therefore it would help me to have a register of customers or a list of clients she visited.'

She straightened her blouse. Stood up. Went over to a machine. Soon a printer was rustling. She tore off the print-out and gave it to him.

The police officer took his leave.

Downstairs, the receptionist was nowhere to be seen. Lisa had said this Kristin Sommerstedt knew the dead girl. Frank glanced at his watch and decided to leave talking to Reidun's friend until later.

So he went out, opened the car door and turned to look at the building he had left. Glass upon glass. Transparent in places. As shiny and impenetrable as metal in others. To hell with them, he thought, getting in the car. What a bunch!

13

The police station door had just shut behind him when he pulled up and turned. Too late. He had been seen. The face of the woman from the temping agency had already lit up. Her stout body undulated towards him.

'Ha, ha. Hi, Frank!'

A bowl of jelly fleeing a children's party, he thought and braced himself. Again he was amazed by this combination of large torso and tiny head. Mauve punky hair up top and slender stiletto heels down below. She waved. Black leggings at bursting point over the stomach. Her whole body pitched and rolled.

'I've been fussing around here for hours on end, worse than a broody hen!'

Between his eyes, he felt his patience being tested.

'And there you are! Just as I've forgotten what it was I wanted to ask you!'

She burst into loud laughter, grabbed his arm and pulled him towards the stairs while stealing furtive glances around her. He tried to free himself but without success. Yawing flesh rubbed against his shoulders and hips.

'It's about that letter you asked me to write to the police officer in the provinces!'

She thrust a few papers into his face, obscuring his view

of the staircase. Someone was coming down and Frank had to squeeze sideways and restrain her on the step below him.

'Ooh!' she exclaimed. 'Let's get physical!'

He continued and tried to put some distance between them. But she followed him up the stairs and down the corridor. Panting two paces behind him. Waving the paper in front of her and speaking while pointing to a word that was misspelt. He grabbed the door handle of his office and turned. 'Absolutely fine,' he bowed. 'Write it your way, no problem.'

The plate of jelly slopped to a standstill. Hands on her hips. 'Do you know what your boss said to me?'

She nodded towards the office door behind his back.

Whatever he said, it can't have been bad enough, Frank thought, and let her steam ahead, glance to both sides, lean back and demonstratively button her mouth as two uniformed officers passed. 'He told me to go to . . .'

She paused for two seconds. 'Hell,' she mouthed. Peering conspiratorially to both sides again.

'I didn't answer,' she assured him. 'But he'll eat his words, mark you me!'

Frank, thinking the suggestion was not a bad one, blinked with heavy eyelids. 'I'm sure you misheard,' he said diplomatically.

'Not me, no. But I know why he's like that!'

Frank could feel his curiosity aroused.

She was nodding her head, in earnest. 'They say he changed when he was widowed. So that's at the heart of the matter.' Head still nodding. 'He isn't getting what he needs, you know! Hasn't done for several years!'

'I beg your pardon?'

'Beg's the word. Begging for it, he is.'

She spun on her thin stiletto heels and the rolls of fat set off a new wave. 'Chance'd be a fine thing though! Ha, ha!'

The next moment she stormed down the corridor. Her backside juddered with each stomp of her calves.

All of a sudden she came to a halt. Turned round. 'Au revoir, *chéri!*'

And rounded the corner.

'Schwenke rang,' Gunnarstranda's voice resounded as he opened the door. A cigarette bobbed up and down in his mouth. Frank slumped on a tatty blue swivel chair and blew out his cheeks.

'Don't be so hard on the clerical staff,' he said.

'Fatty?'

Gunnarstranda rubbed his nose and dropped the cigarette in a faded red ashtray bearing the scarcely legible word *Cinzano* in peeling white letters. He chewed his biro and mumbled. 'She'll have to learn to knock before trampling down people's doors!' And then: 'Tottenham at home to Leeds?'

'Away team wins,' Frank said, switching on the computer.

Gunnarstranda did not agree. 'Isn't there a Norwegian between the sticks at Tottenham?'

'Go for a draw then.'

A few taps on the keyboard. Soon the blue screen came up.

'Executioner have anything new to say?'

'Nothing. Apart from what the girl had eaten. And we knew that anyway. Also, he reckoned he could establish death occurring at somewhere between five and eight on Sunday morning. And that was hardly news, either.'

Frank nodded slowly. Thinking to himself that this piece of information was actually very useful. Nevertheless, he knew his boss well enough to realize that the time had no doubt been underlined in thick red ink in the man's brain.

'What do you reckon about Sigurd Klavestad?' Gunnarstranda asked across the desk. 'Do you think he was telling the truth?'

'Yes.'

'Good,' Gunnarstranda said, nodding to himself as he continued to fill in the pools coupon.

Frank frowned. 'Why?'

Gunnarstranda kept writing and counted the crosses.

'Why?' Frank repeated, louder.

'I let him go,' Gunnarstranda said without looking up. 'I've put Jack Myrberget on his tail for the time being.'

The coupon was finished and he put it in the inside pocket of his suit jacket hanging over the back of the chair. Took another coupon from the pile at the bottom of the drawer. Filled out the squares without any difficulty this time.

'I've used this line of twelve numbers now for twenty-five years,' he said. 'Every week for twenty-five years. Do you know how much I've earned from it?'

'No.'

'Fifty-four kroner. Last Saturday. I got ten right.'

'Is that all you've won in twenty-five years?'

'With that line, yes. But I know it'll do the trick one day!'

'Fifty-two weeks a year. For twenty-five years. Have you ever bothered to work out how much money you've wasted?'

'Whoa there. Just imagine if I win!'

'Fifty-four kroner!'

Gunnarstranda put back the coupon. 'What did you find out about Software Partners?'

Frank swung himself round again. 'Oslo West,' he summed up. 'Nice people, every one over forty with varying risk margins. Expensive clothes, expensive place, computer technology. Five employees. I spoke to three of them. The only oddity was that they had put a new lock on their filing cabinet. A beast of a lock. I'm writing a report on it now.'

He snatched a bag from the floor. 'I was given a whole pile of glossy advertising.'

He lifted the bag of brochures. 'The outfit's small but they boast as if they were IBM. Apparently they're in a period of expansion. I didn't understand all of it, but they're going to increase their equity and get more distributors up and down the country.'

Gunnarstranda took some of the material from the bag. 'I've got some bedtime reading then,' he mumbled.

'Finance Manager,' Frank continued from the chair, 'is someone called Øyvind Bregård, an unmarried bodybuilder. Not very talkative outdoor type who claims he spends his free time hiking in the forests and fields. Admitted, after a lot of fuss, having gone to bed with Reidun, a while back. She gave him the elbow.'

'Anything there?' Gunnarstranda asked.

'Possible – he doesn't have an alibi for the Saturday. Claimed he went to bed early to go walking on the Sunday. Which he also did alone.'

The inspector nodded slowly.

'The Marketing Manager's called Svennebye. Apparently he's vanished into thin air. His wife rang and was very animated while I was there. Her husband hadn't come home from the office after news of the murder was announced. Wife hasn't seen him since.'

Gunnarstranda whistled. Fingers groped for the butt in the ashtray.

'I promised the secretary I would follow this up,' Frank said with some hesitation. 'She seems pretty run-of-the-mill. Oldest one there. Just a bit jumpy.'

He waited until the inspector had lit up.

'Then there's this other woman, Sonja Hager. I mentioned Bregård's fling with the dead girl, and she got all het up.'

'Jealous?'

'Far from it. The woman's married to Engelsviken, the MD. No, not jealous.'

He walked to the sink in the corner. Drank some water. 'But she gets pretty aerated about marriage as an institution,' he concluded. Wiped the back of his hands on his beard.

Gunnarstranda was smoking. 'Anything there?'

'Something I can't put my finger on,' Frank said, walking

back to his place. 'She thought Reidun Rosendal was using other people.'

'How so?'

Frank shrugged. 'Think it's all wrapped up with sex.'

'Using men?'

'Don't know. The woman was generally very vague.'

Gunnarstranda patted his pockets and gripped the door handle.

'You'll have to put that in your report. Take the evening off when you've finished.'

Frank sat staring at the door as it closed, then turned back to his computer. When I've finished, he thought, downhearted, and made a start.

14

Gunnarstranda parked his car at the very top of the ridge, where the gravel road stopped and widened into a turn-around. An hour and a quarter's drive from Oslo, to Hurumlandet, the peninsula to the south. If the gods were with you, that is, because the traffic lights had to be green at various strategic points and Oslo Tunnel free of congestion.

The gods weren't today. He checked his watch with a grim expression. He had been forced to stop the Skoda at least seven or eight times on the road out of Oslo. The engine had been playing up. It died if he did more than seventy. Started spluttering and coughing, and he lost speed, with the result that he had drivers up his backside angrily flashing their lights and honking their horns. Until he felt duty-bound to pull in, to park, nose pointing into the ditch, and to let the worst of the traffic drone past, nervous all the time that the car wouldn't start again. He had gone through the repertoire. Pulled out the choke, put his foot down on the accelerator, hoping that it would manage a few more kilometres until the same thing happened. A dreadful trip. But now at long last he was at his journey's end.

His annoyance at the rigours of the drive had not yet subsided. So he sat calmly looking out of the car window until the familiar feeling announced its arrival. That wonderful feeling of being at home. Private. He thought about Edel. She had managed to make a kind of garden out here. Now, since she was no longer alive, he continued where she had left off. Her whole life she had wanted a place like this and got it in the end. Gunnarstranda did what she could not. Took over. Half his life he had lived not knowing the difference between an ash leaf and a maple leaf. Now he knew a great deal more besides. And four years had passed since she died.

He as good as lived here for six months of the year, from late April till well into October. This was his private haven. Yet he was unable to see the brown pine trunk in front of his cabin without feeling a prickling up his spine. The tingling and the image of Edel in rubber boots with the woven basket over her arm, back from mushrooming. He mused on why it was always that image. Why there were no others and why he got this simultaneous tingling.

From the large pine a little path led twenty-five metres to the cabin which was concealed behind two large rocks. It was at the front that the miracle revealed itself. Spring, summer and autumn. Here she had produced whatever there was to produce in this climate. And he had maintained it. Already now, as he was unloading the files and papers from the car, a worried frown was carved into his forehead. The problem of watering during the summer. You never knew, a case like the murder of Reidun Rosendal could be a protracted affair. For the next few weeks he would not be able to live here at any rate, but what would it be like in May, when perhaps the spring drought would come?

This line of thought was interrupted by heavy steps and the crack of twigs. From the undergrowth by the road came a man dressed in a faded Icelandic sweater and raggedy trousers. Gunnarstranda recognized his neighbour Sørby, who saluted him with a hand to his forehead and a nervous smile.

Gunnarstranda mumbled something incomprehensible in response and concentrated on his luggage.

Sørby belonged to the coterie of pensioners who stuck together out here, partied, played accordion and dressed in rags. The policeman did not like him. The man was an old windbag. Talked about his kids as if he were confiding state secrets.

Gunnarstranda couldn't give a flying fart about people's children or grandchildren. Least of all those this fat bastard was responsible for begetting. Besides, he suspected that the gang of pensioners was talking behind his back at accordion evenings.

Inasmuch as Sørby considered it appropriate to stand there, irresolute and docile, the man could not be on an honest errand.

Gunnarstranda squinted with distaste in the man's direction. Wondered what the fat scarecrow had been doing in the area. Snooping probably. Him and the others.

United, they were such a powerful force. Until they sneaked up one after the other to ask about cuttings and roots. The ones who didn't dare went nosing around when the 'cop' was in Oslo. Gunnarstranda always found evidence of their movements afterwards. Later there were often a few new stalks among the trees by Sørby's plot, before they all died. For neither the wife nor the idiot himself knew what a spade was, or manure, or lime, or anything.

'That's looking good,' the pensioner fawned, waggling his head towards what was visible of a planned extension to the cabin.

Gunnarstranda shrugged and lifted a bag in each hand.

'Cost a bit, won't it?' Fatso chatted.

'It will indeed. A bloody packet. You wouldn't be able to afford it.'

Don't think you're used to being insulted, Gunnarstranda thought, revelling for a moment in the sight of the other man's fallen face before curtly bidding him goodbye and turning his back.

Afterwards he walked along the mountain looking at the tendrils lying across the cliff face, checking the buds and stems. Went on towards the west of the cabin where a five-by-one-metre hole had been scraped out down to the rock, away from the wall, and a line of poles had been cemented in. The footprints from Sørby's tramping around were clearly visible in the wet gravel. Good thing I haven't bought the materials yet, he thought. So the man won't be tempted. Anyway, there won't be time for any building for a while.

He straightened the plastic sheet covering the small cement mixer and walked back. Lit a cigarette on the stool in front of the outside fireplace.

Edel had been the one to attend to social matters. As for him, he met enough people in the course of his job. Too many to waste his free time chatting. Edel would certainly have taken pity on Fatso in the raggedy trousers. Would probably have strolled down to his place with plants and handy tips. Although the advice would have been a waste of breath, anyway.

The air was still. But then you were shielded from the wind up here. It could come only from the south, and that was rare. The lake in the valley lay smooth and shiny and emphasized the silence with its reflections of the bare trees. He stood up. The characteristic squeal of the telephone penetrated the timber walls.

It was Jack Myrberget. Sigurd Klavestad's travelling companion.

Jack, as was his wont, did not beat about the bush:

'Sigurd Klavestad is not on his own any more.'

'Mhm,' grunted Gunnarstranda. He had settled down on the sofa and put his feet on the table; he was relaxed and waiting. It was dark indoors, and outside the dusk was not even capable of bringing a shine to his shoes.

'He caught the bus along Drammensveien and got off at Vækerø. Ambled over to some building called Rent-An-Office. Lots of small businesses.'

'Names?'

'Didn't the woman work for a computer company?'

'Software Partners they call themselves.'

'That's where they are.'

Gunnarstranda gripped the receiver harder. 'More!'

'He went in at three and came out at half past. Together with a woman. About thirty, dressed like an office worker, long dark hair, one seventy tall, nice-looking, black birth-mark between her mouth and chin.'

'And then?'

'I'm looking straight at them now. They're sitting and drinking wine across the street. Fingers interlaced, occasional floods of tears. What do I do if they go separate ways?'

Gunnarstranda deliberated. 'Follow the male,' he decided at length. 'But keep me posted.'

That's it, he thought, putting down the receiver. *Sodding car. It would have to give up the ghost today of all days!*

15

Frank yawned. It was morning. Somewhere between six and half past. Weather grey and cold. The damp mist engulfed houses, trees and cars. The moisture in the air could be morning mist and could be more stubborn fog. Too early to tell as yet. It could be a nice, mild day or downcast and rainy.

Two lines of cars were parked bumper to bumper across the street. It was so early there were few gaps. Most people were sitting at the breakfast table with newspapers spread out and drinking coffee.

The thought of coffee depressed him. No breakfast, no coffee, no shops open anywhere and probably hours of futile waiting on the horizon.

Gunnarstranda had woken him with a telephone call three-quarters of an hour ago. Ordered him up to Lambertseter pronto! Not by car. That was why he was walking along Mellombølgen to locate his boss's position. He was tired. Never got enough sleep. Which, in fact, often affected him until about mid-morning.

Further down the street he could see small smoke clouds escaping from the window of a dark civilian car parked untidily and protruding half a metre into the carriageway. The windows were steamed up and tiny wisps of bluish-white smoke rose skywards. Gunnarstranda had left a crack open. Frank opened the passenger door and stepped in.

'I haven't had any breakfast yet,' he grumbled in an accusatory tone. No greeting.

'Here you are,' said Gunnarstranda, passing him an old-fashioned, shiny Thermos flask. Frank twisted the cap, which sprang open with a pop. And the wonderful aroma of strong, black coffee filled the car. He took a yellow plastic cup with a grubby rim from the dashboard and poured.

'You haven't eaten. I haven't slept.'

Gunnarstranda stubbed out the cigarette in the overfilled ashtray.

'I'll give them twenty minutes, then I'm going in.'

He looked at his watch. Then focused on the middle entrance in a low block ahead of them. A flagstone path stretched twenty metres from the pavement to the entrance. Three entrances to the block in all. The greeny-brown spikes of some large berberis bushes partially concealed the doors. Along the three sections ran parallel lines of verandas. All with raised awnings in a loud yellow colour.

'Who are we waiting for?' Frank asked.

'The man. Sigurd Klavestad primarily, and a woman.'

Gunnarstranda's eyes did not deviate from the front door. 'Jack rang me at half past ten last night, at my cabin! He refused to take responsibility since the man had a woman with him, so I had to come back here. It took me three hours to get to Grønland to change the car. There's something up with the Skoda; it keeps misfiring and dying on me.'

He paused, flicked some ash from the cigarette and continued:

'So I've been sitting here alone all night ensuring that the woman up there is still alive. You don't know a cheap car mechanic, do you, by any chance?'

Frank spared his boss one of the many jokes about Skodas. 'I know of a guy in Kampen,' he said blowing on the coffee and slurping a sip straight afterwards. 'Lives in a collective with a girl I know. Works freelance.'

'No questions asked, know what I mean?'

Frank dismissed his boss's sarcastic tone with a shrug. 'You asked if I knew someone cheap.'

The man at the wheel stroked his chin with a rasp; patchy bristles scraped against his palm. 'Klavestad left the Software Partners building at half past three. With this woman, Kristin Sommerstedt.'

Frank carefully rotated his head. A bit more awake. Remembered her. The long hair and the office outfit, the receptionist.

Gunnarstranda tossed his head. 'That's her flat.'

'Kristin Sommerstedt was supposed to have been friends with Reidun Rosendal.'

'Is that so? Well, they caught the local train to the National Theatre. Went to the restaurant and sat drinking wine for a couple of hours, knocked back quite a bit. Spent most of the time crying and intertwining fingers. Afterwards walked round Aker Brygge, nipped up into town and down to the underground, came here half past seven last night, switched off the light at eleven and that was when Jack phoned me.'

They both stared at the broad, brown front door.

'The man's probably been dipping his wick while I've got one hell of a headache and I'm in a bad mood.'

Gunnarstranda yawned and banged his hands on the wheel.

Frank poured more coffee. Watched his boss check his watch.

'At a quarter to we're going in,' Gunnarstranda repeated, licking his lips. His eyes were red-rimmed.

The door opened. They gave a start, but then relaxed. An unknown man in a brown jacket with cropped hair walked on to the pavement. Unlocked the Opel in front of them.

Gunnarstranda twisted his watch strap as the car drove off.

'They may have decided to have a lie-in,' Frank said in consolation. Feeling the coffee had lit a spark of life somewhere behind his eyes.

'It's only half an hour since the light came on up there, in one window.'

Yet again the door opened. A middle-aged lady stood for a second under the little porch and took a deep breath. Slowly put on a pair of gloves and walked calmly down the road towards the underground.

The windows misted up. It had been bad before, but now it was worse because of the steam from the coffee in the yellow cup. Frank pulled the sleeve of his sweater over his hand and rubbed away the condensation.

This time. The door opened again and Sigurd Klavestad stood there alone. Gunnarstranda already had his mobile phone at the ready, tapped in a number without taking his eyes off the young man on the flagstone.

Sigurd Klavestad was paler than before. The area around his eyes had gone an unhealthy dark colour. This contrasted with his white complexion and gave his face a concave appearance. His long hair was still collected in a pony tail.

Frank heard the mobile phone struggling to find a connection. At last! It rang. The man with the pony tail moved slowly down the road. Calmly, without any undue haste. No one picked up. Frank opened the car door a crack. The phone was still ringing.

'Hello?'

A sleepy woman's gentle voice could now be heard from the inspector's hand. She was alive.

Gunnarstranda carefully rang off. Sigurd Klavestad was quite some way down the street now.

'See you!' Frank said briefly and hauled himself out of the narrow seat and was gone.

16

Gunnarstranda sat staring after them. The mist had lifted enough for Klavestad to be still visible. A slightly built young man in a black reefer jacket with a stiff, somewhat awkward gait. Frølich a way behind. Large, legs astride, rolling gait with both hands in his jacket pockets.

Soon Klavestad was carried along in the stream of passengers hurrying towards the underground. And when the long red worm of a train finally pulled into the station not even Frølich's big body could be distinguished from the others in the throng.

Gunnarstranda waited. The train would have left by now. He got out of the car, went to the front door and up the stairs.

When he rang her doorbell nothing happened. The anger rose to his temples. The exhaustion after hours without sleep provoked him into a terrible rage which he took out on the bell. The bell ding-donged like a pinball flipper. When he finally let go of the button small steps could clearly be heard from indoors.

'Open the door,' he barked with irritation, banging his fist.

'Who is it?'

The voice didn't carry well through the woodwork.

'Police! Open up!'

Again total silence. The policeman, glaring impatiently at the brown wood in front of him, sighed. Raised his hand to pound the door. Refrained. Breathed out with relief as the lock clicked and the door opened a fraction.

'What is it?'

Her face was pale and her skin twitched. The policeman brandished his ID. 'Let me in,' he barked, pushing the door open.

She stepped back, dressed in only her underwear.

'Go and get some clothes on,' he ordered and marched ahead into the flat.

His glare took in the room. Noted lots of little objects, ornaments and figurines in cases and on shelves. Subdued colours. Woven tapestries on the walls. A closed door, presumably to a bedroom. A large loom took up half the sitting room, and a sofa-bed underneath an impressively large weeping fig was unmade. The air was quite stale. The room had obviously been slept in.

She came in, having pulled on some jeans and a short-sleeved jersey, still barefoot but no longer confused.

'Sit down!'

She obeyed. Stared up at him in expectation, no longer afraid. Gunnarstranda's eyes bored into her.

'Who slept here?'

'A friend.'

He seized her arm. Her eyes widened.

'I'm not dangerous,' he assured her in a gentler, husky voice. The words fell on deaf ears.

His headache announced its return, worse than before. The pain made him grimace, then he asked in a gentle voice: 'How well do you know this man you had staying here last night?'

'Know?'

Jesus! He was not in the mood for this. He sat down with a bump on the unmade sofa-bed. 'Sigurd Klavestad. He was with you last night. Are you aware of his involvement in the murder of Reidun Rosendal?'

'Yes, I am.'

'How long have you known him?'

'Since yesterday.'

Good-looking girl. Tall and slim. But eyes a bit bovine. Large, brown and very moist. He remembered the chubby stomach around her navel when she jumped back from the door. Caught himself staring at the black birthmark on her face. Her lips moved. 'He needed someone to talk to. I needed someone to talk to. We . . . talked about . . . Reidun.'

Calm voice. Intense gaze, he assumed she was being honest.

Gunnarstranda bent forwards. 'We cannot rule him out as a suspect.'

She stared back, still calm. 'I know.'

'Yet you bring him back here and let him sleep over?'

'That's none of your business.'

A new gleam took its place in her cow-like expression. Now she was eyeballing him effortlessly.

Gunnarstranda chanced to observe that there were two

pillows next to each other on the sofa. Two pillows but only one duvet.

'And you had never met him before yesterday afternoon,' he remarked sarcastically.

She gave a nod of defiance and he felt his headache return.

'This guest of yours must be a Casanova.'

She held her tongue. But she was on her guard; she had picked up the intonation.

The policeman noted that he liked her decision to remain silent.

'How did you react when you saw him yesterday?'

'React?'

Gunnarstranda tightened his lips in a show of cynicism. 'It must have made some impression on you that the man who was with your deceased friend until minutes before she was murdered was suddenly standing in front of you.'

'I wasn't fazed.'

Her face was pale, expression committed. 'It was nice to be able to talk about her!'

He patted the pillow. 'You must have been very happy,' he said with a cold smile.

She was tight-lipped, but her eyes mocked him.

So that's where you are, he thought. There. In the brown eyes. Condescending disdain for his pathetic attempts to draw her out. He liked that. Liked the strength in her as she appraised him. They glared at each other. She had almost made up her mind to come clean. The pursed lips made her face very beautiful.

'I believe you,' he declared with a hand to his brow. 'Why haven't you gone to work?'

'I didn't feel like it.'

Didn't you, he thought, with a nod. 'You got on with her?'

'I was probably the person she had most in common with, yes.'

'Why were you afraid to open the door just now?'

'I thought someone was there. The telephone rang. Like at Reidun's, and then they put down the phone, and then there was a ring this morning, so early . . .'

'Like at Reidun's?'

'The phone. Sigurd told me someone called her just before he left, someone who rang off on her.'

Gunnarstranda's face went contemplative and he chewed his lower lip. 'Do you know where she lived?'

'Yes.'

'Have you ever been there?'

'Yes.'

'Did she like it there?'

'Yes and no.'

He scented something. 'What was wrong?'

She hesitated.

'Come on.'

'A guy with binoculars.'

The detective nodded. 'Older man? Neighbour?'

'Yes. An old grunter, a peeping tom, so she was forever keeping an eye on the curtains.'

Kristin Sommerstedt paused. Considered. 'I think it tormented her at first. But then she decided she would ignore it.'

'In what way?'

The woman paused again. As if the answer would be hard for him to grasp.

'Go for it,' he urged and winked at the decision-maker in her eyes.

Kristin Sommerstedt lifted her legs on to the chair and crossed them. Red toenails.

'This might sound weird. But she was so fed up with the old pig. Really pissed off.'

The woman searched for words. 'I think she decided this bastard was not going to make her live according to his rules! All the time checking the curtains and what he could see and so on. She had made up her mind to ignore him.'

'In what way?'

The woman shrugged. 'By ignoring him. Letting him peep as much as he liked, to incite him. Opening the curtains every so often. Provoking him, and it must have driven him mad, by all accounts.'

She went into herself again. 'Once he had stood up in the window and . . .'

She studied the floor. 'He had stood masturbating in the window. Reidun had taken a few clothes off . . . and then . . . well . . . opened the curtains after a while.'

Gunnarstranda nodded, his mind elsewhere.

'That was last week. He had rung her up afterwards. Threatening her and being obscene.'

'How did she take that?'

'How do you mean?'

'His call.'

'She just laughed.'

Gunnarstranda frowned, puzzled.

'She did,' the woman on the sofa assured him. 'The old boy oozed with filth. Drivelling on about how he would rape her and cut her into chunks, and he was pretty coarse. But she just laughed at it. I think it had become a kind of war. She was always in an aggressive mood when she talked about it. In fact, it was quite . . . awful.'

'How do you mean awful?'

She flung her arms in the air. 'Maybe wild is a better word. It was all a bit . . . wild listening to the latest in the peeping tom war!'

'She wasn't at all frightened?'

'Nope.'

'And this was last week?'

'Yes. I think she talked to me on Thursday. Yes, it was Thursday.' This was such crucial information that the woman must have known. He studied her features. The sensitive lips and the brown eyes.

She went on: 'We didn't talk about this a lot. But we did talk about our accommodation in general. She didn't have much room and she wanted something more spacious, there were things she wanted to do. And that was when the conversation came back to the war.'

Gunnarstranda listened to Kristin Sommerstedt talking about Reidun's private war. She touched on personal development and awakening. The right to be a woman and dress how you wanted, to live your own life even though you had an old pig living in the adjacent block. 'In a way she felt affronted!'

Kristin Sommerstedt's brown eyes flashed with emotion. 'Affronted by not being allowed to live her life in peace.'

Gunnarstranda nodded. He tried to imagine a long-limbed buxom blonde struggling to rid herself of Arvid Johansen's harassment by opening the curtains and making love all night with this long-haired lad. Listening to her, the detective felt old. So when the woman paused, he said with a cool smile: 'She didn't get any kind of pleasure out of this, did she? It wasn't just that she liked to get the old pig going, was it?'

Her eyes met his. With undisguised disappointment.

'Is that even a remote possibility? That she would get any kind of pleasure from it?'

She stared down at the floor. Her mind boiling with anger.

He waited.

'I should have kept my mouth shut,' she burst out, getting up and pacing to and fro. This was no posturing.

He leaned back. The sofa was unpleasantly soft. It was impossible to sit there and relax. 'Calm down,' he said, clearing his throat and leaning forward. Gave a resigned sigh. 'I asked you if she got any pleasure from inciting the old pig because I consider you sharp-minded enough to answer me if this was the case. Don't trip over your bottom lip! Tell me if she was happy at work.'

Something glinted in her eyes. A connection. Ironic smile

above the birthmark. A sigh. Unarticulated 'All right then'.
She sat down.

'Did Reidun have a steady boyfriend?' he asked.

'Not that I knew of.'

He waited.

'I think there were a few who had a soft spot for her,' she
mumbled.

'But you don't know of anyone in particular?'

She replied with a shrug. 'No one I can think of.'

'She didn't talk about any other neighbours?'

Kristin pondered. 'Don't recall any.'

'A couple with a small child?'

'No.'

'No other men nearby who helped her with odd jobs,
starting the car when temperatures dropped?'

''Fraid not.'

Kristin smiled.

'Was she happy at work?'

'We-ell . . .'

She drew out the pause. 'Have you met them?' she asked

'No.'

'The boss is a bit special.'

'Engelsviken?'

She nodded. 'Over forty. Behaves like twenty-five.
Whizzes round in an open sports car, wearing a silk suit
and sunglasses. Never acknowledges you. Swears a lot and
uses loads of jargon in his speech. Tries to play the millionaire type people find exotic. But he's just a fat adolescent

fixated on tits and ass. Short chubby fingers and a smile full of teeth.'

She shuddered and her shoulders contorted. It wasn't feigned.

'His wife's just the opposite. The fine lady. Bit virtuous like girls in fairy tales. Absolutely amazing that they're married to each other.'

'Amazing?'

She bided her time. 'In fact, I don't think she's very happy,' she said in a quiet voice.

He waited. The woman stared into middle distance. 'Sonja's been through quite a bit. It can't be easy always having to clear up after that shit. Keeping a front.'

'Should they have got divorced?' Gunnarstranda asked. Adding when he saw her expression: 'Perhaps they've got kids who keep them together?'

'Don't know. I don't think they have any children.'

Kristin continued: 'Still I find it hard to imagine Sonja Hager giving up the house on the ridge. Or going out on the town alone. Or . . .'

She grinned. 'To be frank, I don't understand how she sticks it. Ask her.'

He could not sit still any longer. It was his turn to get up and pace the floor.

'The Finance Manager?'

'Hunting-mad fitness junkie.'

'Hunting-mad?'

She nodded. 'Drives round with this big box on the roof

of his car. Whole year round. Keeps a rifle in it twenty-four-seven.'

Gunnarstranda scowled.

'It's true. He's shown me. Suppose he wanted to impress me. He's like that. Shows off his muscles and boasts he sleeps under the stars. Told me he drives to the woods at night to shoot a hare or suchlike. Loves to go on about how easy it is to clean dead animals.'

'To gut.'

'What?'

'It's called gutting an animal when you remove their intestines,' Gunnarstranda said in a low, slightly remote voice. 'He likes going on about that, did you say?'

'Loves making girls recoil with horror. So that he can put his rough arms around them and let them feel his muscles.' She sneered.

'Have you often seen this rifle of his?'

'Once. But everyone knows Bregård drives around with a rifle on the roof.'

'What kind of rifle?'

'Don't know. I'm not very well up on that sort of thing.'

'How many barrels, one or two?'

'Two.'

The police officer held back, and she confirmed with a nod. 'Two,' she repeated.

Gunnarstranda stroked his chin. 'A rifle on the roof,' he muttered.

She peered up at him. 'You seem like an intelligent man,' she said, out of the blue.

He stopped. Their eyes met. This was more difficult.

Kristin Sommerstedt talked about what it was like to be a woman. Playing roles all the time. Gunnarstranda thought of the dead girl who had worked at the Post Office, on the supermarket till and selling computer equipment. *What dreadful roles had she gone around playing,* he mused with a sudden anger. Looking at the attractive woman on the sofa. Full red lips and a fascinating birthmark by her chin. Her lips spoke of what it was like to be a woman among men. Especially if you were smart. Smarter than the men. 'Reidun was smart,' she explained. 'Smarter than most. But she was never acknowledged. Reidun was one of those who adapted to circumstances. Played the dumb blonde, assumed a role, not to stand out, to be accepted.'

The detective nodded slowly. Her self-image. Important. Was Johansen's little rose a small, conceited know-it-all?

'How good was she at this role?'

'Fantastic.'

'Did she challenge those around her?'

'No, she was in total control. She did as she wanted.'

'Did she manipulate people?'

'I wouldn't use a word like that. She did as she wanted.'

'But she angered some people?'

'I didn't say that.'

'You just told me about an old pig who lost his temper.'

She didn't answer.

He tried to visualize her. Reckless. Doing a striptease for a randy old sod hiding behind binoculars.

The woman on the sofa observed him. 'Don't get me wrong,' she said. 'She wasn't like that. She could be like that.'

'Uhuh,' he answered, mind elsewhere. 'This Bregård, did he get lucky with Reidun?'

'I have absolutely no idea!'

'You weren't on intimate terms?'

'Not like that.'

'Like what?'

Kristin laughed as if she had heard a good joke. 'We didn't discuss men!'

Kristin Sommerstedt's mouth was surprisingly broad when she laughed. Her teeth were close together, pointed, with matt patches.

They sat for a while in silence and she it was who broke it eventually. 'Sometimes they went out together, the staff in her office.'

'Where to?'

'I know she mentioned it,' she mumbled.

Gunnarstranda stopped his pacing. 'It wasn't a place called Scarlet, was it?'

Kristin rolled her shoulders. 'I don't remember. We didn't talk about that kind of thing, either.'

Smile.

'Do you know the place?'

'Never been there.'

'Not that Saturday, either?'

'Of course not.'

'Where were you on Saturday?'

She met his eyes with the same smile. As if she had been

expecting the question. 'At the cinema with some good friends. Afterwards we went to Rockefeller's, at about half past eleven, I suppose. Came home at three.'

'Alone?'

'Yes. You can have a couple of phone numbers to corroborate I was at the cinema, and at Rockefeller's.'

'Fine,' he mumbled and resumed his pacing. 'Should it be necessary. By the way, what did you and Reidun talk about mostly?'

She motioned her head towards the loom. 'Weaving.'

He nodded. He didn't have a clue about textiles. 'I rang early this morning,' he said out of the ether. 'Just to check you were alive.'

Smart girl. Thirty-ish and unmarried. Must have a strong will and be very self-assured. Perhaps the same words could describe the dead woman as well. He had an inkling they could.

'Where was Klavestad going?' he asked in a friendly tone.

She shrugged. 'Work, I think. Bit down in the mouth,' she exclaimed with a concerned look in her eyes.

The detective inspector felt his headache getting worse behind his forehead.

'Goodbye,' he said without standing on ceremony, turned on his heel and left.

17

The stream of people leaving the train and making for Eger-torget in the city centre was broad and impenetrable. At the foot of the escalator it became narrower and denser. Commuters with dull eyes. The morning look. Low energy that dissipates into nothing around the head, passengers who don't look around much. Frank Frølich could see that Sigurd Klavestad was not used to taking the Metro. Country boy in town. The man stood on the left up the escalator blocking the way for those in a hurry to catch a bus. The crowd pushed from behind. A blunt fellow with a hat jostled the clod to the right. Klavestad courteously let people pass and then resumed his old position. Idiot, thought Frank Frølich.

Once outside, Sigurd stopped and looked around. In the end, he began to walk, taking long paces, down Karl Johans gate. A bouncing gait with a stiff back. A freak's walk. The policeman could not help comparing him with Finance Manager Bregård. The monkfish with thighs like logs. The Finance Manager next to Sigurd Klavestad. Moustache versus pony tail and black stubble. Frank noticed the girls turning their heads as they passed the man with the pony tail. Sigurd had an effect on women. No doubt about it. *Sensitive type. Women notice that kind of thing,* he supposed.

The guy had trotted off to Reidun's workplace to have someone to talk to. Had sat interlacing fingers with frøken Sommerstedt over a glass of red wine, shed a few tears. Tender soul. Probably talked about his Oedipus complex the way others talk about getting a dose of flu.

Frank Frølich imagined Bregård padding through the forests on a Sunday morning. The Finance Manager on Lake Bjørnsøen. Sitting on a collapsible chair by a borehole in slushy ice, fishing for small trout for hour after hour. Cap with loose ear flaps, then shuffle, shuffle, off to the next hole to pull up a perch or a trout. No. The guy with the thighs was not the type. Was probably a hunter. Yes, that was it, a hunter. That matched the moustache.

And these two totally different men had gained access to the same woman. The woman who blended in everywhere. A chameleon? One day dressed like a schoolgirl, Bregård had said, another like a jailbird's dream. *Sheesh, where did the man get that image from? The way he said it, perhaps this particular fish had been caught once himself?*

Sigurd stopped by a bench in front of the winter-dry fountain in the ornamental lake known as Spikersuppa. Sat down. Frank bought a copy of *Dagbladet* and a Kvikk Lunsj chocolate bar at the corner of Rosenkrantz' gate. Stood leaning against a tree while Sigurd sat happily blowing small clouds of smoke into the ozone layer.

Frank recalled the woman's mutilated upper body and reflected on the lack of a personal touch in her flat. One solitary shelf of Book Club publications. Unread, the paper still stiff. Blue, handmade ceramic wine goblets, placed to decorate the shelf. Nothing on the walls, apart from two broad-brimmed ladies' hats covered with a thick layer of dust. A mirror with a stylish frame. A few records. Divergent taste. House music beside Pavarotti, Randy Crawford and Norwegian folk musician Lillebjørn Nilsen. Probably couldn't call it taste. *What would give you a sense of her personality?*

Clothes, he wondered. Clothes and sketch pad. They had found it in her bag. A sketch pad full of drawings and patterns. Clothes too, jackets and skirts, rough charcoal outlines, skinny bodies. But at least it was hers. Meant nothing to him, but it was human.

He checked his watch. Klavestad hadn't moved for over an hour. He could feel that the chocolate had not filled his stomach. Hunger was making him uneasy. So he joined a group of people setting up banners in Eidsvolls plass.

At last the head appeared over the hedge. Frank bade farewell to the activists and happily followed in the direction of a McDonald's.

Sharp neon lights, garish colours and happy people behind the counter. Few customers. He refrained from looking at himself in the mirror. Instead took a risk and queued behind Klavestad.

In fact, Sigurd ought to have been at work. His workplace wasn't far away, either. A printing house. Obviously the stable type. Not today though. Nervous predisposition. The man's wallet was shaking as he tried to pay. Long, lean, trembling, white fingers. Frølich stared with sympathy at the stiff digits feverishly searching for money. You'll never tie any flies, he thought.

It was almost eleven when he set off on the trail again. He followed about seventy metres behind. The Big Mac in his stomach had sated his needs for the time being.

Up towards the tram lines. They stood waiting for a tram. Which turned out to be a number 11.

The tram wound its way through Storgata at a snail's pace, but soon headed for Thorvald Meyers gate. The bogies creaked and squealed. Frank had taken a seat at the back of the last carriage. Tried to look anonymous. The tram swayed from side to side in rhythm with the irregularity of the rails. The rocking transferred itself to passengers' heads. They swayed gently in rhythm. Same beat. The swaying transferred itself to the loops hanging from the metal poles in the centre of the ceiling. The loops swayed, the heads swayed. Sitting without a ticket in a conductor-less carriage was undisputed evidence that tailing was not his strong suit. He would be teased mercilessly for the rest of his life if he lost the chump because of a ticket inspection.

Klavestad had found a seat at the front. Sat sunken and small in a low single seat. Pony tail hanging down limply over the edge of the seat-rest. It swayed, too.

At last Sigurd raised his arm and pressed the button to get off at the next stop. Got up. Frank didn't move. Glanced out of the window as casually as he could while Sigurd stared back pensively, straight at him. Two men staggered out of a gateway. They were so stoned they were almost walking sideways, both of them. One had had his nose flattened at some time in the past; it was almost level with his cheeks. A hare lip completed the desperado look to perfection. The second was taller, thinner, with glasses perched at an angle. The man's brown teeth revealed a phobia of dentists.

The tram clanked to a halt. Klavestad got out. Frank followed. Colliding with one of the dope-heads, who grunted and spat a gobbet of phlegm on to a parked car.

Familiar territory. The route was in the direction of Reidun Rosendal's address.

Frank hung back, fifty metres behind. Risky turf. Quiet district. To the right a playground before the iron fence of Dælenenga Stadium. Klavestad suddenly stopped. Staring at the ground. Frank had to keep going. Dangerous silence. Some distance ahead, an elderly lady in a grey woollen coat and matching hat weighed down by a carrier bag. He passed Klavestad on the other side of the road and made for a blue door advertising a lottery on the outside. A newsagent's.

What was the guy thinking about? He looked like a poseur in a commercial. Hands thrust deep into his trouser pockets, open jacket hanging becomingly loose.

Frank went in the door and almost bumped into Arvid Johansen. The old fellow was in his own world, exiting the shop the way old folk do when they think the ground is slippery. Using his stick for support. He swore like a trooper when Frank almost knocked into him. But he couldn't be bothered to check out who it was. His eyes were fixed on the ground and he muttered imprecations to himself, unable to interrupt his sidling manoeuvre down the steps.

Inside the newsagent's the peeping tom had left a stench of stale fish offal. The police officer tried to see out. But the window in the blue door was made of wired glass and opaque. Between the shelves of men's magazines he could make out the old boy stomping down the street. Wearing a thick winter overcoat from the fifties, and a broad-brimmed hat which bounced up and down out of rhythm, like a marionette in a puppet theatre.

A Pakistani woman with black hair, a red shop apron and a smile asked Frank what he would like.

'Pools coupons,' he said, and she pointed to a shelf at chest height two metres away. Notepaper and biros lay to hand. Front stall seat. Almost. He had to bend, shield his eyes from several glossy and generously equipped nude models to catch a glimpse. The lady behind him probably considered him mad. He grabbed a stack of coupons from a holder on the shelf.

Outside, the distance between them was narrowing. The grunter was closing up on Klavestad. Actually, he wasn't that stiff, the old boy. Didn't need to support himself on the stick.

The old man stopped. What was going on? The seconds ticked. Suddenly Sigurd recoiled. What the hell! The man had lifted his stick. Sigurd backed away. Walked quickly, as though fleeing, craned his head. Sped round the corner.

The old boy stared after him for a moment. But then followed in pursuit. Back to the corner as well. Now his legs were moving faster. And the stick was turning like a crankshaft. His face was hard and closed.

Frank stuffed the coupons in his pocket, chucked a few coins on the counter, grabbed a newspaper and was off.

18

Gunnarstranda contemplated the ceiling of his office. Blinked, automatically raised his left arm and glanced at his watch. Two and a half hours' sleep. Not bad. The headache was gone. On the other hand, he had a serious crick in his neck. His head had rested at too acute an angle on the arm rest of the old sofa. That would have to be enough. He threw off the tartan plaid, sat up and massaged his neck and throat while trying to keep his head straight. Felt the lack of sleep on his palate. Time for a coffee and a smoke.

Two hours later he was sitting in a police car on his way down Mosseveien. Thinking. The question was: how did the path young Klavestad chose lead to the centre of the drama that had taken place?

The probability that Reidun Rosendal was subjected to sexual abuse before the murder was minimal. Since her flat had not been broken into, Reidun must have let the murderer in through the front door. But what had happened then? And why all the mess inside when no one had heard anything?

The answer was obvious, he supposed. He just didn't know what it was. That was the problem. To find the right answer he would have to ask the right question. *And where is the right question? It's there. It just isn't formulated yet. You*

can see it there, you can't grab it though, because it slips away,
like a tiny beetle you try to catch in a wash basin.

If you can't ask, then you have to observe. And Frølich is a
canny observer.

He passed Katten beach and glanced down at the smooth, wet rock-faces. Deserted. Only one person there. A thin elderly male figure dressed in blue with a black cap on his head and a solitary gull wheeling above him. At the front waddled a plump, ageing cocker spaniel. Panting, it turned its head, with a saliva smile and a patient look at its owner, who was bringing up the rear.

Gunnarstranda left the main road, drove alone through the illuminated tunnel and bore towards Holmlia. Which manoeuvre resulted in him driving in circles. In the end he drew up under a white arrow-shaped sign. His annoyance at getting lost had caused a stabbing pain from the earlier headache to return. The sign showed rows of numbers. It pointed towards a cluster of apartment buildings and small wooden houses where cars were prohibited. He got out and started a methodical search for number 66.

Marketing Manager Svennebye lived in number 66. The detective rang and his wife tore open the door. She was a well-rounded lady. Must have been around fifty. Wearing a blue suit, plus glasses and earrings the same colour as her shoes, mauve.

If she had been excited when she opened the door she was all the more disappointed when she saw the figure on the doorstep. Stared down at him. Tried to make him feel like a maggot with her gaze. That was fine. It matched his mood. He stared up at her. Short reddish hair. Pointed nose, small mouth with unusually thin lips. Nonetheless she had managed to paint a thick layer of brash red lipstick over them. The half-open mouth revealed that one of her front teeth was the same colour as her lipstick. The red stood out against the white.

Gunnarstranda introduced himself and was then asked in, after a moment's considered hesitation. She walked ahead. The tight skirt was taut across her rump and emphasized the excess weight she was carrying. Thick ankles. In the living room she parked herself on a high stool by something vaguely reminiscent of a bar. She chewed on half a celery stick dipped into what seemed to be mayonnaise, glanced down at the inspector and spoke.

'I don't remember having made any kind of approach to the police on this matter!'

It was a proclamation. She wiped her fingers on a cloth on the counter. Her voice was strident and suited her.

'Has your husband gone missing like this before?'

'Who says he's gone missing?' she screeched. The thin top lip followed after a brief delay and rubbed against the lipstick-coloured tooth.

A silence grew as the policeman kept his counsel. The faint noise of children playing between the buildings penetrated through to them. The woman turned, took another stick of celery, crunched it between her teeth and chewed with loud chomping noises. Then she touched her skirt with her fingers this time, as if to wipe them.

'When did you last see your husband?' asked Gunnarstranda when she had finished. He had not sat down; he stood with his hands in his coat pockets inside the door.

'Monday morning, before he went to work.'

'Did you have any reason to expect he would not return from work on Monday?'

'None at all.'

'No rows, no dramatic family events?'

'Not that I know of.'

'He behaved as he always did before going to work?'

'Yes.'

'So let me ask you one more time! Has this happened before?'

Her lips quivered. She removed her glasses and the detective could see she had discarded her mask. Tried to hide the movement, but failed, so the tears made stripes down her over-made-up cheeks.

Gunnarstranda waited patiently, but one finger had started to tap against his left trouser leg. This poorly concealed impatience had a knock-on effect. She took out a handkerchief she had stuffed up her sleeve and feverishly dabbed around her eyes.

'Has he gone on the booze?'

'What?'

'Has he gone on the booze?'

'How dare you!'

'Calm yourself now!'

He had taken a step forward. But without removing his hands from his pockets. 'You are talking to a police officer,' he spelt out coldly. 'Of course something may have happened to your husband. But it is unlikely since you have not reported him missing. So there are three possibilities. Either he is with another woman, or else he is lying somewhere plastered, or he has done a runner from something. It's as simple as that. If it had been a woman you would have known, and you would not have rung his office.'

He turned to the window, looked around the room. 'I'm investigating a murder connected with his workplace. Either your husband's disappearance has something to do with my investigation or it hasn't. So I am asking you: Has he gone on the booze?'

At that moment they heard a key in the front door. The woman looked at her watch. 'Trine and Lene,' she whispered and screamed into the hall:

'I'm in here!'

Her voice cracked. The last word sounded like a scream from a seagull that had just been shot.

Gunnarstranda walked towards the two teenage girls. 'Perhaps you two could fill me in on your father's disappearance,' he said turning to the elder daughter.

She stared back, stunned.

Gunnarstranda introduced himself.

'Has something happened to him?' the younger one asked nervously.

The police officer ignored the question and zeroed in the central issue. 'Is this the first time your father has gone missing like this?'

'No,' she blinked innocently. She had blue eyes, which unfortunately she had inherited from her mother. They weren't

137

deep. They were just squeezed between two folds of skin either side of her nose. Piggy eyes.

The girl's mother slid down off the bar stool and anxiously rubbed her hands against her tight skirt.

'When was the last time he went missing like this?'

'It's what you said!' the mother interrupted before the daughter was able to answer. 'Egil can't take his booze.'

'Why is he on a binge now?'

She shrugged by way of response.

'It's always happening,' the elder daughter interjected, clearly embarrassed.

The three women huddled closer. It happened automatically, they formed a barricade and the police officer smelt hostility in the air. So he relaxed, twinkled his eyes goodnaturedly and clambered up one of the stools at the strange bar. He couldn't even reach down to the foot support. His legs hung in mid-air. This gave him an opportunity to smile and stretch out his legs.

The tight defence loosened. The two young girls exchanged glances and giggled at the man with the short legs.

The detective grabbed his chance and assumed a grave expression.

'Is he normally away for two consecutive nights?' he asked with a worried crease between his eyes. All three shook their heads.

The mother's pale blue eyes suddenly went moist again. 'That's the whole point,' she wailed, gripping her handkerchief tightly. 'This has never happened before.'

19

It was very odd. The old man made no attempt to disguise what he was doing. Not at all. They headed upwards, along Christies gate, towards Lilleborg Church and on to Torshov Park.

Frank Frølich knew where this was leading, he knew where Klavestad lived. So he trailed a fair way behind. For now the task was clear. Tail the tail. And the young man with the hair had all his attention focused on the old codger behind him. Sigurd Klavestad kept turning round, didn't run, but walked faster, apprehensive. At the bottom of Ole Bulls gate he stopped and faced the man, who froze in his tracks. The distance between them was a touch under a hundred metres. Frank Frølich tried to pretend he was waiting for a bus, strode over to the published schedule, stared at the arrival times and scowled at his watch. Nothing happened. The two of them just watched each other. Until Klavestad began to walk slowly towards Johansen. Who didn't move, just poked around with his stick. The distance shrank by twenty metres. Sigurd stopped. Frank Frølich stuffed both hands in his pockets and mooched around the timetable. Nothing happened. Two pairs of eyes glaring at each other.

Until Sigurd finally turned. Took a few steps. The old man

followed. Klavestad spun round. Again Johansen froze in his tracks. Frølich yawned and checked his watch again. Ten minutes had passed. Sigurd was still staring at this man he didn't know. Then slowly turned round again. Went on now without looking back. Though faster. Johansen had to pick up speed. They walked along Torshov Park until they were there.

Journey's end.

Frank strolled at a leisurely pace. Right first time. The door had closed behind Sigurd. The man with the hat and stick stood by the front door studying the name plates.

Soon the policeman found refuge behind a rotary dryer. From there he loped across the road to the block opposite where Klavestad lived. This could have been quite tricky had it not been for a telephone booth hidden amongst some dense bushes.

He slipped in and flicked slowly through the frayed yellow scraps of paper that had once been telephone directories. A blue, a brown and a red wire protruded from the line left bereft of a purpose. The remains of the receiver lay scattered on the ground.

Frank leaned towards the glass and observed the man on the opposite side of the street. He was completely nuts. Talking to himself, scrutinizing the doorbells, shuffling to and fro in front of the entrance. A bent old fellow, his legs and stick jabbing the ground, to and fro outside the door. My God, Frank thought, shaking his head and tut-tutting. You are completely bonkers!

20

'So he left again, did he, without going in?'

Frank nodded and stopped the car at the crossroads between Karl Johans gate and Dronningens gate.

'And you're sure he took the bus back?'

Another nod.

It was evening. It was dark. They were keeping a watch on the pedestrian zone. There were shady figures hanging around on both sides. Most of them dropping comments and aiming disapproving glances at the car. Frank noticed the charmer with the crooked glasses and rotten teeth he'd seen from the tram earlier in the day. Now he was holding a short leash, at its end a Dobermann with restless legs and a pointed snout. At the same time he was chatting to a prostitute with swollen lips and thin thighs that strained to keep her upright. The woman was trying to light a cigarette. So far she had dropped three Marlboros on to the tarmac. They had slipped between her bony white fingers.

Gunnarstranda searched the inside pocket of his coat. 'You had a useful outing,' he continued. 'But I think there's little point doing any more undercover stuff. Except that the old chap worries me a bit.'

'He doesn't exactly seem dangerous.'

'True,' Gunnarstranda conceded, not totally reassured as

he continued his search. 'Nevertheless, there's something funny going on there. Here it is!'

He passed Frølich a passport photo.

Frank stared at the picture of a man in his late forties. Pointed face, thick neck, mouth with a very narrow top lip and pronounced eyebrows. A thick comb-over from his left ear across the crown to hide a shiny bare patch. The man had set the stool too low in the photo booth. Resulting in him stretching his neck and making his eyes seem enlarged.

'Who is it?'

'Egil Svennebye. Marketing Manager for Software Partners. I was given the photo by his wife.'

'Have you been there?'

'Yes, she told me he was having a terrible time with his colleagues and he was fond of a drink. That is, he's always been fond of a drink. So I've asked the boys to check the usual haunts.'

At that moment Glasses-man had to struggle to keep his dog under control. An unshaven rocker wearing jeans and a quilted sleeveless waistcoat came down Skippergata. Strolled towards the car. An Alsatian padded alongside him on a slack leash. It didn't grace the Dobermann with a glance although it had barked up a storm, growling and baring its teeth. Frank rolled down the window.

But the man showed no sign of recognition as he bent down to the window. 'Go to Bankplass,' he said in a low voice, lowering his head to light a fag while talking.

'Totally wrecked! He was chucked out of Original Pilsen

an hour ago and now he's sitting and drinking his own supplies on the steps of the old bank building.'

Message over. The man straightened up and strolled off without looking back. He could have asked the way, seen them or passed on a message. It had happened quickly. It is all a bit speculative when someone bends down to a police car, whether marked or not. You can always recognize the police. The Dobermann shut its mouth when the Alsatian was gone. But a nervous uneasiness had settled over the clientele, which was heightened when Frank switched on the ignition and started the car.

They stopped at the red lights. Frank turned to his side. Gunnarstranda's bald head went red and green as the neon advertising changed colour. Green. The car moved away without a word being said. It was cold outside and the wind had picked up in Tollbugata. The prostitutes huddled in doorways and gateways to get away from the freezing snow. Just one solitary young girl with an open fur coat trudged straddle-legged down the right-hand side. Frank liked the roundness of her thighs between stocking tops and the short skirt. He waved to another undercover man eating a hot dog beside a patrol car. Two drunken men were pushing each other on the pavement in the blue light of a restaurant sign. They stood on either side of a man stretched out with his face in what might have been blood or vomit.

He steered the car into Bankplass, pulled in to the kerb and parked. A woman who had been standing in a doorway turned and slunk back when she saw what kind of car it was. A brief glimpse of silken skin above polished black leather boots could be made out before she merged into the shadows.

Frank cast his eyes around. There wasn't much traffic, and the few cars cruising the street were soon flagged down by bystanders. A guy with blond hair and jeans stood pissing between the rusty railings outside the Museum for Contemporary Art. Beyond that, a mini-skirt sashayed over to a car. She bent down in time-honoured fashion and gave the customer a once-over before getting in. But there was no one on the steps.

His eyes wandered further afield. The officer had said by the steps. If the man had gone, he wouldn't have got far.

'There!'

A man was staggering across Kongens gata away from them. His coat hanging off him and what looked like a half-empty bottle of spirits dangling from his right hand. The man had to use the whole pavement and kept bumping into cars or signposts or other inconveniences.

They opened their car doors and followed him. The man stumbled on. Comb-over flapping. It had fallen the other way and was flying like a flag from his left temple. The two of them set off at speed and caught him up as he fell over a block of stone by the lawn.

'Svennebye!'

Frank crouched down beside him.

The man raised his head. His eyes swimming. His coat and shirt soiled with vomit. Any similarity with the passport photo was minimal. It was the same person, but the face was bloated and this changed his appearance. His lips stuck out from his face like a handle. Two unusually listless eyes swam on either side of a pronounced, pointed nose.

'Police,' Frank stated with authority. Stupid thing to say. He could hear it himself.

The lower lip stuck out even further. Head crashed down. The man tried to rest a forearm on each thigh. Head drooping like a ripe pear between his shoulders. Frank stood up and let Gunnarstranda take his place.

The man put out an arm to move him away but as he did so a gush of white vomit surged from his mouth on to the pavement. The bottle slipped from his fingers and smashed on the ground.

A few chunks of carrot and some green peas enlivened a liquid mass of slime that stank of alcohol. Gunnarstranda had recoiled two paces so as not to get the next jet on his feet. Droopy-Head slowly raised his right hand to wipe away the snot that had collected under his nose. With the support on his thigh taken away he tipped over and fell into the sick, bottom uppermost. At the same time he supported himself on the tarmac and a shard of glass went into his hand, colouring it red with blood.

Gunnarstranda bent down and deftly tied his handkerchief around the bleeding hand that was now quite limp.

'Svennebye!' he said in a low, familiar voice.

The head dangled from side to side.

Gunnarstranda held the man's forehead and pushed it backwards. The face was awash with puke and snot.

'Svennebye!'

No reaction.

Gunnarstranda grabbed the lobe of his left ear and twisted. The head fell back further and his eyes rolled, so that you could see only the whites. The policeman let go, but the head stayed put. Mouth agape. Then suddenly his chest gurgled and another cascade spurted out of his mouth, upwards this time, like a fountain.

The two men stepped back. They let him finish being sick before Gunnarstranda leaned over.

'Reidun,' Gunnarstranda whispered, ever the optimist. 'Reidun Rosendal!'

No reaction.

Frank could see that the vomit had soaked into the man's trousers as he sat on the pavement, with legs apart like a child in a sandpit.

A middle-aged couple hurried past. She gave them a wide berth and both sent the police officers quizzical sidelong glances.

Svennebye tried to whistle. Only air came of the attempt. Then he hiccupped. Snivelled something or other. Twisted his mouth to the right. Things were about to happen.

Svennebye was making noises. Some coarse grunting sounds from down below. He shifted, fell on to his side. The man's head banged into the wing of a parked car. Frank dragged him back into a sitting position. Now he was bleeding from his temple as well. Still grunting. Fiddling with his flies. Soon he was able to jiggle out his apparatus and gave a loud groan as the piss began to run across the tarmac. It didn't get far. It collected in a puddle and was absorbed by his trousers.

They ambled back to the car.

Svennebye sat as before, in his own piss, vomiting with his legs spread out. His head dangling to and fro.

Frank left the radioing to Gunnarstranda.

Soon a vehicle arrived with a flashing blue light and skidded into the square. Two uniformed policemen grabbed the man under the shoulders and dragged him to the van and heaved him into the back where he landed upside down and stayed put, like a ball of dough you smack down on a kitchen worktop.

Gunnarstranda shouted to the nearest uniform:

'Get a doctor to see to his hand!'

The uniform nodded and clambered in the police van with the Marketing Manager of Software Partners.

21

Sigurd Klavestad did not sleep well. He dreamed about white skin against a dawning window, about telephones ringing and no one speaking. And he knew the whole thing was a dream. Knew he ought to wake up and regain consciousness to escape the anxiety that made the dream so horrible and sticky. For that reason he finally gave in and opened his eyes wide.

The first thing he noticed was the sweat making the duvet cold and unpleasantly stiff. But he didn't move. He lay there staring out into the dark. It was night. Grey light from outside. The night dimly illuminated by street lamps. He wondered what the time was. The silence told him it was late. There was a complete absence of traffic noise. So the time had to be somewhere between two and half past four at night. That was when it was still. After the night-taxis had broken the back of their work and before the first shift workers were roaring off to their jobs.

It was always horrible to wake up in the middle of a dream. With a jolt. The feeling you were falling God knows where, without any control. Unsure whether someone was out there in the dark and would attack you.

He was unable to move right away. Scared to make a noise. Scared someone would hear. Idiotic. But it had ever been thus. From when he was a small boy and he thought there was a man waiting with a black hat and a raised sword in the wardrobe. That was how it had always been. Too scared to move, rigid, staring into the darkness, skin tingling. Until he either went back to sleep or forced himself to fight through the barrier and plucked up the courage to switch on the bedside lamp.

Living alone now, he knew very well it was the nightmares of his childhood that tormented him. Nevertheless, the clammy stiffness had succeeded in locking his arms. As indeed it always had.

At last he moved. Heard the soft rustle of the duvet. Managed to stick out his hand and switch on the lamp. A dim light. Barely enough to illuminate the corners of the bedroom. But enough for him to dare to sit up and grab the cigarette packet on the bedside table. No taste. He immediately regretted having taken the first drag. Not because of the taste, but because he had to open the window. For some reason he didn't want to open the window.

He smoked with jumpy, darting movements. Thought of the crazy old man from the day before. The dark eyes. Must have been gay. The town was full of crazy gays. And he was always bumping into them. The old man's mug had reminded him of a face from many years ago. Once he had been sitting and waiting for the tram to leave. Then this man bounded in through the door, and sat on the bench opposite. He said: 'Come to my place and jerk off, and you'll get a thousand kroner.' That was what he had experienced again with the old codger. The dank fear of what sort of

149

nutter he had to deal with. People like that are bloody unpredictable; you can't know what they are capable of doing. Like yesterday. When he turned and stopped. The old man's moist, staring eyes.

The telephone rang.

He wasn't surprised. It was as if he had been expecting it to ring. It was all tied up with the old queer. As if that was why he had woken up, for something like this to happen. He put the cigarette in his mouth and watched the jangling telephone. Answered it. 'Yes,' he said, hardly using his larynx. Cleared his throat. 'Yes,' he repeated.

Not a sound at the other end. He twisted round and wrenched his arm in such a way as to see his watch. Half past three. As he had guessed.

But then he went cold. There was the sound. He had heard it before. Someone smacking down the receiver. A clatter. And then the silence.

A kilo of lead in the pit of his stomach. Legs rigid and numb under the duvet. Mind on the blink.

The image of her. That resigned smile when no one announced their presence. The receiver being banged down. That morning.

Slowly he cradled the phone, too. Even more slowly he lay back and slid down the bed. Remembered the photograph the short, vicious cop had thrown at him. Her mutilated upper body and the transfixed expression on her face. As though she had hurled herself backwards to avoid the lunges with the knife, but had been impeded by the floor, nowhere else to go.

The bedside lamp lit up almost the whole room. Almost. The bedroom door was closed. Now he could hear the silence. It was much too silent.

Was someone there?

His legs ached. The bedroom door shone out at him.

He struggled to restrain the rising panic. He was at home. All alone. The front door was locked. He tried to calm himself.

Someone had called a wrong number. The front door was locked. But the chain? Had he attached the chain? Of course not.

He never did. Security chains are for old dears. He closed his eyes. The door. His legs went heavy again. *There's no one here! Someone dialled the wrong number! There's no one here! Get up, go into the hall and put on the chain.*

This bloody anxiety. Had he locked the door?

He watched his hands lift the duvet. Watched himself get up.

At that moment there was a ring at the door. The lead in his stomach lurched upwards. He felt the cold in his neck, under his chin. His mind froze. His hands seemed to wither, lose strength, go cold and wax-like; they no longer belonged to him.

He didn't feel the clothes as he dressed. He had no contact with his body. A repugnant numb sensation. He sat down on the bed. Didn't move.

Was he imagining things?

The familiar ding-dong. Had he heard it or not?

First the telephone ringing and now this, one ring on the

doorbell. At this hour. Half past three in the morning. He remembered the knife on the policeman's desk. The flash of metal.

He found himself standing in front of the bedroom door. Grasped the handle. Slowly, ever so slowly, he opened the door without making a sound. The sitting room and the kitchen lay before him, silent. The grey night outside allowed him to make out individual contours in the gloom. A yellow strip through the thin crack between the door and the frame told him he had forgotten to turn off the light.

Perfectly still, he stood listening by the front door.

So unbelievably quiet. The doorbell. Had he heard it ring or not? Why didn't he have a peephole in the door? *Everyone had a peephole in the door. Imagine being able to see out!*

There.

Another ring. The sound echoed in the quiet hall. The sound seemed to boom. His knees gave way.

Someone was there. Waiting.

His mouth went dry. Should he say something, ask who was there?

His mind wouldn't work. His voice wouldn't work. He was just breathing, through an open mouth. But he had to change position. His knee cracked. The sound exploded in his ears. It sounded like a twig cracking. *Could it be heard through the door?*

Not a sound from outside. His body ached. His posture was unbearable. How long had he been standing like this? It felt like an eternity.

Then. The sound of footsteps. Someone walking. No

question about it. He closed his eyes, breathed out. Shoulders slumped. Knees gave way. Whole body had been tense. All the muscles that had been straining found peace. He looked at his watch, measured the time and listened. He stood there for ten minutes. Ten minutes. *Couldn't be anyone there now. Not any more.*

His hand went a strange bright white as he unlocked and opened the door.

22

Gunnarstranda had dropped off his car in Kampen, and thus, when, an hour and a half later, he left the bus and strode down to the Grand Hotel, his brow bore a frown of irritation. It had not been easy leaving his car. The garage was not what he had expected. At first, he had not seen a garage at all. The backyard was an empty gravel area containing nothing more than a shed, a clothes line and a bike stand. The shed was a dilapidated garage with cracked grey boards, probably hadn't been painted since the Second World War. A thin metal tube with a cowl on protruded from the crooked roof, a cartoon chimney.

One door at the corner of the yard. He had read the name plates very carefully, without identifying a Gunder Auto there, either. Eventually, he had sneaked out of the yard, looked at the house numbers one more time, double-checked the address. Had cursed, turned towards a short, slight figure in oil-stained overalls padding up the street. 'Gunder Auto? That's me,' the dipstick had said, walked right past him, with a gentle smile. Then he beckoned him into the garage.

There was room for the Skoda. Gunder had beckoned. 'There! There! Over there! Right, straighten up, straighten up, come on, come on.'

Until, sweaty and tired, the detective was finally parked. And he had hardly opened the bloody door when the bean-pole had booted away a jack and moved a metal drum, which was probably full of moonshine. Gunnarstranda inferred that from the feeder pipe and the somewhat shaken expression adorning the mechanic's face for a couple of minutes.

Then the man didn't have any paper. So in the end he had gone upstairs to the toilet to find something to write on. Down he came with two sheets of tissue and a filthy pencil in his hand.

'Hmmm, ignition probs, right, dies when you accelerate, ye-ep, makes a helluva racket, right.'

The inspector had subjected the mechanic to some very sceptical scowls. With some hesitation, he had enquired when he might pick up the car again. But didn't get a proper answer. Just some prattle about what might be wrong and all the things that can go even more wrong with all the electrics nonsense.

On the bus back to town, he had begun to wonder what the hell he had let himself in for. He had briefly considered taking his doubts out on Frølich, who had lured him up there in the first place. Apparently this Gunder lived with Frølich's girlfriend in a collective. Nevertheless, Gunnarstranda came to the conclusion that, whatever happened, he should have reversed his car out of the yard and kept well away. For that reason, he would wait for the bill before he had a confrontation with his colleague.

He trudged into the Grand Hotel Café and stood inside the door on the lookout for his brother-in-law.

A hiss could be heard from the wall with the window facing Karl Johan. It was his brother-in-law. Heard but not seen. Gunnarstranda scanned the café again. There! Suit jacket waving a newspaper.

The policeman bowed to the head waiter who nodded back with cool reserve. Went over to his brother-in-law's table and sat down.

A long life had taught Edel's brother to suppress his laughter. It was dry and shrill, like the lament of a rotating, rusty cogwheel. The sound attracted everyone's attention. On the other hand, on those occasions when it escaped it was contagious. But his brother-in-law didn't like to play the clown. So he hissed like a snake whenever he was going to laugh, say hello, or just catch someone's eye.

'This is a rare treat,' his brother-in-law opened politely, sipping his coffee. Gunnarstranda registered acknowledgement, leaned back and waved for a waitress. 'Coffee,' he mumbled, then faced the table and reciprocated the sentiments.

It was the first time for four years. The first time since Edel's funeral.

Around the room sat well-dressed women chattering over slices of cake and morning coffee. Here and there a few ruddy-cheeked business people toiled over a second breakfast. The brother-in-law blended into this milieu. Round glasses, grey waistcoat over a white shirt. Mild, patronizing expression underlined by two lazy eyelids above a smile that looked more like a grimace. If you didn't know any better, you would think the fellow had had a couple of snifters.

A leather briefcase occupied the chair by the window. An over-sized appointments diary with a plethora of extra pockets and loose papers lay open on the table.

He waved to a becloaked gentleman hurrying past outside.

'Do you know a company called Software Partners?' Gunnarstranda asked.

'No.'

'They make office computer programs.'

'Don't they all?'

Brother-in-law blew on his coffee. But his gaze was less frosty now that he knew the point of the meeting.

The man had been employed by Norsk Data from its inception. Gunnarstranda knew he was somewhere in the top half of the hierarchy. Since he was still there, having survived growth, stagnation and recession he must have been in a position of importance. Apparently on this particular day he was holding a lecture called 'The Future of Norwegian IT', sub-titled 'A Scenario for Information Technology in Norway and the European Union'.

Gunnarstranda had been granted an audience during the interval. The woman with a potato in her mouth, the one who took his brother-in-law's telephone calls, remarked that anyone who was anyone in the industry would be present. The policeman considered the room to be rather too limited for that to be true. However, the Grand did have a large range of facilities, so perhaps the industry was munching its cakes elsewhere.

'Any names?' Brother-in-law asked.

'Terje Engelsviken.'

He recoiled, put down his coffee cup, winced theatrically and shook his hand as if he had burned himself. Hissed aloud and blew on to his hand.

Gunnarstranda waited patiently.

'He studied at the Institute of Technology in Trondheim,' the engineer went on with the coffee cup in his hands again. 'You know, the generation of academics who turned up for their first interview with a sweat band round their foreheads and Mao on their chests.'

Brother-in-law winked. 'And got the job. Engelsviken's a mediocre engineer who for some strange reason found himself in IBM in the early eighties. Left a trifle suddenly, after a couple of years. The official version is that he wanted to start up on his own.'

The waitress came with the coffee. Brother-in-law paused while she transferred the contents of the tray. Resumed after she had gone:

'The unofficial version is that he's a rotten apple.'

'Tell me more.'

'Apparently IBM don't pay well enough.'

'Embezzlement?'

'Not at all, Engelsviken was drawing a wage at a couple of other places as well.' Brother-in-law winked. 'So Engelsviken chose to leave IBM.'

Gunnarstranda guessed that 'leaving IBM suddenly' was open to interpretation.

'Afterwards he started up on his own,' Brother-in-law continued. 'In the eighties when banks thought money procreated money, so long as the company who borrowed it had a project that was couched in enough American jargon.'

Gunnarstranda looked around him, took a cigarette from his pocket. Rolled it between his fingers. Asked:

'Have you met him?'

'Just the once.'

'What's he like?'

He considered for a moment. 'Old problem. Engelsviken can't cut his coat according to the cloth,' he concluded. 'Haven't you met the guy?'

'No. I've only heard that his wife is the elegant type with enough money to play the part.'

'Mmm. Pretty as a picture. Not him though. Eccentric. Likes his liquor, too.' Brother-in-law gave a conspiratorial smile, leaned forward. 'There's a story doing the rounds about Engelsviken. From when he started in the industry.'

He put down the cup with a clink, wiped his mouth with a serviette. 'Business wasn't going too well,' he began. 'But that can't have been down to sales. You see, this was the early eighties when PCs were new and everyone wanted one and companies were computerizing their wage bills and invoices.'

Gunnarstranda leaned back and listened to his brother-in-law's hissy voice. Heard about Engelsviken selling computers like hotcakes, but not paying his bills. 'They were drowning in debt,' Brother-in-law said. 'Creditors were dying for the company to go bankrupt.'

Brother-in-law raised his cup again. Drained the coffee.

Gunnarstranda coughed. 'He sold computers like hotcakes, but couldn't pay his bills?'

Brother-in-law threw his arms in the air with a wry smile. 'They had a place up in Brekke. I went there once. The time I met him.'

He surveyed the room, deep in thought. 'Much too upmarket. Carpets on the floors and a Chesterfield in the dining room. Stock and garage on the lower floor.'

Gunnarstranda was afforded a brief glimpse of the man's two canines before the story went on. His brother-in-law seemed quite clued-up on the details. At any rate, he knew that the lorry in question drove around with bald summer tyres in the winter. And he knew about the weather that day. 'This was the end of the year, either November or December. And on this particular night some fairly unforgiving weather set in. Sledging conditions, freezing rain on the lowlands turning to snow on higher ground.'

Brother-in-law had also heard that Engelsviken had the use of a barn in Brakerøya, outside Drammen. 'You see, that was where the lorry was headed, loaded to the gunnels with computer equipment, office machinery and other expensive items. It happened on the morning when the insolvency administrators were due to come and confiscate all his assets. Engelsviken had obviously been up all night loading the lorry. And after he had finished the bottle was empty. And Engelsviken was pretty pissed. But on these points sources were divided. One version was that Engels-viken had not done any loading, but had been helped by a young lad who had done the job. Another source maintained the boss had done the loading while the lad was going to drive. One thing was certain, however: the solicitor in charge of the bankruptcy proceedings had arrived unexpectedly while the lorry was still in the garage. Here the sources agreed that two things happened. The lad had run like the devil. And Engelsviken, who was well-oiled, hadn't hung around. He sprang up into the cab, started the bloody vehicle and roared off through the garage's double doors on to the road.'

Brother-in-law hissed and reached down in his breast pocket for a cigarillo. Gunnarstranda, who had been fidgeting with a lighter, held up a flame for him.

'It gets a bit sketchy from here on,' Gunnarstranda's brother-in-law, who nevertheless had no trouble imagining the sequence of events, pointed out. 'The vehicle was so heavily laden its road-holding ability was fine for the first kilometres out of town. But when Engelsviken hit Liersko-gen the snow started coming down. The air was thick with flakes and the road so slippery cars were swerving out of control and their wheels spinning as they struggled to get up the hills. The overloaded lorry must have fought its way past Asker and right up to the top of Lierskogen. But then the drunken sot – he's as mean as a pools millionaire – probably didn't have enough money to pay for the toll. So the knucklehead took the old route down the Lier hills to

Drammen. That didn't go so well. The crate took off on one of the hairpin bends.'

Brother-in-law exhaled a thick, blue cloud of smoke. His lazy eyes were amused. 'Engelsviken managed to jump out before the vehicle somersaulted down for something like fifty metres before colliding with a tree. Computers scattered over the whole hillside. Do you reckon he sobered up when he peered over the edge to survey his stock?'

The cogwheel began to rotate. His laughter cut through the café atmosphere and a number of heads turned towards them.

Brother-in-law raised his cup and stopped the creaking noises. Confirmed he had no more coffee and poured himself some more from the flask the waitress had left. 'Then Engelsviken had to thumb a lift home.'

Gunnarstranda was about to say something, but his partner flagged him down.

'We haven't got to the best bit yet,' he said quickly. 'You see, this administrator had seen the boy running away. And he caught a glimpse of the lorry smashing through the garage doors and heading off. So he drew the conclusion that this was a case of simple theft. And the upshot was that the insurance company had to fork out for the stock and the lorry while Engelsviken got off scot-free.'

Gunnarstranda sat deep in thought, smoking. 'How much truth is there in this story?'

Brother-in-law shrugged, didn't answer.

The detective exhaled, still thinking. Someone had made up a story about a man's trickery, intemperance and good fortune. However much truth there was in the story, it said a good deal that the story existed at all.

'I don't think there's any doubt he wanted to clear the warehouse and swindle his creditors,' Brother-in-law mused aloud. 'It's probably also true that he was stopped by ice and a tree. But the insurance bit sounds a trifle far-fetched.'

'Is he an alcoholic?'

'Doubtful. Just a desperado! He's got his name up in a nightclub called Barock because he drank champagne from magnums when it was all the rage.'

The engineer knitted his brows in thought. 'An overgrown schoolboy, drives a sports car and likes wild parties. Afterwards it's back home to the wife, who puts on a nice smile for everyone and pretends nothing has happened.'

'No long face?'

'Of course, but she's a bit aristocratic, in a way. Chooses not to scratch out his eyes. You know, wounds like that are visible, give the hoi-polloi even more to chatter about.'

Brother-in-law glanced at his watch and pushed back his chair. 'I've got a lecture waiting for me,' he apologized and packed away his things. Gunnarstranda waved to the waitress who came and placed the bill on the table. 'I'll pay this one,' he said in a detached though friendly tone, sliding the hundred-krone note back towards his brother-in-law.

'I'll give you another tip,' Brother-in-law said after the waitress had gone. 'I don't know how genuine Engelsviken is today, but I would advise anyone doing business with him to be very cautious.'

He grabbed his briefcase and met the detective's eyes.

'These are only rumours,' he said, leaning over. His brother-in-law's face was as hard and earnest as it was possible to be with such lazy eyelids.

'You'd better check all this out for yourselves, but Engelsviken did go bust. And, let me put it this way, no one is surprised that his companies go belly up. But his creditors have a tendency to pull a face every time his assets are released.'

'Nothing?'

'Nothing is an understatement.'

They left the table, went into the foyer where they stopped to part company.

'On that subject, I've heard the name of a solicitor,' Brother-in-law said. 'But now for the life of me I can't recall what it was!'

The detective took out a notebook and consulted it.

'Brick?' he suggested.

'Possible.' Brother-in-law nodded, putting the briefcase into his other hand. 'What I've heard is that this solicitor sorts matters out for Engelsviken every time he gets into a fix. A kind of legal consultant. Where did you get the name?'

'Software Partners is the kind of set-up whereby you commit yourself to partners for a sum of money, a kind of equity stake,' the policeman answered. 'I understand the concept was devised by Brick.'

Brother-in-law's hiss was eloquent. He proffered his hand.

Gunnarstranda shook hands. 'Thanks for your help,' he mumbled.

23

Then it was off to the courts, where Gunnarstranda went through the archives and made some enquiries. Made some telephone calls. It all took time. Herr Brick was an industrious solicitor on the letter-writing front. A/S Software Partners was involved in no fewer than seven legal claims, and that in just the last six months. In fact, one case had been withdrawn, but Gunnarstranda took the trouble of writing down the names of the litigants on a sheet of paper. Stuffed it in his wallet. Several of the cases concerned demands from companies wanting the sales contract to be rescinded as a result of defaulted payments. One case was between Software Partners and A/S Rent-An-Office, the lessor of Engelsviken and Co.'s rooms. Rent-An-Office demanded a court eviction as no rent had been forthcoming. Brick, on behalf of A/S Software Partners, demanded compensation for what Brick called a scandalous lack of commitment to the lease contract and demonstrable discrepancies between the said contract and actual conditions.

Gunnarstranda was chewing at the inside of his cheek as he left the courthouse on his way to Kafé Justisen.

It was quite crowded. By and large the usual gamblers and jobless drinkers were there knocking back beer, but with the occasional colleague thrown in. Right at the back sat Reier

Davestuen, a detective from the Fraud Unit. Reier shared a table with a fair-haired hobo who kept shouting something over to the gamblers' table and rocked to and fro with a toothless grin. Poor Reier had shrunk into a corner so as not to be jolted. He did not have much success though, he took up a lot of room himself, and the large pink copy of *Dagens Næringsliv* did not make the matter any easier. Reier of the big hands, size 47 shoes and clothes that always seemed too small.

Gunnarstranda wove his way through to the steep staircase to the veranda that formed the first floor and went up. Almost as full here, too. An empty seat by a wrinkled face under an old felt hat. The person had a mouthful left of beer and had already started to point his galoshes towards the staircase.

'Is it free?' the policeman asked.

The man tried to move his lips, but abandoned the attempt and nodded instead, with the result that his hat fell over his face.

'Special!' Gunnarstranda yelled at the young waitress sitting with a lit cigarette in front of the kitchen door.

Today's special consisted of veal, olives, pease pudding, three boiled potatoes with dill on top and an utterly wonderful sauce. He twisted to allow the old boy with the galoshes to dodder off, and he dug in. He relished every bite. Smiled at the waitress who came to the table carrying a bottle of mineral water with a white label because she knew that was the one he wanted. He was of a mind to compliment her on the sauce, but this was beyond him. Instead, in a very effusive way, he ordered a packet of twenty Teddy.

From his seat there was a good view of the tourist deck where Davestuen was still thumbing through the stock exchange listings. Gunnarstranda watched his colleague raise his right arm to disguise a yawn, energetically shake his head and draw breath before looking round with sluggish, withdrawn eyes. Anonymous and grey for as long as he was sedentary. A thin blond fringe and a bony face protruded from a much too small suit jacket around a loud yellow tie that was doing its best to throttle him.

Eventually Gunnarstranda managed to catch his eye and beckon to him. Reier gave a start, then waved back. Got up without knocking over the table, but earned a look of dismay from his toothless neighbour when he drew himself up to his full height.

'Anything new on the stock exchange?' Gunnarstranda asked, still chewing, and held on to his plate as Reier's knees raised the table as he sat down.

'Nothing,' he exclaimed, stretching out his legs and thereby lowering the table. He stared Gunnarstranda in the eye, 'Nothing at all.'

Reier's intensity could on occasion be tricky to negotiate. Gunnarstranda looked down. 'I have a computer company increasing the taxpayer's burden with seven lawsuits all at the same time,' he informed him. 'Plus, to a large extent, panicked demands for compensation reminiscent of distress calls from an empty wallet.'

Davestuen nodded and folded his large hands on the

table in front of him, two pale hams bristling with wiry blond hair.

'The MD is a dubious sort,' Gunnarstranda went on, with the smell of mothballs from Reier's jacket assailing his nostrils. 'Several bankruptcies behind him in the course of very few years.'

He picked up a brochure. 'The company in question is soliciting fresh capital from investors.'

Davestuen took the brochure. Flicked through it and stopped at the picture of the Finance Manager, Bregård. 'This the dubious sort?'

'Nope,' Gunnarstranda answered quickly. 'The dubious MD is not mentioned at all in the booklet. And I was just beginning to reflect that this was a very astute move on their part.'

He slurped the coffee the waitress had put down in front of him unbidden. Smiled at her and she smiled back, not just out of politeness; she winked, too. He liked that, tapped out a cigarette from the packet of Teddy and offered one to the Fraud Unit officer.

'No, thank you,' he answered, raising a deprecatory hand. Gunnarstranda stared at him in amazement. 'You? Given up the fags?'

Reier Davestuen nodded gravely.

'When was that?'

'Yesterday, now that you mention it.'

Gunnarstranda acknowledged his respect, and lit up.

'I know beardy here,' Davestuen continued unruffled and

pointed a stout yellow finger at the photograph of Bregård.

'Øyvind Bregård. Ex-bully boy. Big muscles, right?'

Gunnarstranda nodded slowly.

'Done for GBH at least once.'

Gunnarstranda blew out smoke, waiting.

Davestuen's bony brow creased as he tried to remember.

'He was working for some dodgy debt collection agency we snuffed out a few years ago, but for the moment I can't remember which.'

'And what did he get?'

'A prison sentence. For beating to pulp a Pakistani who ran a shop in Oslo West. Don't remember the man's name or where it happened, but we can find out, of course.'

Gunnarstranda said:

'What he's doing now is definitely not hustling. It's a computer business. I suspect it is not quite kosher though.'

Davestuen nodded.

'Bregård's the Finance Manager.'

Davestuen grinned, displaying pointed teeth. 'Not at all kosher,' he declared and revealed a gold bridge in his lower jaw.

'I'm investigating the murder of a girl working there,' Gunnarstranda went on. 'I don't know if this business is connected with the murder, but it stinks to high heaven.'

Davestuen spat on his hands and straightened his fringe with his palms. 'There's not a lot I can do . . .'

'You could check out the case, find out what these people are actually up to. How can this bully boy possibly be a finance manager?'

Gunnarstranda tapped a nicotine-stained nail on Bregård's photograph.

Reier peered down at Bregård's bearded face, took the brochure and studied it closer. 'Fine,' he said at last. 'Just phone calls for the time being.'

Gunnarstranda stood up. *Major things happen in this world of ours*, he thought. *Europe, the collapse of the Eastern bloc and now bugger me if Reier Davestuen hasn't given up smoking.* He walked towards the telephone on the wall. *Time to reel in Frølich and take a trip to Software Partners*, he thought with satisfaction.

24

Before Frank received a call from his boss, he had been busy studying Sonja Hager's list of Software Partners' business connections. Prospects for a successful trawl did not look too promising. The problem was the range of different commercial activities. Some were shops; some were small businesses you find are obscure broom cupboards in large rental complexes; while others were standard bookshops. Some filtering was necessary.

He summoned up patience and sat down with Bryde's classified telephone directory and Televerket's Yellow Pages. He began to sort names of firms systematically by groups: one for buyers of computer solutions, one for potential company owners and one for both.

After two and a half hours' slog he laced up his boots, put on his green anorak and set off to do some field work.

A bite, first cast of the rod.

The drive where he found himself was at the back of a side street off Rådhusgata. The place was a vacuum. In Rådhusgata cars and people sped to and fro without even so much as a sidelong glance at the quiet nooks and crannies, it was like being behind a breakwater. Here.

The business could not be very interested in having customers because the shop window was characterless, coated in dust, its presence only marked by a worn awning that flapped and creaked to the movement of the heavy traffic beyond. The sun had successfully removed almost all the colour from the posters. Box files, electric typewriters and unwieldy calculators behind the glass.

He went in. A bell jangled. Pure tea-shop stuff. Well, almost. The aroma of freshly baked buns was missing. No comely wench behind the counter, either. The absence of staff was conspicuous. He looked around. Alone. Not a soul to be seen. Dry air. The buzz of a photocopier and the faint drone outside were the only sounds to fill the room.

He shook the door again. Shrill jangle of the bell.

Something stirred.

Then he was there. The man was getting on in years. Erect back. Short and plump with a wig that was as black as the bristles on a paint brush. Tiny tufts of genuine hair, of the thin, grey variety, stuck out of his ears.

'Morning!' the man smiled in welcome with an outstretched hand.

Frank showed his ID.

The happy expression on his features was gone, but he politely offered Frølich a seat behind a room-divider where he had set up a little office overflowing with newspapers and unfinished crosswords.

The police officer passed him the photograph of Reidun Rosendal without uttering a word.

The shop-owner ran his hands across the table, lifting piles of paper until he found his glasses. They had black plastic rims and thick lenses. With these on his nose, he nodded again and again at the girl in the photograph.

'She's dead,' Frank said to make him stop. 'Murdered, and I'm investigating her death.'

The news had an impact. The man chewed the ends of his glasses. 'Dead?'

'Did she often come here?'

It took the man quite some time to compose himself. 'Very often. Last week she was here,' he began, fidgeting, disorientated. 'No, no, no,' he sighed. Strange look in his eyes.

The policeman leaned back in his chair and waited.

'She handled the co-ownership.'

'Co-ownership?'

'I've become a co-owner of Software Partners.'

His face suddenly creased. A kind of reaction to the officer's curiosity.

'We're interested in anything to do with Reidun during the last weeks of her life,' Frølich explained reassuringly. 'Absolutely everything. We don't want to go on tapping in the dark.'

The man surveyed him over the edge of his glasses.

Frølich inclined his head with a jovial smile. Wondering at the same time how come this creep with the sixties staplers in the shop window could be a co-owner of a yuppy firm in prestigious Oslo West.

The man stopped staring over his glasses and declared: 'I own this block where we are now.'

He paused for reflection as though the whole thing was a long story.

'Over the last few years this shop has been a loss-maker ... I've kept myself afloat with the rents I earn from the block. And that is how I would have continued, had it not been for the biggest tenant.'

The shop-owner named a technical journal. Frank recalled the dusty rows of empty windows on the floors above. He doubted the rental income would make this guy fat.

'They served notice. You see, without them I would actually have gone bust.'

The eyes under the wig were doleful. 'Everything's tight now, the rental market's at its zenith and there have been too many office blocks built over the last few years. It's impossible to get new tenants, so the outlook for increasing your income is grim.'

He stared into the distance, then suddenly brightened up.

'Had it not been for this offer from frøken Rosendal, well, I don't know what I would have done!'

'What offer was that?'

'I've become a dealer. Of a new series of commodities. I've bought myself into a company ... and I'm now a co-owner.'

Another partner for Software Partners! The logic was all in the name.

'How did you become a co-owner?'

'I bought a share of the firm and thereby an automatic right to sell their products.'

'A kind of franchising?'

'No, no, co-ownership.'

'But isn't competition fierce in the computer market?'

'Yes, it is.'

A smile flickered around the man's mouth. His eyes sparkled as he exclaimed:

'But now Software Partners have launched a commodity they have sole rights to throughout Norway!'

As if the competition would be any the less for that, the policeman thought.

'So you've bought shares in Software Partners?'

A shadow of doubt crossed the man's face again.

'Shares? I suppose I have . . .'

'Haven't you received them?'

Apologetic smile. 'I gather there's a technical innovation here, to avoid red tape. A-shares and B-shares or something like that.'

Not completely happy with his answer. Shifted uneasily in his chair.

'Is it permitted to ask how much this partnership has cost you?'

Defensive furrows above the glasses.

'I can't see the logical connection with the case.'

Time to let a silence get under his skin, thought Frank. Met the man's gaze and allowed a silence to pervade the room. The eyes across the table roamed.

'Two hundred and fifty thousand!'

'That was bold!'

His surprise was sincere. Two hundred and fifty thousand kroner was a lot of money, at least for this man.

The shop-owner didn't like the surprised tone. 'Calculated risk,' he boasted. 'You're never too old to take a risk.'

Pause. Thoughtful examination of the ceiling. 'But there

is no risk here, either. This new software will have people banging down the doors of whoever has the rights. Software Partners have the monopoly in the country. I'll be killing two birds with one stone, reaping the benefits from the mother company and getting the profit through the shop!'

The policeman stretched out his legs.

Knew the arguments. They were the same as in Bregård's glossy brochure.

The guy was a pipe smoker. The pipe had once been red and shiny, made from briar root wood. Now it was stained and matt. The mouthpiece was worn, green at the tip and chipped from a firm bite. The man filled it with tobacco from a tin on the table. Rød Orlich.

'You're never . . .' *puff puff* . . . 'too old . . .' *puff* . . . 'to take a risk . . .' *puff puff.*

Blue smoke wafted upwards. Nice aroma. Used match in the ashtray. Another match.

'I had the choice . . .' *puff* . . . 'either to buy myself a life annuity which was not index-linked . . . or . . .' *puff* . . . 'you see, I'm thinking about my pension – ahh, tobacco is where I like to indulge myself . . . or invest in a risky project, use my savings to make an investment. I chose the latter. I put in everything I had!'

He is content now. Pipe between his teeth. Thumb in his waistcoat pocket. Rounded stomach straining against his waistcoat. Wig with the Hitler haircut.

'That's what the problem is today of course! The private sector needs venture capital. Solid companies like Software

Partners have problems when they approach ordinary financial institutions.'

He had forgotten his pipe, waved it around. 'Tell me why I should hesitate? Why shouldn't I grab the chance while it's there? Frøken Rosendal personally calculated a return on my investment that no one would dare dream about in today's market.'

'Frøken Rosendal?'

The man nodded. 'Yes, indeed. Frøken Rosendal in person!'

Frank gasped internally. A/S Software Partners: the revue act woman in flat shoes, Bluto and the snob from the house on the hill. Reidun with a tight skirt and a background in the Post Office. Would these characters provide this gentleman the returns no one would dare dream about? Something jarred.

'Are there enough funds for others to get in?'

Pipe back in his mouth. Business-like expression, matter of fact. 'The company has set a ceiling for the number of partners and the minimum stake is a hundred thousand kroner.'

He pondered. Puffed on his pipe. To the policeman's amazement, he got the pipe going immediately. Nice smell.

'I must say I'm glad I signed up early.'

'You really do have faith in this, don't you.'

A light brown drip of saliva from the pipe stem dropped on to Reidun's photograph. 'If you had met her you would have known this business was the real McCoy.'

He had assumed the dreamy expression he had had before. 'She was from another world.'

'Another world?'

The detective wiped the photograph with the sleeve of his jumper. The stain would not go away and blurred the girl's face.

'Yes, how can I put it, not just tall and attractive, but, well, look around you!'

'Yes?'

'I saw it on your face the minute you stepped in here. You saw it straight away, didn't you! A bankruptcy. Look around you! What sort of turnover do you think I can boast? Nothing. Every summer I have letters from the tax office because they can't believe my figures! What do you think I could buy from this woman who loyally drops round with her brochures and spends valuable time here? Nothing! But she came! Again and again and again. She was a woman from another world!'

Frank knew he wasn't going to get his questions answered.

Time to hit the road.

Luckily his pager bleeped.

25

'So this is where you are,' Frølich said.

Gunnarstranda studied the façade. *Oslo West*, he thought. And mumbled: 'This building is no more than five years old, max.'

'And not fully occupied,' Frølich added. He pointed to a row of empty windows on one wing.

'The rent must cost an arm and a leg,' Gunnarstranda remarked and went in first.

Kristin Sommerstedt nodded with a blank expression. 'No one up there,' she informed them.

'But the Finance Manager's in the fitness room, I suppose,' she hastened to say when she saw Gunnarstranda's look. 'That's what he said anyway as he dashed past half an hour ago.'

The policeman, taken aback, glanced at the clock. It was half past twelve.

The fitness room was in the cellar. Down there you were spared the luxury with which the rest of the building appeared to be saturated. The corridor walls were not painted and the concrete floor was untreated. They had to pass through some large steel doors that rumbled and a hollow echo reverberated along the bare walls. From somewhere deeper in the bowels they could hear the sounds of someone doing weight-training.

Gunnarstranda first stepped over the high threshold. Bregård was lying on an exercise bench forcing up a bar with a considerable number of weights attached. He was in the middle of a routine and showed no signs of stopping. The man was panting like a hippo. His face was red and dripping with sweat, and the mouth with the impressive moustache inflated like a frog's every time he sucked in air for the next press.

At last. With a huge clang the man dropped the bar and sat up on the bench. The veins in his temples were bulging. His pectoral muscles were clearly outlined under his T-shirt.

'That looked hard,' Frølich said. 'Nice to see you again, by the way.'

Gunnarstranda, though, was looking for somewhere to sit.

Bregård puffed, ignoring Frølich's small talk. Gunnarstranda glanced at them. Both big men. Bregård was most concerned with the palms of his hands.

The room was sparsely furnished. The police inspector clambered up on to the seat of an ergometer bike. Smiled, did a couple of circuits on the pedals and leaned forward over the handlebars.

'Probably harder steering the finances of A/S Software Partners, isn't it,' he stated in a measured tone.

Bregård got up and stretched both arms back.

'You're unknown to the Company Register,' Gunnarstranda went on.

Bregård placed his right hand against the wall and did a long stretch with his upper arm. First right, then left. His heavy breathing was all there was to hear in the small fitness room. The man immediately started a new round of stretching, first right, then left.

Frølich, who had found some barbells to play with, whistled a tune.

The athlete bent down to pick up his towel from the floor.

'The Brønnøysund Register Centre is always late,' he panted into his towel.

'But Brønnøysund didn't register anything last year, either.'

Bregård turned to Gunnarstranda while drying his neck. The police officer smiled.

Frølich was whistling.

The Finance Manager raised his voice imperceptibly. 'We only set up the business last year.'

Continued drying himself. 'So we'll be sending our first year's accounts this year.'

'So you haven't sent them yet?'

'No!'

'Well, then you can't blame the Centre for not being up to date!'

Bregård was annoyed. 'I'm not blaming them for anything!'

'But you just gave us to understand that all the accounts had been sent and that Brønnøysund was not up to date.'

Gunnarstranda pedalled round three times, stopped and waited for an answer.

Bregård sat down with a rigid grin.

'Fine,' he said and raised his hands in defence. 'Come upstairs with me! Nothing in this business is secret. Our accounts are quite public.'

'All accounts are public,' Gunnarstranda corrected him.

'Why is there no one upstairs?'

Bregård craned his head in annoyance towards the man who was whistling, then sent Gunnarstranda another bad-tempered glower, but said nothing.

The latter dismounted from the bike and walked towards Bregård. Stopped in front of him. 'How come you can lie down here grunting in the middle of a working day?'

Bregård put on a resigned smile. Keeping it there was a strain.

'Why don't Software Partners want to pay their rent?'

An attempt was made to convert the smile into an aloof grin but it failed. 'Don't want to pay,' he mimicked with a grimace. 'If you've got any questions about that, you'll have to talk to my boss.'

'Aren't you responsible for the company's finances?'

'Yes, indeed I am.'

Bregård's eyes flashed again, and again the blood vessels in his temples were visible.

'Then answer me!'

The man's mouth was contorted and sullen beneath the moustache. 'Will you shut up!' he screamed at the officer who was still whistling.

Frølich shut up.

There was a heavy silence.

Bregård grabbed the towel hanging over his shoulder and dried his neck angrily.

'You've already dried that bit,' Frølich informed him.

Bregård spun round. But Gunnarstranda darted between them. 'How come your boss is never available?'

'How should I know?'

A metallic timbre had coated his voice. His face was redder than before.

'He's never here when we come!'

'No one survives in this industry by sitting on their ass in the office eight hours a day!'

'But there ought to be someone in the office! If you were intending to survive! Where's Engelsviken?'

'I don't know, I told you!'

Bregård's voice cracked with fury. His knuckles around the towel were white.

'You've already dried your hands, too!'

This came from Frølich, leaning against the brick wall, with a smile. But Gunnarstranda didn't let Bregård answer. 'Why is there no one in this business who can answer anything,' he hissed close to the man's face. 'Why do you hide behind your boss?'

'I haven't been bloody hiding!'

'So tell me why you won't stump up the rent!'

For a moment Gunnarstranda thought that Bregård was going to throttle him. Time for a smile, he thought.

All at sea, Bregård stared at his hands.

Gunnarstranda went a step closer. 'Your sole success in

the finance industry,' he whispered, 'is that you almost killed a man who couldn't pay his rent.'

Bregård scowled.

'So how come you, of all people, pop up here as the Finance Manager of a company that is going to conquer half the kingdom?'

'I've mended my ways,' Bregård said unconvincingly.

'Doubtless.'

'I've paid my debt to society!'

'Of course you have.'

Gunnarstranda signalled to Frølich. Girded himself to go, then addressed the gentleman with the moustache one last time: 'But you know as much about financial management as I know about fox-hunting in England!'

He smiled again. 'Absolutely nothing.'

With that, he turned his back on Bregård and took Frølich along with him.

'How's Svennebye getting on in the drunk cell?' Frølich asked as they got back into their car.

'He's probably sleeping,' the inspector mumbled, disorientated, and the squeal of his pager made him start. He fumbled around trying to switch it off and grabbed his mobile phone. 'We'll talk to him afterwards,' he said in a low voice with his hand over the speaker before bending down to hear the message.

'Well?'

Gunnarstranda wondered whether to tell him right away. Decided to wait. Groped around for a roll-up.

'Drive to Torshov,' he said and could hear the agitation in his voice.

26

The two detectives had to enter where the staircase went round and round in long corkscrew spirals. It was tight. A uniformed policeman stood with his hands on his hips on the second-floor landing. He was trying to appear unruffled but was not succeeding. The Adam's apple over the blue collar was bobbing up and down nervously. By the feet of his incredibly long thin legs lay a body beneath a stiff plastic sheet that bore the signs of having been used before. It was full of holes and dirty. A powerful floodlight cast sharply delineated shadows and emphasized all the brutal details. The streaks of blood on the wall turned black in the white light.

Gunnarstranda peered up at the uniformed officer. 'Nausea?' he asked.

The man with the Adam's apple had placed his hands behind his back and focused his gaze somewhere ahead of him. The thin, pale face appeared unusually small under the cap. His answer was lost in the clatter of people on the stairs.

'Who found him?'

'Elise Engebregtsen, a pensioner, first floor.'

This time he had taken a run at it. His voice thundered and echoed off the walls. Everyone stopped, turned round and stared at him. His Adam's apple accelerated. His nervous eyes, bird-like and small, looked to the right.

'Any murder weapon?'

'Sharp object. Not accounted for at the crime scene.'

The photographer who had wedged himself further up the stairs sniggered. Gunnarstranda glowered at him, turned back to the body. He sighed, nodding to himself. Peered up the stairs. Blood on the wall and steps. Like a fine spray, here and there a broad stripe as well, where a thicker jet had splashed.

He bent down, pulled a plastic glove off the roll standing upright on one of the steps, walked over to a pool of blood and lifted the plastic to look closer. It wasn't easy. He had to hitch up his coat so as not to get it soiled while lifting the blood-stained plastic.

He cursed. Removed his coat. 'Hold this, will you,' he said to the uniformed officer who avoided looking at the floor. Gunnarstranda folded the sheet over to one side.

The face of Sigurd Klavestad was whiter than it had ever been. His eyes looked up, vacant and glassy. They were like marbles, Gunnarstranda thought as he met the gaze. He could hear loud gulps from the tin soldier behind him as he felt his stomach go queasy at the sight of the clean, deep cut that had almost beheaded the victim. Slowly he let go of the head and let it roll back to where it had been.

For a moment he surveyed the dead body. Bare feet. Bare arms. The dead man had put on light clothing in a hurry. The long pony tail was rigid and sticky.

He turned back to the tin soldier with the Adam's apple. Collected his coat.

'You can run along,' he said under his breath. 'Tell the

187

boys to get the names of everyone who is in the block, or who was here from yesterday afternoon until now.'

Gunnarstranda stood still. Tried to absorb the atmosphere that was no longer there. Strode towards the floodlight and switched it off. Those who had been working busily until now stopped. No one said a word. Slowly their eyes got used to the new light. A yellowish-grey glimmer from a bare bulb on the staircase wall.

He had fallen here. Frightened.

Gunnarstranda closed his eyes. Opened them. The others had not moved. Just stared at him. Unrolled the plastic glove. Dropped it on to the floor. Put the roll under his arm. Buried both hands in his coat pockets and took a deep breath before walking past Frølich and leaving.

On the ground floor they were met by Bernt Kampenhaug, the Unit leader. Actually quite a likeable musician, Bernt was. Someone who played the squeezebox three nights a week for the whole of November and December and, not only that, he had a collection of vintage automobiles. Three old police saloon cars. Nice bloke provided that he was not at work. And that you weren't discussing anything that resembled politics. Bernt was a man with strong opinions regarding stricter uniform regulations and weapons. Now he had slotted his sunglasses into his hair and was chewing gum, one hundred per cent tourist, and seemed happy with the fit of his overalls. A radio with a short aerial crackled in his hand. For the occasion the man had requisitioned a handgun that made his backside even broader than usual. Gunnarstranda could feel the sight of him beginning to get under his skin.

Kampenhaug stuffed the radio under his arm and accompanied them out with one hand on his belt. In the sun, he flicked the sunglasses on to his nose, nudged them into position with a finger, got the radio to crackle and tried to look his best for the press photographers outside the cordons.

One journalist shouted something to Gunnarstranda, who ignored him.

'The body was found by an old dear on the first floor,' Kampenhaug drawled, pointing with a thumb. 'She seems pretty dazed.'

Then he was off to give a journalist who had strayed across the cordon an earful. Came strutting back with the sun on his face.

'The old boiler was wittering on about the wrong person having been killed because the right one wasn't there. Senile if you ask me! He lives on the floor above her. The door's open!'

'Great,' said the police inspector.

The tin soldier with the bird-eyes crossed the rope.

'You're a police officer, man!' Kampenhaug screamed as if he were in the army. 'Wipe that vomit off your face before you talk to people!'

27

Gunnarstranda established that Sigurd Klavestad's flat told him no more than he already knew. Two rooms, a kitchen and a combined toilet and shower with a door to the hall. Loads of mirrors in the hall. Funny ones. One made your nose look like a swede and another distorted your face into a figure eight, making it look like something from a cartoon.

Chaos. Comics, shoes and a variety of clothes, jackets and jumpers lay scattered across the floor. The man was not acquainted with the shelving principle, it struck Gunnarstranda. Or at least tidying up. He left the hall of mirrors to his intelligent colleague and studied the two posters on the wall. One a copy of a French poster from the nineteenth century. A can-can dancer with flapping clothes, a painting. The other was a bird's-eye view of a short-sighted Marilyn Monroe. She lay reclined over a curtain, gloss lips slightly apart.

He continued into the bathroom and pulled up inside the door. The white washstand was spattered with blood on the inside. The floor was wet. Without a word, he stepped back into the sitting room.

Put on two thin plastic gloves from the roll he had in his pocket. Opened a window and called down to Klampenhaug.

There was something that bothered him about Klavestad's death. He ransacked his brain. Realized it wasn't Klavestad's passage to the beyond that annoyed him but the new perspective. Something was niggling him at the back of his mind. A nagging doubt. The fear of having to change hypothesis.

Two cue words for the moment. Knife and night. He liked that. But he didn't like the cut. The slash to the victim's neck. He didn't like that at all. What a damned nuisance that the man had been killed!

The murder would bring the stuffed shirts out of the woodwork, the schooled suits and ties who still felt a need to say aloud what everyone else was thinking. Hassle was brewing. Demands for statements and perhaps the odd press conference. Formalities. They irked him. But there was one positive side. He could feel himself getting angry. A good omen, he confirmed to himself and turned. Stood inspecting the stove. A slightly dusty tiled corner stove with a marble top and a nickel-plate handle. The old type.

Imbued with a sudden inspiration, he crouched down in front of it. Ran his hand warily along the iron. Stroked it again without the plastic glove this time. Hm. Possible.

Cautiously, so cautiously, he coaxed open the stove door. 'Frølich,' he called quietly.

Frølich came in from the hall. 'I suppose he was in bed sleeping,' he said. 'The reading lamp was on and the bed unmade.'

'Look here,' Gunnarstranda whispered.

Frølich stooped down and peered into the smoking ashes.

'He must have been heating the room,' he commented lightly.

'Not him,' Gunnarstranda said thoughtfully. 'Not him. And this is not wood. It's smouldering. This is material. Clothing! If there's anything left.'

28

Elise Engebregtsen was waiting for them with the door open when they appeared outside the lift doors. She was fat. Unusually fat. And the grey smile revealed an ageing set of dentures.

'Morning,' she said. 'I don't know anything, so you can just go again. I don't know anything.'

Frank smiled courteously, inclined his head. Looked down at her. A checked apron. Stout upper arms and an imposing backside, thick ankles that flowed over her slippers. Sixty maybe. Maybe sixty-five. Her dentures were catching flies. Clicking sounds caused by a nervous tongue. *What a bite on her! Like a trout's*, he thought, fascinated.

Gunnarstranda coughed.

'All right, come in then! But I've told you! I don't know anything.'

She waggled in front of them. As broad as a sumo wrestler. Small head with greasy, auburn wispy hair, cut close to her ears. Heavy, rhythmical breathing. She was a wrestler, a real one. Her teeth clicked.

'Aahhh,' she groaned, slumping into a chair. 'Goodness me.'

She pulled over a flower-pattern Thermos jug. Poured coffee.

'Goodness me!'

Small cups with roses on. 'Sugar in your coffee?'

Frank shook his head.

A somewhat muggy smell. As though you might expect to find moss inside the walls. A kind of grandmother smell. Small, round pictures. Light blue wallpaper with neutral white flowers. Needlework. Embroidery and knitting. The lady herself in the middle of the wall. A baby on each arm and a happy dentures smile on her face.

'I told you, I don't know anything.'

Nerves. Teeth clicking.

Gunnarstranda sipped the coffee. 'When did you find him?'

'Today, this morning.'

'What time was it?'

'Half past eight. After the morning service on the radio.'

Gunnarstranda nodded slowly.

'Mm,' she sighed. 'Goodness me!'

'It must have been terrible,' the policeman said sympathetically.

'I told the man with the pisstool! I don't know anything.'

'Pisstool? Pistol!' Frank spluttered.

Gunnarstranda nodded. 'He said you'd seen Sigurd Klavestad leaving last night!'

She breathed in. Scratched her forearms. 'Yes, that's right. He did leave, that's for certain!'

'When was that?'

'Four o'clock in the morning.'

'It was night. You noticed the time?'

Energetic shake of the head. Wispy hair lashing her face.

'I was up. I sleep so badly I was up and heard him running down the stairs!'

'He ran down the stairs?'

'Yes, first time.'

'He ran down the stairs and came back up again?'

Elise Engebregtsen breathed in and nodded.

'How do you know it was him?'

Shrug of the shoulders. 'Just think it was.'

'But you're not sure it was him?'

'I told you, I don't know anything!'

'But something made you think it was him running down the stairs!'

'Yes, he usually makes a lot of noise.'

'It's happened before?'

Another nod.

'So he came down again, after he ran up?'

Nod.

'Did he run then, too?'

'No, I didn't hear him until he was out of the house.'

'So he walked down slowly the second time?'

Nod.

'How much time had passed?'

'Ten minutes, fifteen maybe.'

'Did you see him leaving the building?'

'Yes.'

'How? Did you see his face?'

'I saw it was him.'

'But you didn't see his face?'

'Saw his coat, his body.'

'So it could have been someone else?'

'It was him!'

Angry now. Her mouth was a straight line and there was a deep furrow between her eyes which disappeared as her face contracted.

Gunnarstranda nodded. Sipped more coffee.

'What were you going to do outside?'

'Get rid of the rubbish!'

'What happened?'

'Couldn't open the door.'

'You couldn't open the door?'

'No.'

Gunnarstranda waited patiently.

'Managed to open it a tiny crack.'

She shivered. Scratched her forearms again.

'A crack.'

Very ill at ease now. Wandering eyes.

Gunnarstranda waited.

'Just saw this tiny white hand!'

'The hand, yes . . .'

Gunnarstranda nodded, his gaze fixed on her; it was like extracting words from a child that would not stop scratching.

'And on the floor . . .'

'On the floor, yes . . .'

'Blood on the floor . . .'

'Blood, yes, a hand and blood . . .'

'Then I saw it in the crack!'

'Saw the dead man, the body on the floor. Mhm.'

Gunnarstranda leaned back. 'Was he blocking your way? I mean, was his body blocking the door?'

She nodded.

'Close your eyes now,' the policeman said.

She obediently followed his instructions.

'And try to imagine Klavestad as he was leaving last night.'

She nodded.

'Can you see his face?'

'No.'

'But you can see his body?'

'Yes.'

Gunnarstranda got up. Stared out. The town lay grey and dull beneath him. 'Did he walk down the road?'

'Yes, down.'

'Keep your eyes closed, fru Engebregtsen. You can see him walking down the road. You can see his body in the light of the street lamps. Black, full-length coat, right?'

'Yes, the black coat. Yes, yes.'

'His hair? Did he have a pony tail or not?'

'Don't know.'

'Why not?'

'I can't see.'

'Does he turn round?'

'No. I leave the window and go to bed.'

She sat as before, with her eyes open.

Gunnarstranda was staring, serious. 'Are you sure it was Klavestad you saw?'

Irritated now. 'Yes, I told you I was.'

'But you didn't see a pony tail?'

'No, I think he was wearing a hood.'

The detective nodded. 'A hood,' he mumbled. 'Have you often seen this neighbour without a pony tail?'

Shrug of the shoulders.

The inspector is serious. 'You know, fru Engebregtsen, I've never seen him without his pony tail. Can you remember if you've ever seen him like that?'

Another shrug.

'Fru Engebregtsen?'

Another shrug. Scratched. Scratch marks on her arms. 'Goodness me!'

Gunnarstranda sighed. Fiddled with his coffee cup. He sighed again. 'Thank you very much for helping us, fru Engebregtsen.'

She didn't answer, just went on scratching her arms nervously. Her dentures clicked.

Gunnarstranda got to his feet, nodded to Frank. 'Soon, some other officers will come and take a statement. I hope you won't mind telling them what you've just told me.'

She didn't answer.

The two detectives turned and left. The last thing they heard was the click as Trout-Mouth went catching flies that weren't there.

29

'The racket she heard must have been Sigurd Klavestad falling down the stairs,' Gunnarstranda said to Frank in the car afterwards.

He nodded without taking his eyes off the road.

'The murderer must have gone back up,' the inspector continued. 'Cleaned off the blood in the bathroom. Gone into the sitting room, burned his outdoor clothes, which were stained with blood, to remove any evidence, put on some of Sigurd's clothes and left.'

'So it was the murderer she saw leaving, not Sigurd?'

'I presume so.'

'How did the bastard lure the victim on to the stairs?'

'Sigurd must have been woken up. The telephone was used as a warning with the girl. Presumably the murderer rings and warns them before coming. At any rate, I doubt he stands ding-a-linging the doorbell for hours. It would be too risky. But after phoning he rang the bell. Klavestad opened up, fine, but it's a job to know what happened afterwards.'

'The murderer may have hidden on the stairs.'

'Or he was someone Klavestad had no reason to fear,' Gunnarstranda suggested.

'An execution.'

'Right!'

The police inspector waved his hand in annoyance.

'But why on the stairs?'

Gunnarstranda stared out of the window, rapt in thought. 'Suggests nerves. It would have been safer inside the flat.'

Frank couldn't make that add up. 'Whoever did this cannot be nervous!'

'That's exactly what he was,' Gunnarstranda objected calmly. 'Scared shitless. The fact that the murder took place at all suggests the murderer knows he has to be quick. The whole sequence of events reeks of panic.'

Frank said nothing.

'For the time being,' Gunnarstranda broke the silence. 'I'm keen to find out what the peeping tom was doing last night. So, let's take a drive down there.'

30

Today there was more life in Johansen's block. A strong, agreeable smell of curry met them on the stairs, causing Frank's stomach to issue soft rumbles of lament, but they were not audible over all the shouts and laughter of games emanating from the open door of one flat.

These sounds grew fainter as they ascended. At the top the children's noise could hardly be heard and the stink of stale staircase dominated the food aromas from downstairs.

The old-timer showed them in, sat down in the battered chair and indicated the sofa while flicking his old Zippo into life. Frank cleared away the rubbish and freed up a spot to sit down. Took out his notepad and pencil. Signalled to Gunnarstranda that he was ready.

'I'm going to talk now,' the inspector said from the window, 'and you tell me if you agree or disagree afterwards. Is that all right?'

Johansen didn't say a word, just sent the little man by the window a dismissive glare. Inhaled smoke with a rattle of the throat.

'Reidun Rosendal was killed in her flat.'

Johansen glanced over at Frank. 'Bright sort, your boss, isn't he,' he sneered.

Gunnarstranda ignored the comment and continued:

'The place was turned upside down as if there had been a burglary. But no everyday objects of value were touched. Hence there is a good chance the evidence left after the burglary was intended to be a red herring. A ruse carried out by the murderer to mislead the investigation. If this proves to be correct then the murderer, even though the intention was to kill her, must have had an ulterior motive. In which case potential suspects can be limited to the circle we might call Rosendal's network. Family, friends, enemies and admirers.'

The latter was pronounced with especial irony. 'You,' Gunnarstranda emphasized, 'You are a part of this network. And from here you have a view of her flat.'

'A witness,' Johansen interrupted with firmness. 'I am a witness you have already established saw nothing at all.'

He burst into a coughing fit, but still had to have a few more drags of his cigarette when it was over. The cigarette was a moist brown colour between the man's nicotine-stained fingers. The bloodshot left eye had improved to such an extent that now only the network of veins in the corner was visible.

'How many people did you see go through the gate on Sunday morning?'

'I've already told you!'

'Which other men did you see in her flat?'

Johansen said nothing.

'Who visited her recently?'

'Nice weather today, isn't it?'

Johansen's tone was if possible even drier than before,

and he stubbed out the cigarette in an overflowing ashtray before meeting Gunnarstranda's eye, unwilling to yield an inch. He sat breathing asthmatically through a half-open mouth.

Silence descended.

'Did you ever ring Reidun Rosendal?'

'No.'

'Did you ring her last week?'

'No!'

'And if I insist you spoke to her on the phone last week?'

Johansen sat still, staring into space.

'You're lying to me, Johansen.'

'No, I am not!' the old man barked. He shifted uncomfortably in his chair. Even the bags under his eyes moved. 'I had forgotten.'

'Did you also forget that you were tossing yourself off in this window as well?'

Johansen breathed in.

'Have you forgotten what you said on the phone?'

Johansen didn't answer.

'You threatened her.'

Johansen's shoulders began to twitch.

'What did you say to her, Johansen?'

The twitches in the man's shoulder subsided. His eyes had gone hard. 'You don't know, do you,' he confirmed with a triumphant laugh. 'You haven't a bloody clue what I said!'

The inspector's voice repeated the question, this time with a metallic tone: 'What did you say to her, Johansen?'

'Wouldn't you like to know!'

Frank could see Johansen was mentally there, or close, but then he retreated, into his own head. He unleashed a grin and revealed a row of bad teeth.

'I told her how she should be fucked!'

The two policemen's eyes bulged.

'How she should be fucked up the arse!' he crowed with a manic cackle and slapped his thigh. The laughter degenerated into coughing.

The two detectives didn't move.

The old boy had to take out a handkerchief. Soon his breathing was a heavy rattle, back to normal. It was clear he felt he had scored a victory. Still he slanted his watery eyes towards the inspector as though expecting him to fall to the floor.

'I believe you,' Gunnarstranda said. 'That is what you told her. But *she* didn't agree!'

Again the room went silent. Johansen's breathing was a gurgle.

'*She* didn't agree,' the detective repeated. 'That was why she left the curtains open on Saturday, to show you how it should be done!'

'You're lying!' Johansen whispered, without looking up.

'She let you have a real eyeful,' Gunnarstranda hissed. 'She lay on her back wriggling under the lad, teasing you, poking you with a stick the way she would have poked a little rat in a cage to death!'

'No!'

Johansen jumped up from the chair with a wrinkled fist ready for a fight. Instantly Frank was up and grabbed his arm. It was dry and uneven to hold, like corrugated card-board.

'You're lying!' Johansen screamed as the policeman forced him back into the chair. He didn't feel anything, just stared manically at the bald little man moving from the window towards him with narrow, flashing eyes.

'She was teasing you,' the detective laughed. 'She brought out the devil in you, Johansen. The devil that couldn't bear to be led on. The devil that screamed the little whore down there should burn. She should be brought to her knees! She should burn! Burn in hell! So that was why you didn't give in until she was lying on the floor with no breath left in her body!'

Johansen didn't answer. He hid his face in his large creased hands.

The inspector watched him for a while. Then returned to the window.

Frank peered up and met his boss's eyes. Both waited.

At last the man removed his hands from his face.

'What were you doing in Torshov on Wednesday?' Gunnarstranda asked.

'Afternoon stroll,' Johansen answered. He had recovered some of the cold cynicism he displayed at first.

'Where were you last night?'

'Here.'

'Can anyone confirm that?'

'No.'

'You were observed walking in Agathe Grøndahls gate at half past twelve on Wednesday. Were you there?'

'You know everything already,' came a meeker response.

'Yes or no!' the officer barked.

'Yes.'

'Did you go to Agathe Grøndals gate at a later point, Wednesday afternoon, Wednesday evening or last night?'

'No.'

The old boy took a stub from the ashtray, managed to light it with some difficulty, his right hand trembled as he smoked. Johansen held it with his left to stop the trembling. Gave up. Put down the cigarette.

'Old injury,' he tried to explain.

'Are you aware that Sigurd Klavestad lived there, in the house in Agathe Grøndals gate where you were observed on Wednesday?'

'Who the hell is Sigurd Klavestad?' the man scowled in a barely audible voice. His neck had suddenly become very stiff.

'The young man with the pony tail you followed from here all the way up to Agathe Grøndals gate.'

Johansen didn't answer now. He was staring at the floor.

'He's been murdered.'

The old man's head embarked on a slow movement. His gaze rose from the floor.

'Someone cut the young man's throat last night.'

Johansen was breathing heavily. 'Murdered?'

His mouth hung open. A drop of saliva had collected on his lower lip. Like a sleepwalker he got up and began to pace to and fro. 'So he's dead, is he?'

He rubbed his right thigh as he walked.

'Did you know that, Johansen?'

The old man continued to pace the room in silence.

'Answer the question!'

'No.' Johansen's voice sounded tame. 'I didn't know.'

He stopped, took a deep breath and pressed down his right leg.

'Work injury. The nerves just go now and then.'

Frank could not keep his eyes away from the uncontrolled twitching in the old man's hands and legs.

'The only thing that helps is to walk a bit, to do something,' he continued.

'Why did you follow him?' Gunnarstranda asked in a more friendly tone.

Johansen sat down. 'He was here,' he sighed in a weary voice. 'Down there.'

The man tossed his head towards the window. Took the pouch on the table. Removed some tobacco and a rolling paper. But the trembling index and middle fingers caused him to tear the paper. Johansen stared dejectedly at the mess and the tobacco on the floor.

'Here you are!' Gunnarstranda passed him one of his roll-ups and held out the lighter.

Johansen inhaled. 'I followed him because I wanted . . . I think I wanted to do him in,' he said blowing out the smoke. But he straightened up when he saw Gunnarstranda's look. 'I said I thought I wanted to do it,' he stressed. 'In my head I wanted to kill him or something like that.'

He stared at Frank. Turned to address Gunnarstranda.

'He was here,' he repeated in a panic. 'Down by the Dælen-enga fence! Round here!'

He got up, made a scramble for the window and looked out. 'He stabbed her,' he insisted with vehemence. 'Cut her up!'

His voice cracked and he had to clear his throat. 'I wanted to do him in. I followed him, found out where he lived!'

'What other men have you seen in her flat?'

Silence.

'You did see some, didn't you.'

Silence.

'You've been watching this rose of yours for two years, Johansen. You saw people there!'

Nod.

'Who?'

The old-timer stumped back to his chair and sat down. His hands gripped both arm rests.

Gunnarstranda followed. 'Who?'

No answer.

'Who?'

Frank noticed the bags under his eyes. The sallow hue of his skin. The round shoulders and the mass of dandruff on his faded clothes. He contemplated a very small man sunken in the chair.

Johansen cleared his throat. 'No one.'

His composure was back. 'No one,' he repeated evasively, with his eyes closed. 'Just her.'

The old man drifted off. Mumbling something incomprehensible.

Gunnarstranda moved. 'You'll have to come with us to the station in Grønland. We have to take your fingerprints.'

Johansen lowered his head.

'We're going to search your premises.'

Frank got up wearily and at once started to open the drawers of an old bureau leaning gently against the wall. The inspector bent over the old man. 'You're hiding something, Johansen,' he whispered. 'You're keeping your mouth shut about far too many things! But I can promise you one thing! If we find a single knife or anything sharper than a fish slice in this dump, there won't be any bus trips home for you afterwards!'

Frank rummaged through the drawer. Pencils, biros and a bit of fishing line. A rusty nut was the only metal object he found. *This is going to take time,* he thought patiently, picking up a beer cap.

31

Gunnarstranda gazed out of the window, watching the old man with the stick staggering down the long hill towards Grønlandsleiret. Arvid Johansen, peeping tom. Bent figure, wearing a coat and a hat with a brim. The man turned and shook his stick at Police HQ. A spiteful guest. A gesture that symbolized the man's willingness to co-operate. A stubborn silence. *I wonder if that is all you can do*, the policeman by the window thought. *Can this shaking fist cut into flesh? Living human flesh? It would be a convenient solution to think it could. Easy. But probably wrong. So count your lucky stars we didn't find any weapons in your flat.*

The door was opened behind him. A man shuffled in, followed by an officer who turned, went out and closed the door without a word.

The silhouette of the new arrival was outlined in the window. Jesus! The man's face was redder than a Pink Lady apple. Gunnarstranda stared alternately from the face in the reflection to Johansen on the street until he disappeared behind Grønland Church.

Then he swung round and asked Svennebye to sit down. He didn't comply with the request and sluggishly remained standing where he was, in front of the desk. Gunnarstranda was forced to realize that the man had probably not been through the best of times recently. A sorry sight. The un-buttoned coat revealed stained trousers with the fly open where a shirt tail had got stuck. The tie hung like a loosely coiled skipping rope. The inspector sniffed the air and decided he would open the window.

'Take a seat,' he repeated, indicating with one hand a spindleback chair in the middle of the room, one and a half metres from his desk.

The man coughed and fumbled around with his right hand which was wrapped in a large white bandage. In the end he succeeded in hanging his coat over the back of the chair. Sat down gingerly, still with the tip of his tongue making swift forays up and down his lips.

'Name?'

'Egil Svennebye.'

'Job?'

'Unemployed.'

'I beg your pardon?'

'Unemployed!'

The policeman sat down with a thoughtful furrow on his brow. Opted for the formal approach. Pulled out a drawer from the desk and rigged up a microphone. 'Now, everything that is said in this room will be recorded,' he explained, fidgeting with the mike which at first would not stand up and kept tipping over on to the table.

There. He caught the man's eye. He was scowling. Pale blue irises floating from side to side in bright yellow albumen.

'Your name is Egil Svennebye. Your last registered workplace was A/S Software Partners where your position was Marketing Manager. Is that correct?'

The man nodded.

The detective pointed to the microphone.

'Yes.'

The man mopped his forehead with the bandage.

'I'll be quite honest with you,' Gunnarstranda promised after a pause of a few seconds. 'Drinking and public disorder offences are not my province. I deal with murder cases.'

The irises stopped floating.

'How come A/S Software Partners still consider you an employee?'

'Management has not yet received my resignation.'

'So you are resigning?'

'Yes.'

'Why?'

Svennebye cast down his eyes and sighed. 'I've had a few days to mull this over and I've come to the conclusion it's the only thing I can do.'

Gunnarstranda leaned back, pulled out the lowest drawer with the tip of one shoe and rested his foot. His trousers rode up, baring a pasty white leg with a mass of light blue veins across a red tractor rut made by the elasticated top of his sock.

Svennebye's eyes were drawn by the sight.

'What is your view of Software Partners as a place of work?'

'May I have some water?'

The policeman got up and went to a white sink by the

door. Flicked the tap which straight away made howling noises. He let the water run while testing the temperature with his fingers every now and then. Observed the profile of the man in the chair. His forehead was damp with droplets of sweat. He could not remember being that hung-over or fragile, ever. 'I have taken the liberty of contacting your family,' he informed him, reaching for a paper cup that was not entirely clean, and rinsing it. 'Your wife says you were not happy there, at Software Partners.'

Svennebye took the cup with trembling fingers and greedily gulped down the water.

'I've started looking for another job, yes.'

His voice had become breathless.

The inspector sat down. Placed both arms on the desk.

'Why?'

'I didn't like it there.'

'Why not?'

'Too small, not enough responsibility.'

'That's not the kind of answer I want.'

Svennebye went quiet. His red face bore an uncertain expression.

'I want details. Your wife told me about a strange business trip you went on a few weeks ago.'

Svennebye mustered a wry smile. 'Strange is the word,' he mumbled with a shiver and flipped the coat on to his shoulders. Folded his arms in front. 'We were supposed to present our software at a fair in London. That is, Engelsviken, Bregård . . . me and . . .'

'Reidun Rosendal,' Gunnarstranda completed deftly. 'When?'

'Exactly seven weeks ago.'

'And there we touch on something else that bothers me.'

The policeman deliberated. 'Did you, you old soak, manage to keep off the booze in London's pubs?'

Svennebye assented with a composed nod. It seemed that the inspector's sudden informal tone had allowed him to relax.

'I had a few problems dealing with the system,' he answered, stressing 'deal'. 'At work, that is.'

There was a frozen grimace on the man's lips. This was not easy for him.

'Put it into words,' the detective urged and saw his request strike home. The man nodded, as though to himself. 'The whole enterprise was random, no planning. There was something peculiar about it from the word go.'

Gunnarstranda played with a cigarette and did not interrupt.

'As long as you bow and scrape you're everyone's best friend, but the minute you make demands there's resistance. Sarcasm and barbed comments rain down on you.'

'What kind of demands?'

Svennebye wasn't listening. He was still dealing with the sarcasm. 'The more I think about it, the clearer I can see. There were two camps at work. Those who were in the know and those who weren't. I belonged to the latter category.'

The man looked across the desk. 'What kind of demands?' he echoed with rising intonation, his mind else-where. Then he became serious. 'The kind that expect to see results from the work you're doing!'

Gunnarstranda was beginning to enjoy the conversation. 'Was that why you went to pieces?'

Svennebye closed his eyes and leaned back so far the chair creaked. The inspector let him take his time. 'Reidun and I started on the same day,' he said with a solemn face. 'Software Partners was becoming something, we were told. They were seeking sales staff and a Marketing Manager. I'm over fifty.'

His eyes twinkled with more life now. You could read the irony in his expression. 'Early retirement was beckoning.'

Gunnarstranda stared at him. The ruddy complexion and the bags under his eyes. The coat and trousers that smelt of dried urine and vomit but which were quality garments. The policeman could easily imagine him on the way to a morning meeting with a project group, though in clean clothes, of course. Svennebye talked about his line of work. The hoarse voice reeled off key terms like creativity and youth. He had never believed he would get the job. But when it was in the bag he had felt like a dynamo. 'I'm over fifty,' he repeated with a smile. 'I had beaten off competition from younger political and business economists and God knows what!'

'But then,' the dehydrated voice continued. 'Let me put it like this: the job was a challenge.'

Gunnarstranda was told that Svennebye's role was to develop a sales mechanism and a distribution network for the company. By Sonja Hager and Brick, their lawyer. Was the latter on the board of directors? Svennebye wasn't sure; he thought he was. The whole bunch of those who were apparently 'in the know' had given a solid impression during the interview. But then nothing happened. 'Can you imagine what that is like?' he asked. 'To want to do a job of work, to make a contribution, and then you're just confronted with waffle! No specific planning. Just sporadic telephone calls at home late in the evening.'

Svennebye heaved a sigh of despair. 'Engelsviken ringing with rock music in the background. Asking me to go to a meeting at half past eleven at night.'

He sighed. 'So you go there, without an ounce of enthusiasm, but because you have to. And there's Engelsviken, sitting half-pissed with this lawyer and he sets out these visions of the future that are crazier than the tower of Babylon.'

He paused for breath. 'In the end you're forced to wonder, to examine what you are doing and to ask yourself: Will any money come from this? How am I spending my time? What the hell are we doing?'

The man clenched his good hand. 'And you can do nothing about it! You don't even have the guts to quit.'

Svennebye lowered his voice. 'I felt I was caught in a rat trap. When the police phoned on Monday I couldn't stand it any longer. I was too thirsty.'

The detective nodded. 'The trip to London? Was it a waste of time?'

'I just went along,' the man continued with the same intonation. 'I had my suspicions, you see.'

'What sort of suspicions?'

'That it would be a failure. No one was prepared. All the advance planning degenerated into chat about pubs and beer and . . .'

He smiled for as long as his dry lips let him. 'I joined them the first night, only had a Coke and went back to the hotel.'

Gunnarstranda trod water.

'Absolutely hopeless it was! The Managing Director came on to Reidun, made some dubious suggestions to her, while Bregård was knocking it back and scowling like a jilted suitor in an American B-film.'

Svennebye mopped his sweaty brow with his bandage. 'The next morning I had breakfast on my own. I sat in the lobby waiting for them for a couple of hours. We were supposed to be going to this fair. No one turned up. Can you believe it? No one. I went looking. Found Reidun and the MD in the jacuzzi wrapped around each other, oblivious to anyone else, most of all to me, standing there with my briefcase and indicating my watch.'

He wiped his brow again. 'I thought it best to turn a blind eye. It wasn't any of my business where she slept at night. But I was pretty annoyed that the MD wasn't interested in doing any business. So I knocked on Bregård's door instead.'

Svennebye angled another ironic smile. 'Øyvind had just woken up when I arrived. Unshaven, and with a king-size hangover. The guy was only interested in where the others were. When I told him where I had seen them, he went ballistic.'

Svennebye's lips forced a smile. 'The big guy set off in his underpants. At the end of the corridor we met the lovers coming arm in arm. Bregård said nothing. Just pasted one on Engelsviken, who fell to the floor. The guy went completely beserk. Øyvind, that is. Called Reidun a tart.'

Svennebye paused.

Gunnarstranda lit a cigarette, removed a flake of tobacco stuck to his lip. Inhaled and blew out a cloud of blue smoke.

Svennebye stared at the cigarette poking out between the inspector's fingers. Gunnarstranda reached into his pocket for a crumpled pack of non-filter Teddys, tapped out a creased one and offered it.

The man accepted and smoked greedily. Got up, went to the sink and spat. Drank some more water and sat down again.

'You were saying?' Gunnarstranda prompted. 'What did Engelsviken do?'

'Struggled to his feet. They flew at each other. Uneven contest. Engelsviken is a bit podgy and not exactly fit. And have you seen Bregård? The weightlifter. Engelsviken was back on the floor within two seconds.'

Svennebye gave a weak smile. 'A cleaner down the corridor ran off in a complete panic. Shouting and dragging her Hoover. Straight afterwards two security men appeared with bulges under their jackets. Big guys who spoke some weird English no one understood. Could have been Scottish or Irish or something. I tried to calm everyone down. Seemed to work, anyway the security boys carried off Engelsviken and laid him on his bed. Reidun, the poor thing, was so embarrassed she fled to her room. Bregård went back to bed, and I went to the fair alone.'

'Engelsviken is married, isn't he?'

'Mm.'

'She's in the office as well, isn't she? Sonja Hager? How did that work?'

'Sonja didn't go to London.'

'But afterwards, between Reidun and the MD?'

Svennebye shrugged. 'Nothing to do with me. But I really don't know what the young woman was thinking about back in Norway. Having fun on an office trip is one thing. Continuing with it at home is quite another. Have you met Engelsviken?'

'I'm afraid not.'

'You haven't missed much.'

He raised his hands in defence. 'OK, stupid thing to say. The point is I don't like him. But it's personal. The guy's all right.'

He nodded.

'Very all right. That's why he's dangerous. He doesn't look much.'

He tilted his head. 'A man in the panic years. Silk suit, sports car and a roving eye when his wife isn't looking. But he's got charisma. Energy, immense energy. Friendly manner with people and dominates groups with his personality. So I didn't think it was very strange when he checked out Reidun for a night. She was fresh and new and out for a bit of fun.'

He snuffed his cigarette. Leaned forward and grabbed the

pack Gunnarstranda pushed across the desk. Lit up. Took a few drags with a contemplative pucker in his brow.

'But I don't understand why she persisted.'

'The two of them were having a relationship?'

'Mhm. For a while.'

The man on the chair closed his eyes. 'Things turned nasty after the trip. That was how I perceived it. I'd seen them in London and observed the odd incident afterwards that maybe others hadn't.'

'Sonja Hager knew nothing?'

'Nothing.'

He hesitated. 'Perhaps she did. I don't know.'

He gave another weak smile. One of the sores on his top lip cracked. 'If she had known . . .'

'Yes?'

'Then she would not have had an easy time. I mean, they all worked together . . .'

Gunnarstranda, in a brown study, stared into space. 'How long did the relationship last?'

'Don't know.'

'How can you be sure it did finish?'

Svennebye licked the sore lip. 'There was a break-in at the office about a fortnight ago.'

He bent forward and rested his chin on one fist.

Gunnarstranda's ears pricked up. The word 'break-in' had caused a bell to ring at the back of his mind. He listened to Svennebye describing all the mess. The drawers that had been emptied and slung across the floor. Svennebye said no other tenants in the block had been affected, only Software

Partners. He had been the first to arrive that morning. He had been the one to discover it and had immediately rung Engelsviken. To tell him what had happened and warn him he was going to ring the police. The MD had got into quite a flap. Started to give him a bollocking, as good as. It ended up with Svennebye being forbidden to do anything at all until Engelsviken was present. When he did eventually come Svennebye and Reidun Rosendal were instructed to clear everything up. Thenceforward all employees were banned from mentioning the break-in to anyone else.

Svennebye extinguished his cigarette and leaned back. 'For almost six months they had been running down to the law courts on trivial matters! But when it came to the break-in . . . they weren't even willing to entertain the bloody idea!'

He jerked his head. 'That's what I meant by two camps in the place. It was as if Reidun, Lisa Stenersen and I were being kept in the dark. As if there were a secret connected with this break-in.'

The man sighed. 'It all culminated in a row, and this led to quite a drama between the two of them, Reidun and Engelsviken.'

He sighed in despair. 'Just imagine, the middle-aged MD pinches the girl's bum, wants to drag her into his office and no one is supposed to see what's going on. Absolutely hopeless.'

Svennebye licked his lips again. 'So she told him what he could do with his pinches!'

'It wasn't just a lovers' tiff?'

'Far from it! Reidun had had enough of being a mattress

for her boss, there's not a doubt in my mind. She was livid with him. This strange reaction of his is what triggered the avalanche!'

'How did he take it?'

'It was pretty embarrassing at first. But later . . . I think he would have liked to keep the relationship alive.'

'You mean he was still hankering after Reidun?'

'Yes.'

'And you could see that?'

'Well, I could, anyway.'

'And the others?'

'Don't know.'

'What was stolen in the break-in?'

'Nothing.'

Svennebye snorted in annoyance. 'But that's not the point. It's the principle of the thing. A break-in is a break-in.'

Gunnarstranda raised an arm to pacify him. 'How can you be so sure nothing was stolen?'

'We talked about it for ages.'

'What was said?'

'Well, first of all we checked everything. Among other things I had a few hundred-krone notes in a cup on the desk. Untouched. Reidun went through everything else. We all agreed nothing had been stolen.'

'But who was talking? Everyone? Or just those not in the know?'

Svennebye sat staring at the policeman. Chewing his bottom lip.

Silence descended over the room. Gunnarstranda gave

him space to reflect. Got up and went to the window from where he surveyed the traffic in Grønlandsleiret.

'Yes,' came the gruff voice from behind him. 'In fact it was just us. Reidun, Lisa and I.'

'Had the filing cabinet been opened?'

'Yes. It had been broken into and everything was scattered on the floor. Sonja flipped. I suppose she must have been . . . frightened of something.'

'So you don't know if anything was stolen from the cabinet?'

'No.'

Gunnarstranda sat down again. 'Why is the cabinet always locked?' he asked.

'Don't ask me. I didn't have permission to use the cabinet. All the filing went through Sonja Hager. If I needed any material it had to be ordered in good time via her. The fusspot!'

He sighed, ruminated. 'Nope,' he continued. 'Sonja's all right, too. But she should have dealt with her husband. That's perhaps the nub of the matter. She pranced around dispensing vacuous phrases. I was fed up with her.

'I suppose she deserves some sympathy,' he added without much generosity in his voice. 'The husband hits the town every single weekend while she stays at home. Reigning from the hill like a queen, with her house help.'

'Servant?'

'Yes. A young Filipina or Thai poppet who helps Sonja to wash, tidy and cook.'

A quiet grin spread across his cracked lips. 'The woman's a laughing stock!'

Gunnarstranda watched him release a sequence of small smoke rings from his mouth.

A laughing stock, he mused, and asked:

'Have you got anything specific in mind when you say she's a laughing stock?'

Svennebye grinned again. 'No, in fact, now that you're asking me she has always seemed a laughing stock to me. Pathetic. Stupid. Don't ask me why.'

Gunnarstranda changed subject: 'How did Bregård get on after your trip?'

Svennebye shrugged. 'Think he calmed down. He'd got it out of his system. Sent her the goo-goo look whenever she flashed her legs.'

He chuckled. 'And that was not so infrequent.'

'Bregård's a bit of a hothead, is he?'

The man considered that. 'Can't really say he is. He's a great guy, head mostly full of hunting and sport. I saw him lose control that one time, but he had a hangover.'

'I've heard he drives around with a rifle in the ski box on top of his car.'

'That's right.'

'Why does he do that?'

'He goes off into the country after work, shooting wood pigeons and crows. Hoping to hit a grouse or a hare.'

'What do you think about that?'

Svennebye took his time to answer. 'Lots of people are like that, aren't they? Hunting and outdoor freaks.'

'But this rifle's in the car ski box the whole time.'

The man nodded.

'Is the box locked?'

'No idea. In fact, I've never given it a moment's thought. That's just the way Bregård is. He's got a rifle on the car roof. He's always going on about his nature experiences. Sunsets and coffee round the campfire. That sort of thing.'

The inspector leaned back in his chair, watching the man withdraw into himself, his head bowed. Svennebye was struggling with a problem. When, at last, he raised his head, his eyes were hard and implacable. 'Now I'll tell you something that ought to interest you preservers of law and order,' he announced. 'After we returned from London I was tasked with making a catalogue for a product I do not begin to understand.'

He left an eloquent pause, then continued: 'The others partied for days over there.'

The man tapped a white index finger on his chest. 'I went to the fair. Not the others. Yet Engelsviken claimed afterwards he had returned with a contract!'

The finger tapped faster. 'I'm the Marketing Manager! The person responsible for sales. And Engelsviken demanded that I sell this concept of his in a brochure to be distributed country-wide. But he didn't bloody tell me what it was based on. He just gave me a load of computer chit-chat I didn't understand. As a result I couldn't sell the products properly in the catalogue, either. So I wrote a lot of meaningless twaddle.'

The finger came to a rest in the man's pocket, then he leaned across the table and formed his sore lips into a smirk. 'For seven weeks Reidun Rosendal and Engelsviken and

Bregård went around selling something they didn't understand.'

'Which means what exactly?' the policeman snapped.

Svennebye smirked again. His dry lips had cracked in several places and now he was licking blood off his top lip.

'Just what I say.'

'But some people have actually invested!'

'Possibly. I don't know. But have you seen a registered trade mark anywhere?'

'No,' Gunnarstranda was forced to concede. Reclining, sunk in thought. Intake of breath. 'I've read a lot of fancy words.'

'I wrote those words.'

The inspector studied him, watched him smoking, but he didn't pursue the matter.

'From now on Software Partners don't have a Marketing Manager. Since Reidun's dead, officially they don't have any sales staff, either,' Svennebye continued. 'But I doubt that will stop them selling. It's the emperor's new clothes.'

They sat in silence for a while. Until the policeman pulled out the drawer and switched off the tape recorder. 'Now I just need your signature on this,' he said, still lost in thought, and got up. 'Not much more and you can go.'

32

It was early morning. Gunnarstranda had got up at half past six. In the usual sequence he had quickly devoured his portion of porridge, drunk two glasses of skimmed milk and consumed half a jug of hot coffee. Now he was sitting in a taxi on his way to Kampen, a suburb of Oslo. The driver's tongue was going nineteen to the dozen. They had been through the whole repertoire. From the Olympic Winter Sports committee in Lillehammer to the Government, EU opposition in the Centre Party to the old dears who hadn't twigged that they should be lying in bed gasping for air instead of trying to cross Vogtsgate on green.

Not that the police inspector cared. He just stared out of the window with his mind elsewhere.

Gunnarstranda asked the driver to pull over by the church in Kampen main square. He wanted to walk the last few metres. It was still early. Gunnarstranda liked the sleepy tranquillity that settled over the timber houses in Kampen. He liked to walk there, to breathe in the idyll of brightly coloured houses and the wooden fences that enclosed small gardens. An article he had read about Oslo came to mind as he strolled down towards the blocks of flats in Kjølberggata. It had been written by some dusty bureaucrat whose considered opinion was that it was possible to influence politicians' decisions with sensible discussion. At any rate, the main gist was that Oslo's most striking hallmark was its painted houses. Gunnarstranda had to concede the bright spark was right. Kampen was like a bouquet of flowers, even in April before the grass had turned green.

He was soon at his destination. Ambled in through the gate. The Skoda was nowhere to be seen. But there was a strong smell of paint coming from the yard. And shrill whining sounds from the garage. He walked round the garage and opened the little door at the back where the padlock hung open.

It wasn't possible to see anything clearly. The outline of a light blue van could be glimpsed through a grey mist of paint and solvents. Something moved in the mist. Soon a black, oil-stained face appeared. The man bared a row of white teeth. Gunder.

'Come in,' he bawled.

The policeman instinctively retreated. Stepped back over the half-metre-high threshold and into the open air.

'You can't go in there without a mask,' he gasped to the man who followed him out. The same friendly smile. Gunder's eyes were large and white. Four flat wrinkles bedecked his forehead.

'It's the purest mountain air in there now,' he claimed. 'You should have been here an hour ago, then you might have had to cut your way through the fog!'

They stood in the yard, outside the garage with the crooked walls and corrugated tin roof that threatened to collapse.

Gunnarstranda said nothing and held out a lighter flame. The mechanic had poked a recycled dog-end the size of a fingernail between his lips and managed masterfully to light it without burning himself. They trudged through the yard and on to the dark drive. Gunder led the way. The man's two worn-down black clogs hastened across the tarmac with a clatter. Round the street corner and across to the white Skoda parked by the kerb.

'I changed the distributor cap because it was knackered. Changed the pins, the fan belt, plugs and two plug cables.'

The man was speaking with the dog-end glued to his lower lip.

'The car's only three years old!' the policeman protested with his arms outstretched.

The mechanic in the stained overalls responded with a kindly look.

'Three years?' He motioned towards the Skoda. 'You have to count the age of this crate in dog-years.'

Gunnarstranda scowled. 'Is it all right?'

'Now it is.'

'How much?'

'Invoice?'

Gunnarstranda frowned at Oil-Face, who was now sporting five wrinkles. Something was going on inside.

'It's all tied up with VAT.'

'Tell me how much!' Gunnarstranda remonstrated.

Oil-Face examined his hands. 'Wouldn't have been much of an invoice anyway,' he sighed. 'Six hundred!'

The policeman rolled back his shoulders and stuck a

hand in his inside pocket. Took six hundred-krone notes from his wallet.

Oil-Face produced a friendly smile. 'Bit of body rust,' he said, stuffing the notes into the back pocket of his overalls. 'Round the door handle.'

Gunnarstranda accepted the car key without a word.

'I do body work as well,' Oil-Face informed him.

The police inspector turned and went towards the car.

Oil-Face smiled and wandered back to the garage. 'Just give me a buzz,' he shouted as he rounded the corner. The car started with a roar. Gunnarstranda smiled with satisfaction, manoeuvred the car away from the kerb and drove a few metres. Stopped and got out. The engine was purring like a cat. He opened the rear bonnet. Perfect. New cables. New distributor cap. He was happy. Straightened up and closed the bonnet. Searched his pockets for a cigarette. Found one, found the lighter, glanced up in the air and froze. Filthy windows with white lettering. Talk about a co-incidence. Every other pane. SOLICITOR written on the glass. Wall. The name BRICK written in white letters. Wall, and then SOLICITOR again.

He switched off the ignition. Closed the door and strode across the street and into the gateway. Nice back garden. Evergreen thuja bushes in a tidy flowerbed. Table for scoffing packed lunch in a corner. Brass name plate. Perfect. Etched with acid into the metal: Brick, Solicitor. So this was where Engelsviken's business manager lived.

The inspector stood and considered. Finally made up his mind. Turned and sauntered back to his car.

33

It was Friday morning. The car was fixed. But there would not be a trip to the cabin this weekend, either. Nor next weekend probably. Nor the weekend after that, probably. It didn't bear thinking about. He just got irritated. Somewhere further east, over Sweden, there was grey cloud cover. It would bring rain in the course of the day, according to the weather forecast on the news last night. On the desk lay Marketing Manager Svennebye's statement. The man who didn't know what his employer was selling. The man who didn't know how the company could sell anything at all. Because his superior had not done any business deals when they should have done.

Gunnarstranda was smoking. The ash fluttered down on to a glitzy brochure from the same company. The brochure in which an ex-bully boy, convicted for having beaten up a businessman in Hovseter, was enticing potential investors with large capital returns. Trust Software Partners, it said, pay with ready cash. Money in the bank for whom? A group of unknown shareholders? Or Terje Engelsviken? The bankruptcy king with a hungry wallet and a dubious reputation?

The inspector had lots of questions he would like to ask the solicitor with the brass name plate in Kampen. But he wasn't ready yet. And he may not be the right man to ask them. This might be better left to someone else.

Gunnarstranda blew the ash off Bregård's face, crushed the cigarette in the ashtray, picked up the phone and dialled a number.

'Davestuen,' a voice said, chewing something.

'Gunnarstranda.'

'Ah, right,' the voice continued to chew. Gunnarstranda was irked, gave a measured cough. 'Software Partners.'

'Guessed as much.'

Davestuen was still chewing. Slow, wet mastication, like a child playing in mud.

'Got anything?'

'Well . . .'

Gunnarstranda put the receiver under his chin to hunt for another cigarette. 'You're having breakfast, are you?' he asked in calibrated courteous tones.

'Nope,' Reier said, smacking his lips. 'I'm coming to terms with withdrawal symptoms. We've got a pretty thick file on this Engelsviken.' He munched on, unruffled.

Gunnarstranda nodded. Wondered about the withdrawal symptoms but let the subject go.

'Dropped cases,' Reier slurped. 'Creditors who have reported the guy for fraud. They reckon that before and during the bankruptcy he was trading with the money owned by companies he headed up.'

Gunnarstranda grunted. 'What have you got in your gob?'

'Nicotine.'

The frown on Gunnarstranda's forehead deepened. Hoping the man would stop. But Davestuen chewed on:

'Engelsviken emptied the coffers before the bankruptcy, you see? All the cases were dropped for lack of evidence. Everything ended up in a row over dates. Engelsviken could vouch for things having been sold well before legally set deadlines. There's a pattern here that reeks of hanky-panky, if you want my opinion.'

Gunnarstranda grunted again. He had finally found the cigarette he had been hunting for.

'But this case is different. Now his firm, which he has called Software Partners, wants to increase the share capital.'

Davestuen went quiet. Gunnarstranda could hear his big hands fumbling with the receiver. The sound of squelching sludge returned.

'But, you know, this solicitor of theirs, this Brick, has devised a new trick to raise capital. And this is actually a trifle complicated.'

'How can you eat nicotine?'

'In chewing gum. Flat bugger. Pretty hard and it does not taste good.' Davestuen chuckled. 'Modern chewing tobacco. You remember the old fellas cycling up Markveien with half a bottle of vodka in their back pockets and two slimy rivulets of tobacco dribbling down their chins?'

Gunnarstranda nodded. 'Yes,' he mumbled, disorientated, scanning the desk for his lighter.

Davestuen cleared his throat. 'Now they make chewing gum instead, supposed to satisfy the craving for nicotine. We're thinking about the environment here, you know.'

'Right . . .'

'Protecting the environment!'

'Yes, yes, but we were talking about the tricks Engelsviken and Co. are getting up to!'

'OK. Instead of borrowing money, Software Partners go out and ask small businesses to become co-owners, thus increasing their share capital, which in itself ought to be fine. However, it happens in a rather odd way.'

'Oh?'

Gunnarstranda registered the mounting silence.

'Great,' Davestuen burst out. 'Finished chewing that crap. Anyway, this financing is distinctly fishy.'

He explained: 'The way Software Partners acquires capital is not strictly legal. The shares are sold in tranches with a minimum cash investment of something like a hundred thousand and no one sanctions the arrangement. Furthermore, the new owners do not have the usual say in the company because the shares they have bought are B-shares, which provide limited rights. All they receive is a dividend and a kind of entitlement to sell the company's products.'

Gunnarstranda listened patiently. Familiar ground. The shop-owner Frølich had spoken to in Rådhusgata had banged on about a minimum investment. He had seen some advantages to being able to sell Software Partner products. Gunnarstranda lit up.

'Legally speaking a grey area,' his colleague went on. 'Since parts of this arrangement are not covered in law. This solicitor, Brick, maintains therefore that the potentially obstructive regulations stipulated by the securities law are no longer valid.'

Davestuen paused for a while, coughed again, emitted a sneeze accompanied by tiny chewing sounds. 'On the other hand, there could be big money in this, as the minimum investment is a hundred thousand. Ten takers would give you a million. Think what fifty would mean, or for that matter a hundred!'

He coughed louder. 'And it's this financial side that I think could be the most interesting for us.'

'Oh?'

The voice in the receiver was lost in a paroxysm of coughing. 'Christ, this nicotine shit does something to your throat!'

Gunnarstranda stared at the receiver. Bloody hell, there was no end to this man's physical noises. He blew the ash off the cigarette glow. Took another puff and patiently burned a ring of black scorch marks on the paper around the photograph of ex-bully boy Bregård to pass the time.

Davestuen was back. 'You see, the money isn't paid into Software Partners but to a finance company called Partner Finance.'

'What's wrong with that?' asked Gunnarstranda.

'The problem is that no one can say who owns Partner Finance. So no one knows what happens to the money that has been paid in. What's even more peculiar is that it transpires that this company has given its address as Guernsey, a so-called tax haven.'

The faint smell of scorched paper merged with the aroma

of tobacco in Gunnarstranda's nostrils. Bregård's halo of burn marks was half-finished. 'But this is probably not illegal, is it,' he said.

'No, it isn't,' Davestuen agreed and explained. The point was that no one he had contacted in the finance market knew about Partner Finance. It was peculiar, to put it mildly. Alarm bells were ringing. The bells that presaged fraud. But to establish whether something illegal had really taken place, more investigation was required.

Gunnarstranda chewed his cheek.

'For the moment someone is acquiring capital for a firm,' Reier continued. 'The new co-owners can sell a new product and everything looks hunky-dory.'

Gunnarstranda let Davestuen finish what he was saying. He added a few more scorch marks. Blew the glow until it was red and clear before breathing in. 'These new sellers,' he said and paused to catch Davestuen's attention.

Davestuen didn't answer. There weren't even mastication sounds in the receiver.

'Are you there?'

'Yep.'

'I was just wondering,' Gunnarstranda proceeded. 'What would these new sellers be selling?'

'How do you mean selling?'

'Well, they pay a sum of money, more than a hundred thousand in readies, to buy the right to sell something, don't they? What do they sell?'

'I haven't found out yet.'

'Isn't that odd?'

'Well . . .'

'The point is,' Gunnarstranda interrupted with emotion. 'The Marketing Manager doesn't even know what they're selling.'

'Oh?'

'He really doesn't. His name's Svennebye. He did the prospectus, the brochures, all the paperwork that we and these speculators have been burdened with. But he hasn't a clue what he's selling. Of course he knows it's about computer software, but why it would be attractive for people in the industry to have an agreement with Software Partners, he doesn't know. Simply because he doubts very much whether Software Partners have anything new or exciting to sell at all.'

'What!'

'It's true.' Gunnarstranda smiled. 'You heard correctly. What's more, I can tell you that this Marketing Manager has decided to resign. He thinks Engelsviken and Co. are working a scam, and he wants to jump ship before the rats.'

He inhaled and blew out a cloud of blue smoke. Let the information sink in.

'Hmm,' Davestuen said at length.

'Food for thought, eh?'

He poked at Bregård's head, which still hadn't quite come away yet.

Davestuen gave a little cough. 'If that's the case and Software Partners don't have any money,' he summarized, 'and if at the same time money is coming into the company from the market, then the money's disappearing somewhere.'

'Exactly.'

'If the money's disappearing somewhere,' Davestuen concluded, 'it's a crime.'

Gunnarstranda gave a nod of satisfaction. He liked the edge that had crept into the voice in the receiver.

'Since Software Partners have not submitted their accounts to the public register as the law requires,' Reier argued, 'nothing can be checked in the usual way.'

Gunnarstranda said nothing. He smoked quietly and allowed his colleague to set the pace.

'That means it's time for a bit of action.'

Gunnarstranda still said nothing, letting his colleague think aloud.

'Right,' decided Davestuen. 'But we'll have to talk to this Marketing Manager of yours first. Svennebye, wasn't it?'

'Mhm.'

'By the way, do you know what the worst thing about giving up fags is?'

'No,' answered Gunnarstranda, who couldn't care less.

'You miss lighting a cigarette when the telephone rings. Taking a piece of chewing gum is not quite the same.'

'Mm, I can believe that,' Gunnarstranda answered politely.

'I take it you still smoke, Gunnarstranda?'

Gunnarstranda chuckled at the tone in Davestuen's voice.

'That I do,' he answered softly and said goodbye. Sat drumming his fingers before repeatedly pressing the cigarette-end in the overflowing ashtray. 'That I do,' he reiterated to himself under his breath, and threw away Bregård's head, which had now come loose from the paper.

34

At that moment Frølich shoved his large body in through the door.

Gunnarstranda allowed himself the luxury of a self-satisfied expression on his face, then straightened up and glanced at the clock.

'What's the matter with you?'

'Davestuen's found out why Software Partners locks up its files,' replied Gunnarstranda gently and placed the tape recorder on the desk.

'But that's another matter.' He wound forward and played the conversation with Marketing Manager Svennebye.

They listened in silence. Gunnarstranda supported his head on his right hand. Occasionally he was unable to resist the temptation of playing with bit of scorched paper. Frølich sat back on the sofa with both hands behind his head and his eyes fixed on a point in the ceiling.

'Love triangle,' said the man with the beard after Gunnarstranda had switched off the machine.

'Love polygon,' Gunnarstranda corrected. 'Love was all around, as they say. Our little girl was with Bregård for a while, a while longer with the MD, a while here and a while there, in the end she was with Sigurd Klavestad for a while. Until she was killed. Until Klavestad was slashed.'

The inspector interrupted his reflections and anticipated Frølich: 'Yes, exactly. And in the midst of all this sits the dirty old man messing everything up! Where the hell does Johansen fit in?'

'Perhaps he doesn't fit in at all?' suggested Frølich.

Gunnarstranda breathed in. *Johansen's keeping something quiet,* he thought. *Dead certain.* 'Do you know what he reminds me of?'

'No.'

'A little boy who's done something naughty. He's as happy as hell that he's pulled the wool over our eyes. Regarding one point. One single bloody point. It makes him feel powerful.'

They sat in silence for a while, until Frølich cleared his throat.

'This break-in at Software Partners . . .'

'Yes?'

'Apparently nothing was stolen.'

'That's right.'

'Apparently nothing was stolen from Reidun, either.'

'Correct.'

'Is that a coincidence?'

'I don't believe so.'

Gunnarstranda's fingers galloped up and down the desk edge in impatience. 'We have lots of good reasons to pursue Software Partners now,' he said.

Frølich nodded.

'But we have to take a closer look at this restaurant place, too. Scarlet. I want you to pop by.'

'Fine,' Frølich growled. 'But what now?'

Gunnarstranda lifted the telephone and dialled a number. 'Terje Engelsviken,' he said to the voice in his ear. 'OK,' he answered when the voice couldn't help.

'For a change,' he grumbled and rang off.

'Not in, as usual?'

'At a meeting. Wonder if it's with himself at home,' he speculated.

Frank nodded. 'Not inconceivable.'

'Then we should be there, so we could have a chat with him.'

'Would be good. Shame he hasn't invited us.'

Gunnarstranda smiled and got up. 'If no one invites us, I think we will be obliged to invite ourselves!'

35

Engelsviken and Hager had an address in Hoffsjef Løvenskiolds vei.

Gunnarstranda sat in the passenger seat quietly gazing
out of the window. Examining the bare branches of the
birch trees, the dirty grey patches of ground between the
ochre remains of last year's foliage by the roadside. (Spring
is always dirty grey and mucky at first.)

At last the car started the laborious climb over Uller
Ridge. Bare trees with bare branches here, too. Posh areas
don't look much without the colour afforded by grass and
leaves. Largely uninterested, Gunnarstranda surveyed the
towering residences in the shadows of large leafless deciduous trees, black bark against blue sky.

Engelsviken's house was not at the top. Though not at the
bottom, either. It was an edifice that gave the impression of
something other than frugality.

Frank Frølich parked in front of one of the three garage
doors facing the road. Gunnarstranda sat studying the
design of the house. Chocolate brown with white window
frames, a hipped roof covered with blue glass tiles that glinted in the sun. Panoramic glass panes reflected the views to
the south and west. A magnificent hillside garden in front
of the cellar wall set off the rocks from the house down to

a lawn at street level. Now, so early in the year, you could only see the spongy winter-green growth and occasional dry twigs that would explode into life once summer was here.

The still yellowish lawn beneath the house was part of a landscape design in which large shrubs were planted between a few fruit trees. He recognized the red twigs of Tartar dogwood and the characteristic horny bark of a few forsythia bushes where the yellow flowers had formed full buds but had not yet blossomed. Between branches they caught glimpses of a narrow path made with quarry dust.

No shortage of work here, he thought. A park-like area, developed and maintained by a trained workforce, not an Oslo West lady with a hand-weeder.

The black wrought-iron gate screamed on rusty hinges behind them as they slogged their way through the shingle up to the house.

The entrance at the back was not particularly interesting and did not live up to the house front facing the street. An ordinary bare step of expanded metal led to a standard teak brown door. Gunnarstranda pressed a button in the mouth of a bronze lion's head.

Not a sound to be heard. Either there was no bell or they had been fortunate with their insulation. No one came, so he pressed again.

Oceans of time passed.

At last. The door was opened slowly by a smiling girl with obvious oriental features. 'Morning?' she queried in a thick voice.

Dressed in a servant's uniform. Short, black skirt and

matching blouse with a white pinafore. The girl mustered a tentative smile. Her hair was collected in a bun at the back. A few strands had slipped out of the bun and hung down beside her ears.

Gunnarstranda left the conversation to Frølich. His eyes above the beard were fixed on the girl's breasts. His voice asked after Engelsviken. No answer. 'Engelsviken,' Frølich repeated, in frustration.

The girl stared from one to the other. Then slammed the door.

Gunnarstranda looked from the door to Frølich, who raised his hand to the lion's head and kept his finger on the bell.

Time passed.

At last the door was opened again. Same girl. But with a different expression now. There was fear in her eyes.

'Nobody home!' she stuttered. 'Nobody!'

And, with that, slammed the door again.

'Did you notice?' asked Frølich.

'Notice what?'

'The buttons!'

Gunnarstranda didn't understand.

'When she opened the door first her blouse was buttoned up wrongly.'

'I thought you were ogling her tits!'

'The second time it was done up properly.'

'How the maid dresses has got nothing to do with us!'

Frølich turned and stepped down. 'That depends on whether she's alone or not,' he said.

On the road a grey Mercedes was flashing a yellow indicator and wanted to go into the garage where the police vehicle was parked. A silver saloon from the exclusive range. An irritated honk on the horn followed by flashing headlights told them the driver was waiting.

The car door opened. An elegant, dark-haired lady placed one foot on the ground and leaned out of the vehicle, eyeing Gunnarstranda. Her face was semi-hidden by her round mirror sunglasses. Some wisps of her long hair were blown into her mouth. As she stroked them away, she looked very attractive.

The inspector realized who she was. Hand outstretched, he went over to introduce himself. 'Sonja Hager, I presume,' he chuckled.

'You're blocking my drive!'

Disdainful tone.

Gunnarstranda waved to Frølich, who was back in the car. He reversed.

'We have a few questions,' the policeman said, as amiable as before, 'but please do park first.'

The lady got back into her car. Seconds later the middle garage door opened. The Mercedes engine raced as it covered the few metres into the gap between the polished body of a low-slung sports car and a more unassuming Japanese model.

Gunnarstranda waited by the unmarked dark police car and held open the rear door for her.

'Wouldn't you prefer to come inside?' she asked with a hasty glance at the house. Gunnarstranda followed her eyes.

A figure could be discerned behind the large expanse of glass. Looked like a man. At any rate someone taller than the uniformed maid.

He looked into Sonja Hager's eyes. The next moment, when he looked back at the window, there was no one to be seen upstairs.

'We've just come from the house,' he said with a friendly smile. 'No one at home, I'm afraid.'

He pronounced the last word with extra stress. 'Take a seat in here.'

He closed the car door after her, gathered his coat around him and entered from the other side.

'I believe you've met before, haven't you?' Gunnarstranda said, motioning to the back of the head behind the wheel. 'Frank Frølich.' The woman didn't respond. She was clutching her bag and staring coldly out of the window.

'He asked you whether you knew if there was anyone Reidun Rosendal was particularly attached to.'

'We all knew her a bit,' she answered offhand.

'Are you aware of any men she had a more intimate relationship with?'

'Øyvind,' she said in the same curt manner. 'That is to say, I didn't know, but I was informed this was the case by your colleague.'

'No one else apart from Bregård?'

'No.'

'You two were close?'

'Not that I was aware of.'

'We've been told you were.'

'You shouldn't listen to everything you're told.'

'Reidun was an attractive woman, wasn't she?'

'Certainly.'

'No cold sweats or pats on the bottom?'

'I beg your pardon.'

Gunnarstranda held her arm. 'Six months at the same workplace and you can't remember anyone who had a crush on her?'

She looked down her nose at the policeman's hand. Gunnarstranda didn't let go. 'Tasty morsel . . . no appeal for the boys?'

'Let's stop beating about the bush, shall we,' she said, ice cold.

The detective agreed, and became serious.

'Let me make the following quite clear: I don't know how often Reidun chose to make herself available. Or with whom. And I don't want to know. That's not what interests me.'

The door shut with a bang. They sat and watched her stomp towards the house. Not very easy. High heels are not practical on shingle. Especially not uphill.

'Temperamental,' Frølich mumbled.

Gunnarstranda grunted.

'What do we do?'

Gunnarstranda was quiet. 'I'm not sure,' he said at length.

Frølich whistled. 'Look right!'

Gunnarstranda observed a male figure standing with a woman behind one of the large window panes staring down at them. The woman was wearing Sonja Hager's elegant

248

outfit. The man was the same person he had seen a few minutes ago. A grey-clad gentleman with slightly glittery suit trousers.

'I suppose we knew that,' the man at the wheel confirmed. 'We knew he was at home.'

Gunnarstranda sat thinking. 'There's only one pattern I can see here for the time being,' he concluded. 'And that is that those two are floating in money. While all the evidence suggests that they shouldn't be.'

'Floating,' he mumbled after a while. 'Swimming in it!'

He smiled to himself. 'Swimmers treading water knowing there is a jellyfish nearby. It might be to the right, to the left, or just beneath them. They don't know where. They can smell the danger and are kicking out. Move! Fast!'

Frølich started the car.

Gunnarstranda leaned back. Looked at his watch. Gone four. So it would be evening before he had finished the day's routines. 'Now we'll see,' he said, 'whether this panic will bear fruit. I wonder why this snob doesn't want to talk to us.'

'Let's imagine for the sake of argument it's true that Software Partners is a scam, as we believe,' came the voice from the front seat. 'Suppose that Bregård and Engelsviken got together after we had a word with Bregård in the fitness room. Suppose also that this Brick received a few telephone calls from Davestuen at Fraud Squad.'

Gunnarstranda listened, thinking.

'It's no wonder Engelsviken is keeping well away from us,' Frølich continued.

'Well,' Gunnarstranda objected, only half in agreement.

'This scam of theirs should be able to withstand a bit of nibbling at the edges from the cops. Engelsviken has experience of this kind of thing . . .'

He paused. 'Perhaps the jellyfish is beginning to tickle their feet.'

He felt his lips forming into a smile. *That is, if it wasn't the smoke from the bonfire we were forever walking round and stoking up*, he thought, crossing his legs.

36

Queueing always made Frank Frølich go soporific. It was like sitting on the tram. Your brain latched on to a thought you had filed away, you withdrew into yourself and patiently watched the world go by waiting until it was all over.

Not Eva-Britt. She thrived in queues, construed them as a social event and was already in conversation with two bald-headed guys from Oslo West. Both on top form. Loud young men with a strong need to tell everyone around them what they felt.

Eva-Britt screeched with laughter at the boys' corny jokes, was treated to swigs of the beer they had brought along and an all-out charm attack. Clinging on to his arm, as if fearful she might get into deep water.

Frank listened with half an ear, gazing patiently into the distance. The red wine in his stomach dulled the inane chat of the society boys. He preferred to concentrate on the door ahead of them, which kept opening and closing without making any impression on the length of the queue. Some customers seemed to be more popular than others, he mused. Watched a couple who fitted in that category. A babe in tart costume inched her way out of a taxi, revealingly, legs first. Grabbed the outstretched hand of her escort with highlights in his hair. Both wriggled their way sideways through the queue, the woman with bashful, downcast eyes, as though she were walking topless on the beach. Both struggled in through the glass door where a self-assured bouncer with a tattoo on the back of his hand took care of them.

When Frank and Eva-Britt finally forced their way inside they had been waiting for three-quarters of an hour. The West End boys left them for two scantily clad girls beckoning and gesturing from a table by the dance floor. Frank and Eva-Britt found themselves a table at the back, a long way from the bar, but with a good view of the dance floor and the entrance. A free table cluttered with dead glasses and dirty plates.

It was difficult to talk. The music was so loud. Frank looked around and let Eva-Britt do the ordering from the menu. The room was dark, the dance floor spacious. A lot of attractive people. Men and women who could tell the difference between a backhand and a forehand on the centre court.

Eva-Britt wanted to know what he was going to drink.

'Well, let's see,' he smiled, at a loss. 'Anything that costs less than a thousand kroner a bottle.'

Eventually the table was cleared by a girl who rationed her eye-contact. She appeared to take their orders without being aware anyone was sitting there. However, the drinks came faster than expected.

Frank held the glass and considered whether to make a fuss. There was definitely not more than four decilitres of beer in the half-litre glass. Perhaps you would notice me if

I chucked the beer in your face, he reflected, sending her a happy smile. At that moment something happened at the table with the West End kids. The boys got up and waggled their backsides as if they had just scored the winning goal in a final. The girls waved and shouted. It was a kind of ceremony. The group was welcoming a guest. Frank leaned back against the wall and sipped his beer. There was something familiar about this guest. The glittery suit. A middle-aged, bloated man on skinny legs. Grey suit that glittered when he moved.

He followed the man with his eyes. Moist, slightly wan face with a rigid smile. Strong voice that carried. The waitress was on the spot at once with champagne. Frank watched the man giving people around high fives. This person was well known. Very well known. He even got a hug from the waitress with the niggardly eyes.

Frank Frølich was in no doubt.

The West End table had become a cheery party. The new arrival was the focus of everyone's attention and gesticulated as he spoke. He was so drunk he didn't even notice when he knocked a glass off the table. After he came to the punchline he tucked his lower lip under his teeth, raised his cheeks and guffawed. Everyone laughed. Fell over the table laughing.

The idiot seemed to be amusing, Frank thought, and started playing footsie with Eva-Britt. She was eating spaghetti with lots of sauce. Glanced up, winked and sucked pasta. Sexy lips. She looked down again. Kicked off a shoe under the table and put her foot in his lap. He looked down in his glass. Empty. He waved to the waitress who was still acting as if there weren't any customers sitting around.

'Another half-litre please!'

She was gone.

'Hey!'

He caught her arm.

She stopped, half-turned.

'The guy you hugged before, is that Terje Engelsviken?'

She turned right round. Viewed him with more interest. Nodded.

'That's what I thought,' he smiled. 'I just wasn't sure.'

Eva-Britt's eyes questioned him.

'The guy taking off his jacket over there,' Frank explained.

Both watched him struggle with his jacket, stagger backwards and knock over another glass. It was funny. The whole group howled with laughter again. Engelsviken laughed loudest. Raised the empty bottle and roared. The sound carried across the room. The waitress, who was now behind the bar, gave a nod of the head.

'That's how the big boys order drinks,' Frank said.

'Has he killed someone?'

Eva-Britt was sitting with her back to the group again and rotating her fork.

'I don't know.'

He studied Engelsviken as he lurched between tables. Slapped people's backs on the way. Stopped and spoke to a man. Straightened up, threw back his head and laughed. Lurched onwards, round the corner to the gentlemen's toilet.

Frank carefully removed the foot that was still resting on his thigh. 'Just going to the loo,' he mumbled and followed.

The toilet was large and light. There were white tiles on the floor and the air was perfumed with the faint smell of vomit.

The man in the silk suit stood combing his hair in front of a mirror. His knees were bent and he was going to a lot of trouble to comb his hair back with the right flick. Concentrated expression. Frank went to the urinal. He thought about Reidun Rosendal with the nice mouth. The man by the sink was sweaty and a bit too fat round the belly. Not exactly good-looking. But sociable. Obviously had a lot of friends. Could tell jokes and laugh out loud. So, someone who could dominate social groups. Like now. The dude was warbling a tune.

'I'm just a gigolo,' he crooned. 'Just a gigolo.'

Out of key.

Someone flushed in one of the cubicles, unlocked the door, went to the sink to wet their hands. And was gone.

They were alone.

The policeman washed. Stood beside Engelsviken who was finally happy with the flick of his hair, put the comb in his back pocket and found his eyes in the mirror.

'Engelsviken?'

The man nodded. Turned. The swollen face still had the vestiges of a forced smile hanging there.

'Frank Frølich.' Frank passed him his hand. 'I'm investigating the murder of Reidun Rosendal.'

37

It was late at night. Already well into Saturday, officially a free day. He should have gone to bed hours ago, but had kept postponing it. Knew he wouldn't be able to sleep. His brain was churning.

Gunnarstranda sat at the living room table flicking half-heartedly through Emil Korsmo's illustrated plates of weeds. Sometimes botany helped his brain to focus on other things. So he had snatched sporadic looks throughout the evening. The mint problem. Last year's garden pest at the cabin. It could have been corn mint or cat mint. Determining which wasn't crucial. But it was annoying that he couldn't establish which it was.

The thing was, it threatened a rare *Clematis sibirica* that he and Edel had planted, and it had survived until now.

The plant was more than ten years old. The seeds were harvested one summer eleven years ago when they still had the old VW Beetle. They had come from collecting plants in Jotunheimen. Stopped at Fåberg and found where the clematis grew wild. The white bells had withered long ago, but the fine tassels of the seed pods alongside the mountain were unmistakable. He thumbed through the weed book, turning over the pages with the back of his hand. Looking from the dried example in the herbarium and down to the book's neat drawings. Notwithstanding the artist's fabulous lines, the task was impossible without fresh material. He sipped at a half-empty bottle of low-alcohol beer, uninspired. Emil Korsmo and Volume Two of Fægri's *Norwegian Plants* lay on the table with sheets of dried plants from his own herbarium.

Sod this knife-wielding murderer. The unfeeling bastard who could not be smoked out because his crimes weren't visible from the outside. It was just in films that murderers shuffled around like escaped inmates from a nut-house.

He rolled the bottle between his hands, sighed and raised a dry, wrinkled Petterøe from the ashtray. Didn't light it. Reached for the remote control for the TV and switched it on. There was a blue gleam from the opposite corner of the room where a man with pocked skin, hollow cheeks and sunglasses walked unannounced into the sitting room of a naked woman with an angelic white face. The scene was so stupid he was annoyed. The weak point in the case. Reidun Rosendal had not made any noise. Infernal riddle. Anyway, he wouldn't find the answer in this film. He got up. Glanced at his watch. Past two o'clock in the morning. He ought to go to bed. Stood ruminating and staring into the air while the man with the sunglasses on TV was making the woman scream.

He yawned. Turned. Christ, the racket she was making! He switched off, held his right hand against his sciatic nerve while stretching. Went over to the window and looked out.

That, too. Films always have screaming victims. What sounds had there been in Reidun's flat?

Violence. Of course violence leaves traces in a man's character. The point is that they aren't immediately obvious. At least not to him. But it had happened. In the dock. Long, pale clerical fingers. And a look. Eyes: two small slits behind thick lenses. Then he had finally known what she had seen, the victim the man had strangled with his pale fingers.

Two windows in the block across the street shone warm and yellow against the dark wall. Inside, the man got up. String vest and loose braces today. The old boy opened the window and blew out cigarette smoke while talking to his wife who appeared behind him. *Soon be in tears again,* thought Gunnarstranda when he saw her. The tight black brassière squeezed her flesh into rolls all the way down her body.

A marriage can become damned restrictive within two rooms and a kitchen. Gunnarstranda could not count all the times she had sworn at the man as he strolled off on Friday evenings. Routine. The man had had someone else for years.

She joined him where he stood smoking. Stroked his back. *I don't know what's worse,* the policeman philosophized. *The thought that he's deceiving her, or the thought that everyone knows. She can take it anyway,* he thought with a grin. *She hasn't killed him yet.*

He felt the smile stiffen on his lips as he turned from the window and tugged at his tie.

Turned back. Watched the unfaithful husband putting his arms around his plump spouse. She hadn't killed him yet. Gunnarstranda gave a malicious grin. Not him. Why on earth would she kill him?

The tie fell over the back of the chair and slipped down on to the cushion.

Of course she wouldn't do anything to him!

Gunnarstranda watched as the light in the couple's flat was switched off. Tried to organize his thoughts as a taxi with a yellow roof light splashed through the rain on its way to the city-centre night clubs that were still open.

He unbuttoned his shirt. Had got halfway when the telephone rang. Inhaled, deep, but didn't answer. Started to button up his shirt again. They would ring for a long time. They always did when something important happened at night.

38

The first thing Frank noticed was the dregs of Gunder's moonshine fizzing somewhere in his head. Then, far away, he heard the telephone, like in a bad dream. He moved his head and got a nose full of hair. Lifted his hand, stroked the hair to the side. Almost woke up. Rolled on to his side. Let her slide off. The telephone droned on. But Eva-Britt was still fast asleep. Her head was just blonde hair and her nipples two dark blue beacons in the dark. He writhed backwards, groped for the telephone. Stretched. Grabbed the receiver, lifted it up and put it back down.

Silence at last. A gentle breeze wafted through the partly open window. Her perfume sweetened the air. By some happy chance he had had only one glass of home brew. To hell with Gunder. The mechanic always managed to saddle Eva-Britt with a bottle. As a rule she emptied it down the pan. Yesterday she had spared it, and he had been foolish enough to sample it when they came home.

He felt her turning on to her side. Her heart-shaped bottom smiled at him. He stroked her hip. She stirred and grunted from miles away. Carefully he spread the duvet over both of them and turned on his side to continue sleeping.

Then the telephone rang again.

He opened his eyes wide and stared into the dark. Examined the crack between the mattress and the wooden frame of the damaged bed. Had to get up on his knees. Grabbed the receiver. Crackles. Boss on the line. Gunnarstranda's abrupt voice injected energy into the room.

Frank drew down the arm with the receiver. 'Are you aware this is the middle of the night?' he whispered groggily.

'Yes,' the line crackled. 'Get dressed.'

He tripped over the bedstead. Wasn't used to having the mattress on the floor. That hurt! He rolled across the floor. Bloody phone. Working at this hour! Why the hell didn't I pull out the jack-plug?

He was upright. On all fours anyway. Less enthusiastic than a mediator in pay discussions. Brain hiding behind the sofa like a tortoise. Dreaded thought of standing on two legs. Did it. Dizzy. Thank you, Lord. No nausea. His mouth tasted of beer, garlic and Christmas cake.

Staggered into the bathroom. Threw water over his face. Head felt like it was under a pile of wooden boards. Cleaned his teeth. Held a hand in front of his mouth afterwards, tested his breath without fainting. Got clothes on, trudged into the kitchen and wrote a note to Eva-Britt on a corner of the loaf paper. Tore it off. Dithered outside the bedroom door.

The bed framed the mattress and her. She lay on her side facing him, no duvet. Lying in a box. Dark nipples. Smooth tummy, rounded legs and a thin line of hair curling towards her groin.

And I can't even put this down as bloody overtime, he thought bitterly. Folded the note in the middle and placed it on the bedside table by the telephone like a tent. Quietly closed the door after him.

Felt dizzy on his way down the stairs. Rain outside. Paused for a moment before unlocking his car. Looked at his watch. A quarter to three. Pangs of conscience, which he instantly dismissed. Found some chewing gum in his jacket pocket and unwrapped it. It tasted like a sheet of A4.

The car shot across the Ring Road. It was night and it was raining. The windscreen wipers beat a steady rhythm, and Sinsen intersection was reflected in the glistening wet tarmac, vast and empty. A husky woman's voice was speaking on the radio. She was gone, played 'When the Night Comes' with Joe Cocker, after the obligatory howl the guitar solo that made his spine tingle. The traffic lights on amber in deserted Hans Nielsen Hauges gate. A blonde bird rubbing up against a guy in the telephone booth on the corner of Sandakerveien. It must have been cold. Middle of April. The gleam of the lights seemed dark in the rain, almost orange.

Frank drove into the taxi rank in advokat Dehlis plass and parked. Got out of the car, stood inhaling the fresh air in the drizzle. The paving stones in the turnaround glistened and the light from the jeweller's made everything sparkle.

He could feel his jaws aching and spat the chewing gum into the conveniently nearby litter bin. A stooped figure was coming down Bergensgata. It was Gunnarstranda. Without an umbrella, with a wet coat. The grey material had begun to darken over the shoulders.

'You'd better drive,' Frank said in welcome and occupied the passenger seat.

Gunnarstranda pulled up at the red lights in the crossing with Arendalsgata. Frank yawned aloud, unembarrassed. Gunnarstranda glared to his right. 'Weren't you working last night?'

'Can't sit for four to five hours drinking coffee in a place like that!'

'There is such a thing as moderation! You smell of vomit.'

'That's why I asked you to drive.'

'Did you find anything?'

Frank indicated the lights. 'It's green.'

The inspector gunned the engine and set off with a kangaroo hop.

'I met Engelsviken.'

Gunnarstranda drove in silence.

'Silk suit and Italian shoes. Pretty plastered. We met by the urinals.'

'Did you talk to him?'

'Bit. He boasted he had screwed her.'

'Whom?'

'Reidun. And in fact that was all he said.'

'Nothing else?'

'He started to shout his mouth off. Asked what the fuck the cops were doing following him to the toilet.' Frank sighed. 'He was already drunk when he arrived. Joined a group of younger socialites he must have known. Two men and two women who put on one hell of a show when he appeared in the doorway. The guy was pouring champagne down them.'

He yawned and went on: 'The guy's face was drenched

with sweat, he was loud and waving his arms about. Dragged the girls on to the dance floor. Where he tried to stuff his fingers down the knickers of one of them. With people watching.'

Gunnarstranda nodded slowly to himself, slowed down and looked right before crossing on amber. The wipers scraped across the window. He pushed in the cigarette lighter.

Frank resumed:

'That happened right after he and I had been talking in the toilet. But the girl wouldn't stand for it. She made quite a scene. Slapped him so hard you could hear it over the disco music.'

The lighter clicked and jumped out. Frank rolled down the window as his boss lit up.

'Then Engelsviken spotted me,' Frank continued. 'It was quite embarrassing. The girls left, so Engelsviken was alone on the dance floor. Legs akimbo, spine arched backwards. A sick smile on his mug. Suddenly he started slapping himself in the face. Ten, eleven, twelve real stingers. With the red and green disco lights flashing above his head and the music pounding. And he wasn't holding back, his head shook from the slaps. Crazy stuff!'

Frank yawned aloud. 'After he had finished slapping himself his nose was bleeding. But the man didn't notice; he just teetered back to the table with his shirt tail hanging out and the same sick smile on his face. He looked dreadful. Blood from his nose was running into his mouth, discolouring his teeth. Then he finished off the bottle of champagne, jumped up on the table and yelled.'

Gunnarstranda smoked with a dry smile on his lips.

'Then Eva-Britt couldn't take any more.'

'Eva-Britt?'

'Girlfriend came along. She reckoned this madness was because of me, and began to feel uncomfortable. So we left. In fact, that's not long ago.'

'And was the madness because of you?'

'He looked over between slaps.' Frank grinned, and stifled another yawn.

'The conversation in the toilet . . .'

'Yes?'

Gunnarstranda tapped the ash off the cigarette through the rolled-down window.

'The drunken chat?'

'He wasn't confused, if that's what you think. He seemed jovial at first. I followed him in to make contact. Told him who I was, told him I'd spoken to his wife during the investigation.'

Frank yawned. 'He got pretty upset, didn't give me time to finish what I was saying. He called Reidun a mattress. Nerd-speak.'

Frank sighed. 'Afterwards he turned and began to have a leak, then he suddenly screamed: 'What sort of fucking whisky do they sell here? My piss smells like lager!'

Frank adjusted his jacket. 'And so on,' he groaned. 'Then he calmed down and commented to me over his shoulder: "Yeah, I gave her a seeing-to now and again. That's what you want to know, isn't it." I didn't answer, and he zipped up. Then leaned back and hollered: "I'm just a gigolo!" I just watched. Then he kicked the condom machine, shook it and laughed out loud before going all personal, as if we were old friends. Put his arm round my shoulders, eyes went all gooey. Good and pissed he was. He was going to let me into some secrets. "Do you know what I remember best of all," he said. "Well, when she came she twittered like a little canary!" "You don't say," I said. But he didn't like that. Lost his rag and yelled at me: "What the hell do you think this is, following me into the piss house, you bloody perv. Are you a homo?" And with that he was gone.'

Gunnarstranda chewed his lower lip. 'And that was before the performance on the dance floor?'

'Yes, immediately before. He rolled straight from the toilet to the yuppie table, dragged both girls on to the floor and there was no stopping him.'

'And he didn't have to queue to get in?'

'That's right. Scarlet has a so-called club for the more regular guests, and I suppose he's a member.'

'Was he celebrating something last night?'

'Haven't a clue.'

Gunnarstranda pulled in and came to a halt. 'You'll have to go to Scarlet again.'

'I had planned to.'

'But during the day when the bar's closed.'

Frank smiled quietly, turned his head, glanced across the road and recognized where they were. 'Why are we here?'

'There's been another burglary in Reidun Rosendal's flat,' answered his boss, opening the door his side.

'Tonight?'

Gunnarstranda nodded. 'And it seems this masochist, the MD of Software Partners, has found himself an alibi for this particular number,' he added drily.

39

The gate was open. The lock had been smashed to pieces. Gunnarstranda examined the remains. Ran his fingers over the metal. Heard Frølich come from behind. The sweet smell of vomit filled his nostrils.

'The guy must have used a crowbar,' Frølich opined.

They advanced further through the dark arched gateway. The front door didn't seem to be damaged at all. Curious, thought Gunnarstranda. And stopped.

'It might have been open,' the man behind him suggested. 'The guy broke open the gate, but the front door could have been unlocked.'

'Hm.'

Gunnarstranda swivelled and retraced his steps, into the gateway. Opened the gate wide until it hit the wall.

'Hm,' he repeated, groping along the wall with his fingers. Felt a scar in the wall.

Frølich reacted. Strode back to the car and returned with a torch. Shone it on the wall where you could see the plaster had been damaged. Pulled the gate wide open again. The lock hit the scar in the wall.

'That does not come from prolonged wear and tear,' Frølich stated.

'If so, we would have seen peeling paint at most. This is from a blow or blows.'

Gunnarstranda agreed. 'You mean someone smashed the lock to pieces and used the wall as a base?'

'Looks like it.'

Gunnarstranda didn't answer at once, stroked his lips, thinking that it might not have happened like that. The gate could have slammed open when the lock was smashed. And then the lock case would have damaged the wall when it struck. But whatever the reason the result was the same. He heard Frølich's voice:

'Our boys'll have to examine the wall.'

Gunnarstranda nodded, opened the door and went up the stairs first. The flat door had been levered open with a crowbar. The whole frame had been torn off so the white wood in the splinters shone like spilt paint.

The small flat was hardly recognizable. The last time books and papers had been scattered everywhere, this time it was worse. The mattress had been slashed and stood sideways against the wall. Its innards were strewn across the floor. Duvet and pillow had met the same fate. The room was deep in brown and white feathers from the bedding. All the cupboards were open, the contents spewed out.

Someone had systematically worked their way through all the objects in the flat.

Gunnarstranda experienced an urge to swear. 'This was thorough,' he mumbled, going over to the window and drawing the curtains. The walls outside were in darkness.

More or less. On the opposite side of the street two panes were illuminated.

Frølich wiped his forehead.

'I think it's time to have another little chat with Arvid Johansen,' said Gunnarstranda softly, letting go of the curtain.

They ran down the stairs at speed. The rain had got heavier in the street. A stream was running down the gutters.

Gunnarstranda flipped up his coat collar and ran across. Stormed up the steps with Frølich at his heels. Rang Johansen's bell.

No one answered.

Frølich stood with his ear to the glass in the old-fashioned double door. 'It's quiet in there,' he whispered. 'Perhaps he saw us?'

Gunnarstranda rang again. Pounded on the door with his fist. Nothing happened. One more time. Three long, firm rings on the silent staircase. No reaction.

Frank Frølich raised his right leg and kicked in the door. The bolt securing it to the floor cracked like a piece of chalk. Both doors burst open with a bang.

Neither of them moved.

The light in the flat came from a door in the hall. The bathroom. The rest was in the dark.

Gunnarstranda went in first. Switched on the light in the sitting room. The chair was empty. The sofa was empty. The bathroom was empty. Johansen's flat was empty.

They began to carry out a sporadic search of the flat. Opening random cupboards that were crammed with the same clothes they had found on the floor the last time they had ransacked his place.

On the kitchen worktop there was a half a loaf and half a can of liver paste that had gone dark and crusty at the edges. A stained coffee jug was half full of black coffee. In the fridge there was a carton of buttermilk past its sell-by-date. Two bottles of export beer were in the door with a half-empty bottle of cod-liver oil. On the top shelf there was a piece of lightly salted bacon in a plastic packet, as well as a bag of potatoes. Kerr's Pink, thought Gunnarstranda when he saw the reddish skin and the deep eyes.

On top of the fridge there were some blue prescriptions and a number of unpaid bills with an uncashed social security form showing that Johansen was not living off the fat of the land.

In the middle of the worktop lay Johansen's wallet. It was thick, brown and the leather was very worn. Gunnarstranda picked it up, weighed it in his hand. Opened it. In one pocket there was a stiff identity card issued by the Post Office. The card showed a picture of Johansen wearing a shirt and tie. The bags under his eyes were less conspicuous than in reality. The card revealed that the man had retired five years ago.

The police inspector cast a brief glance at the picture, then removed what was causing the wallet to bulge. A wad of paper, as thick as a book. Bluish white with pink and purple hues. A wad of one-thousand-krone notes with an elastic band round them.

'Either he's out and up to mischief,' Frølich said from the sofa, 'or something's happened to him.'

'I fear it's the latter,' answered Gunnarstranda. Shook out a transparent plastic bag from the bunch he had in his pocket. 'We'll have to be careful.'

He dropped the pile of money into the bag. 'I don't think we'll find a single fingerprint in Reidun's flat.'

'That wasn't here on Thursday!' Frølich said referring to the money. He had got to his feet and was studying the contents of the bag.

'Nor the wallet,' replied Gunnarstranda stroking his mouth, thoughtful. 'Although the money may have been here. If he had had it on him.'

40

The two detectives were back at Police HQ. It was early morning and this wing of the station was dead. They were the only ones in the corridor. Frank Frølich slumped against the wall and watched Gunnarstranda fumbling in his pockets, looking for the keys. In the end, he couldn't be bothered to wait any longer and unlocked the door himself. Went in first, threw himself into a swivel chair, swung round and took two cups from the window sill. Stifled a yawn.

'I wonder what this bloody thief was after,' Gunnarstranda mused aloud from the sofa while Frølich attended to coffee.

'There's a pattern here,' the inspector reasoned in vexed mood. 'Someone broke into Software Partners three weeks ago. He turned everything upside down, but apparently he didn't steal anything. Someone searched Reidun's place on the night of the murder. No easily fenceable items stolen. Someone went through her flat a second time with a fine-tooth comb, last night. Odds are it was the same man.'

'Mmm,' agreed Frank without much enthusiasm. Put a foot on the floor. Swung round and regarded himself in the window. Could see a little frown growing in the dip between nose and forehead. 'This break-in seems very peculiar to me,' he exclaimed and could not restrain the burgeoning yawn. 'I don't see the link with the murder. I don't see why whoever burgled Software Partners would burgle Reidun. And I'm buggered if I understand why she had to die as a result.'

'She didn't die because of a break-in,' the inspector answered, his mind elsewhere, hiding behind a drowsy veil in front of his eyes.

Silence descended. The coffee machine coughed and spluttered. Gunnarstranda got up, lifted the lid impatiently, stared down at the brown liquid that had not yet seeped through the filter.

Bet he won't be able to wait, thought Frank. Right first time. Gunnarstranda had to pour himself a cup. He cursed aloud when the coffee splashed and burned his fingers. He dried his hand on his coat and sipped the coffee. Sat down. Blew on the coffee and took another sip. His little head was almost concealed by the cup. Only his bald crown with the cotton-like hair and the slightly curled ears were visible.

He looked up. Eyes clear now. Banged the cup down on the table. 'Let's take one thing at a time, shall we,' Gunnarstranda proposed. 'No one climbed in her window the night of the murder. That's obvious. And Sigurd Klavestad was willing to swear he heard her lock click behind when he left. But Mia Bjerke found her door unlocked. It isn't a latch lock. The door has to be locked with a key from the outside or the handle on the inside. So how did this thief get into her flat on the night of the murder?'

'She let him in.'

'Or he had a key.'

Frank objected. 'Reidun would never ever lend her flat key to anyone.'

'No?' Gunnarstranda queried, taken aback. 'Why not?'

'I just know she wouldn't.' Frank leaned forward. 'Her personality,' he argued quietly. 'I envisage a girl with some distance from people, a girl who does as she wants! For her it was important that she was in control of her fate. That she could spend her time as she wished.' He straightened up in his chair again. 'We've just seen that the murderer had to break in. So why would he have had a key on the night of the murder and not now?'

Gunnarstranda nodded slowly.

'No one had a key on the night of the murder,' Frank stated with conviction.

Gunnarstranda's eyes lit up. 'Let's assume you're right,' he continued eagerly. 'No one had a key and no one caught her by surprise. We know she locked up after Sigurd Klavestad. They had hardly fallen asleep when Sigurd got up to go. She went over to the window where she drew the curtains as Johansen said. Afterwards she went back to bed. Sigurd told Kristin Sommerstedt that Reidun's telephone rang just before he left. It was an anonymous caller. No one spoke. Let's assume it was the murderer who called.'

Gunnarstranda paused, got up and surveyed the town as the grey dawn began to break.

'At first Sigurd Klavestad couldn't get out of the yard,' he continued, facing the town. 'It took him time to clamber out. Johansen confirmed that. Reidun, who had gone back to bed, was probably asleep. At least we know some time passed. Johansen said it was a quarter of an hour. Sigurd maintained it was ten minutes tops.'

Frank glanced instinctively at the clock himself. It was half past five. He imagined Eva-Britt sleeping at home in his bed. She would probably have gone back to Julie by the time he had finished here, fairly annoyed with him, he assumed. So he had better ring her afterwards and arrange a morning walk or something to pacify her.

'In the end, Sigurd manages to scramble over the bloody fence and into the street,' Gunnarstranda's voice came from the window.

'Mm.'

Gunnarstranda nodded and turned to Frølich.

'I think the old boy saw the murderer, too,' he concluded. 'The old codger wouldn't concede he'd seen the two hippies arrive by taxi before Sigurd Klavestad went home. They unlocked the gate and the door to the stairs. Johansen kept mum about them until we pressed him. So he must have seen the murderer go the same way. That was why he was so bloody high-handed with us. He was messing us around, he knew what we wanted to know and kept it close to his chest. He was so pleased with himself. Because he had followed Klavestad, knew who he was and where he lived.'

Gunnarstranda gave a tight-lipped smile. 'He exchanged the information for a wad of one-thousand-krone notes. He could do that because he had seen the murderer and knew who he was! You saw yourself how his face changed when he heard that Sigurd Klavestad was dead. If it was Johansen who sold Klavestad's name and address to the murderer it's no wonder he got het up when we pressed him.'

'Hm,' Frank pondered. 'How did Johansen find the murderer?'

Gunnarstranda shrugged. Seeming to lose confidence.

'Hard to say,' he said, dismissing the question. 'We know he had been watching Reidun for more than a year. He must have seen most people who visited her last year. That's a possibility. He recognized the murderer, knew who it was.'

Frank wasn't impressed by his boss's tentative response. 'Thin,' he contended. 'There must be a better explanation than that.'

'Maybe. Let's leave that for the time being.'

The inspector faced the town again. 'We know Sigurd Klavestad met the murderer outside the gateway. That's why he's lying on Schwenke's slab now. He met this person who killed Reidun.'

Frank closed his eyes. Opened them. Pulled the hold-all on the table towards him. Took out the bag of bank notes. Held the plastic up to the light, let it dangle in front of his face.

'Would the old idiot try anything so stupid?'

Gunnarstranda eyed him. 'Have you got a better suggestion?'

Frank cleared his throat. 'The jogger, this big-mouth upstairs. We could put the squeeze on him, find out if he really knows as little as he claims.'

Gunnarstranda wrinkled his nose. 'Bjerke,' he mumbled,

lost in thought. Nodded to himself. 'It's true the man noticed precious little on his jog.'

Faint smile. 'Would be interesting to hear what he has to
say about the burglary last night.'

The smile broadened into a big grin. 'Good idea, Frølich!'

He snatched the telephone. 'What about if a couple of
boys toddle over to Bjerke now and spoil the morning jog?'

Gunarstranda picked up the receiver, rang and got what
he wanted. Leaned back in his chair afterwards with coffee
cup in hand.

'That's done then,' he said under his breath. Raised the
cup to his mouth, but put it down quickly. Pulled a grimace
at the confrontation with cold coffee. Lit a cigarette instead,
exhaled a cloud of blue smoke.

I'll remember that smell for ever, thought Frank, closing
his eyes. *Smoke, coffee and the boss's Aqua Velva aftershave.
The smell of night in this room.*

'There are still several loose threads,' Gunnarstranda
mulled aloud. 'But let's unravel the knotted ones we know.
The murderer,' he began. 'The person Klavestad met and Johansen saw going into the block of flats. The gate was open.
It had been opened by the freaks on the top floor with the
half-dead cannabis plant on the window sill. The murderer
went upstairs and rang Reidun's doorbell.'

Gunnarstranda took a break. Frank inhaled and continued for him:

'Reidun must have thought it was Sigurd coming back!'

'Presumably,' Gunnarstranda concurred with a nod. 'She
got out of bed, went over to the door . . .'

He hesitated.

Neither of them said anything. Frank rose to his feet, walked over to the sink with the coffee jug and filled it with fresh water. Gunnarstranda sat with his elbows on the desk. Staring ahead, puffing on his cigarette without removing it from his mouth.

For the second time they sat listening to the chug of the coffee machine as the water trickled through.

'This is where we have to tread with great caution,' Gunnarstranda mumbled to himself.

'We know the knife came from the flat,' Frank affirmed.

His colleague nodded.

'So the murderer didn't take the weapon with him.'

Gunnarstranda nodded slowly. 'That's important,' he nodded. 'No weapon.'

He stubbed out the cigarette, interlaced fingers and put them under his chin. Rested his head on his hands with his elbows on the table. 'She opened the door a fraction,' he said softly. 'Because she wasn't wearing any clothes. She thought it was Sigurd coming back, but then someone else was standing there.'

'She knew him,' Frank said. 'He was unarmed.'

'Yes,' Gunnarstranda nodded. 'She knew him. The murder was not an accident. It was committed in passion. The murderer exploded in there. But how well did she know the person who rang? Suppose it had been you standing there, what then?'

'Then she would have asked what the hell I wanted.'

'And you would have said you wanted to talk to her.'

'"Talk then," she would have said.'

'"Let me in," you would have said.'

'She would have told me to piss off. But if I had known her I assume she would have closed the door in my face and kept me waiting in the corridor while she put on some togs.'

'That could have happened,' Gunnarstranda decided, extinguishing another cigarette. He sat with his head lowered. 'It could have happened like that,' he repeated softly. 'Except that she put on a loose dressing gown without a belt, and nothing else.'

Frank raised one foot on to the edge of the desk. 'It could have happened like that until she tried to close the door!' He fought another yawn, lost the battle, his jaw clicked. 'But the person standing there never let her close it. He just shoved open the door and went in before she could react.'

'But that doesn't make any bloody sense!'

Gunnarstranda got up with his coffee cup, poured the cold slop into the sink, came back and poured himself another cup from the fresh brew. 'If whoever-it-was forced his way in,' he argued, 'then some time must have passed before the murder was committed! After all, she was wearing this dressing gown. And the man who was there had to locate the knife first, the murder weapon. Since he came unarmed he would have had to lose his temper enough to kill her, to grab the knife in passion. That takes time, too. In addition, he managed to make a terrible mess of her flat! That takes time. And in all this time that just ticked away none of the neighbours heard a single sound. There's something very bloody wrong here!'

He thumped his fist on the desk and rubbed the edge of his hand afterwards. He'd hit it so hard he hurt himself.

'Fine,' Frølich said with diplomacy. 'Let's drop that one then. And go on. We're assuming that Sigurd Klavestad met the killer outside. He died because he had seen the killer there. But why the hell would the killer feel threatened by him?'

'Because Sigurd saw him again.'

'Where?'

'At Software Partners when he was searching for someone to share his grief with and found Kristin Sommerstedt.'

Frank whistled. Stared at his colleague. 'If Sigurd was murdered because he recognized the killer at Software Partners, then the murderer is one of those connected with the business. As far as we know, Reidun had a close relationship with most people there. I assume a knock at the door from someone there would not especially alarm the woman.'

Gunnarstranda nodded and heaved a sigh.

Frank smiled without opening his mouth. 'So we know the murderer was connected with Software Partners,' he beamed, unable to curb the laughter creeping up on him. 'Why for pity's sake would the guy break in at Software Partners then?'

'That's it,' roared Gunnarstranda. 'Of course!'

He jumped up. His lips were trembling and he nervously ran his long fingers over his bald patch. 'That's how it has to be,' he whispered, excited.

Frank felt he was hanging on by his fingernails. 'How what has to be?' he shouted testily.

'You're right!'

Gunnarstranda's voice was still a whisper. His eyes sharpened neurotically. 'The thief doesn't work there. Only the murderer!'

Frank was none the wiser.

'Use your grey matter, Frølich!'

Gunnarstranda sat down slowly and managed to find his mouth with the cigarette. But when he lifted the lighter his hands were calm and his eyes shone across the table, cold and triumphant. 'There were two people, of course!'

He grinned with a barely concealed supercilious expression on his face. Lit the cigarette, leaned back in his chair and lectured:

'The thief used a crowbar to break into Software Partners a fortnight ago. But he didn't find what he was looking for. One Saturday two weeks later Reidun is picked up at Scarlet. A place where we know these computer people hang out. She takes Sigurd home to her place. They spend the night together. He leaves at the crack of dawn. Then the murderer comes. Speaks to Reidun. Speaks about something that is incredibly important to the visitor. The time suggests that. Whoever drops by at six o'clock on a Sunday morning must be fairly agitated. As Reidun is standing there without any clothes on she can't be all that interested. She's tired and is just waiting for her guest to piss off. In the end, the guest grabs the knife that's lying around and takes out his rage on Reidun's chest. Then the murderer runs away. Doesn't even bother to close the door.'

Gunnarstranda got up.

'Later the burglar comes along, the one with the Software Partners' break-in on his conscience. The door's open and he can walk right in.'

The little man sat down again. 'For some reason he's got it into his head that whatever he's looking for is in Reidun's flat. He finds the dead girl on the floor, but doesn't give a damn about her. Starts looking, but then panics. It must be the morning, before Mia Bjerke has returned from her Sunday promenade with husband and child and decides to wash the stairs. The thief clears off without finding anything, but also without having a thorough look. So he is fairly desperate. Has to go back and finish the job. Which he did last night. The body has been removed and he feels safe. Things have calmed down and he can break in at his leisure and search for hours undisturbed.'

'That can't be right,' Frank interrupted with a thick voice. Had to clear his throat. 'Give me one good reason why this burglar would be passing that particular door on that particular morning with Reidun lying dead inside.'

'I can give you several,' Frølich's colleague replied. 'She could have arranged to meet him for all we know. Or the burglar may have some arrangement with the murderer. Perhaps he was tailing him. There are several possibilities. But that's not the main point.'

He smiled. 'The most important thing for us is to find what he was looking for. Then we've got him!'

Frank stared at him. The older policeman with the cigarette and coffee cup had blue bags under his eyes. The thread-like hair lay in unruly tufts across his balding head, his coat was creased and his face sallow under the grey stubble.

Goodness, he thought. *Then we've got him!*

He turned to the window and saw that day had broken. The sky above the street called Grønlandsleiret was blue.

41

Later Frank was better, but nowhere near in top form as he walked through the glass door and entered the restaurant known as Scarlet. The darkened room was completely still. Chairs hung from tables with their legs in the air. There was the sweet smell of beer and many smoked cigarettes.

He crossed the room, passed the small dance floor where Terje Engelsviken had inflicted punishment on himself a few hours earlier, and went over to the brown counter in front of the shelves lined with bottles. Behind the bar, beyond two swing doors to the kitchen, he could hear someone banging around.

'Hello!' he shouted.

A man appeared in the doorway. He leaned against one of the swing doors with an inquisitive yet unsympathetic expression on his round, unshaven face.

'I'm looking for the owner.'

'That's me.'

'Police.'

Frølich showed his ID. The man came from the door to the bar. Looked at the ID. His mood was serious.

'What's this about?'

The policeman lifted a chair from one of the tables and sat down. 'A customer,' he said casually and studied the man taking a half-litre glass from a plastic dishwasher tray on the bar. Drew off beer from a tap and kept scraping away the rolling mass of white froth. Ordinary sort of person. Knitted blue waistcoat over a plain blue shirt. About fifty. A round and slightly bloated restaurant face with perma-bags under his eyes, which were dull and expressionless until the content of the glass was brown and clear. 'Fancy a beer?' he asked, concentrating on his work.

Frank hesitated. 'No, thanks.'

The man fished out a packet of cigarettes and a box of matches from his breast pocket. Put them all on a tray and joined the policeman at the table. Opened the packet and lit what smelt like a cigar.

'Terje Engelsviken!'

The man nodded. 'We know him,' he answered, crossing one leg over the other in business-like fashion. 'We call him the Kaiser. Gives generous tips,' he explained.

'Saturday, the 13th of April.'

The man deliberated. 'Just a mo.'

He put the cigarette in the ashtray, got up and left.

The cigarette went out after four minutes. Two minutes later the man returned with a receipt. 'This is dated the 15th of April,' he said and sat down. 'That means Engelsviken was here that Saturday. The receipt is for a sheet of glass we had to replace.'

A question formed on Frank Frølich's furrowed brow.

'He kicked in the glass,' the man explained with a dry smile, pointing over his shoulder to the glass door. 'Expensive business.'

'When did he arrive?'

'He usually comes at about eleven. He's got a card, and comes right in. Doesn't have to queue.'

'And on that Saturday?'

The man rested his chin on his hands with a fresh cigarette, and cast his mind back. Took a last drag and crushed the butt in the ashtray. 'I came here at twelve, so I can't say when because he was already here.'

'How so? Did you notice him or what?'

The man glowered. Then his eyes went blank. 'What's this about?'

The policeman didn't answer.

'For me Engelsviken's a good customer, that's all,' the man continued and took a swig of his beer. Smacked his lips. 'Nothing personal.'

'Terje Engelsviken was here that Saturday. He told us,' Frank lied, focusing on the man's eyes. 'Look at it this way: what you say confirms what we already know. But I'm interested to hear your version of events.'

The man nodded. 'It was the same as always,' he said, cracking a match in the ashtray. Began to poke around in his teeth with the sharpest fragment. 'The usual mayhem.'

'Who was he with?'

'Don't know. He's all over the place. Feels comfortable, knows people. Sometimes he comes with someone but . . .'

He took something out of his mouth and examined it. 'I don't know. The Kaiser's not the kind to refuse a drink, let me put it like that. And I suppose he had a skinful then, too.'

'More than usual?'

'Possibly. But it's hard to say.'

'Do you know the name Øyvind Bregård?'

'No.'

'Big fellow, bodybuilder type, blond hair, ring in the ear and a big moustache, droops down on both sides.'

The man nodded and chewed the matchstick. 'A gent with a moustache. We know him. Pal of Engelsviken's.'

'Right. Was he here that Saturday?'

The man rolled the match from side to side in his mouth. 'Don't know,' he said in the end. 'I didn't notice him anyway.'

Frank rummaged in his inside pocket. Passed the man the photograph of Reidun Rosendal. 'Seen her?'

The man studied the picture. Tilted his head. Tried to rub off the brown stain that obscured the face. Gave up. 'Hard to say,' he mumbled. 'Looks pretty standard, doesn't she?'

'She was here that Saturday.'

The man shot the policeman a glance, waiting.

'She must have left the place between half past eleven and half twelve,' the policeman said. 'With a boyfriend. Slim, good-looking lad with his hair in a pony tail, I think, about twenty-five. Dressed appropriately. I mean, the artist type, black clothes and nose in the air.'

The man nodded. 'That could fit,' he mumbled, head bent back, stroking the stubble under his chin. 'The time could well fit!'

'Oh yes?'

'I arrived at about twelve. Long queue. Not many people leaving. Straight after that there was a bit of a fuss. The Kaiser was stirring it. I had a peep to check how it was going, but everything was back to normal. Engelsviken was sitting by the bar and called out something to a long-haired bloke on his way out with a cool blonde.'

'What kind of bloke?'

'Well, nose in the air a bit, as you said. Long, black hair.'

'Pony tail?'

'No.'

'Engelsviken yelled. Was that all that happened?'

'Yep. The bloke gave him the finger, and left with the woman.'

'Could it have been her?'

The man studied the picture again. 'Possibly. I had my eyes on her bum. But it could have been this babe, yes, it could.'

'Tall?'

'Yes, long legs, black, tight-fitting clothes, mini-skirt.'

'How tall?'

'About one seventy-five.'

'What was her hair like?'

'Blonde.'

'I mean, permed curls or what?'

The man looked at the picture of Reidun with permed curls.

'No,' he concluded. 'This one had thick, blonde hair. Cut at a sharp angle over her ears.'

Reidun! Frank coughed. 'Are you sure?'

'Yes, indeed, that's why I remember. The woman had style, she was hot. The short hair and the figure.'

'What did Engelsviken call out?'

'Haven't a clue. He was pissed off with them!'

'And then?'

'Nothing, it was all peaceful again. Some chick wrapped herself around Engelsviken to get him in a better mood. The woman was gone.'

'But Engelsviken didn't move?'

'Right.'

'And?'

The man smiled and stroked his mouth.

'The receipt! Engelsviken held out until half past three. When we were closing up he was asleep. Seemed unconscious. The boys had to carry him out. This can happen.'

The man smiled apologetically. 'Not that often, it's true to say, but a few customers have a glass too many. We bundle them in a taxi as a rule. But we had our work cut out this time.'

He thumbed over his shoulder to the glass door again. 'You see when they tried to take him through the doors he went berserk, put up a fight and smashed the whole door with a couple of kicks.'

He sighed. 'Fantastic. Half past three in the morning and you can't lock the door.'

'And then?'

The man studied the day's catch on the matchstick. Sucked it back. 'I suppose I should have called your colleagues,' he summarized. 'The cops.'

He chewed the matchstick. 'But I rang for his wife instead. She drove up in a fat Mercedes and stumped up four thousand for the glass. Four smooth one-thousand-krone notes straight from her purse, without a murmur.'

'I was here yesterday,' Frank said absentmindedly.

'Hope you enjoyed it.'

'Yes, I did,' nodded the detective, and paused. Pulled himself together. 'Engelsviken was here.'

The man didn't answer at once. 'I definitely wasn't here,' he replied, indifferent. Drained his glass.

'Engelsviken was on the dance floor, alone, hitting himself in the face,' the detective declared.

The owner stared at the empty tankard he was holding.

'Have you ever seen him do anything like that?'

'Never.'

'Why would he hit himself in the face all those times?' Frølich wondered aloud.

The owner smirked. 'He might have been angry with someone.'

'Then he must have been angry with himself.'

The owner put down his tankard and stood up.

'Sounds like a good bet,' he agreed, shook Frank's hand and accompanied him to the door.

Outside the double glass doors Frølich stood thinking and staring at a rusty red rubbish bin. He was thinking about a long-haired guy giving Engelsviken the finger one Saturday evening shortly before twelve. Arvid Johansen had seen Sigurd and Reidun entering the flat at half past twelve. Reidun with short thick hair, around one seventy tall. It could fit.

He turned. Inside, behind the bar, the owner was drawing

another beer. Frank tore himself away and hurried back to the car. It was a Saturday and he wanted to go home and sleep. Wonderful, he thought, a warm duvet, an Asterix comic to send him off and sleep – sleep – sleep until he woke up of his own accord in the afternoon and felt like a beer.

He had hardly articulated the thought when he was called over the radio.

42

He drove halfway on to the pavement at the corner of Markveien. Strolled up the street. A crowd of people had collected in the area around Foss School. But they were not pressing. Straggly bunches of youths mostly. Groups of twos and threes chatting. Shivering in the cold weather and laughing nervously to each other. If you didn't cast curious glances over towards the square by the bridge.

A few journalists nodded to him. Frank recognized Ivar Bøgerud, a former student friend who was leaning against a tree on the slope down to the river. Bøgerud was puffing at a roll-up and deep in conversation with some skirt from another paper. Ivar had acquired a centre parting since they last met, Frank confirmed, and nodded to him. Strangely enough, the guy didn't seem particularly interested in latching on to the detective on his way down. Had learned the ropes, he thought. Waiting until there is enough to ladle from the source.

He pushed through. Was exhausted. Almost collided with Bernt Kampenhaug. Same sunglasses, same crackly radio. Loads of teeth under the glasses.

'Wasn't exactly a high-quality fish we caught in the river this time, Frølich!'

Frølich smiled back politely and continued towards the

bundle lying on the river path. Further away, a dog lay on the ground, dead as well. The man was partly covered by a plastic sheet. An older man, that much was obvious. Overshoes, brown trousers and a battered coat. The wet clothes gleamed in the sharp light. It could be Johansen lying there. But the man's face was hidden under the plastic.

'Was it gruesome?' he asked, with a thumb.

'Too early to say anything.'

Kampenhaug had a look around. 'Someone had dragged the body half on to the bank, and when we came there was just a dog here.'

He angled the radio aerial towards the dead dog. It had been shot. A long, pink tongue hung like a tie from the half-open jaws. The shiny coat was disfigured by a red wound in the stomach. A civilian with a bobble hat was kneeling over it.

Frank stared back at the corpse on the river bank. Two black reinforced plastic overshoes pointed heavenwards.

'Wondered perhaps if he was the witness we were after,' he mumbled. 'Arvid Johansen. A pensioner.'

'So I heard. Well, it's not easy to recognize that face!'

Kampenhaug bent down and pulled back a corner of the sheet. Frank turned away. Kampenhaug grinned. Replaced the sheet and straightened up. 'The dog was obstructing the investigation,' he sniggered. Addressed the civilian and called in a louder voice. 'Did you hear that?'

Then marched the few metres over to the man and kicked him in the back. 'Next time you buy a dog make sure you keep it on a lead.'

The man turned his head. A tear-streaked face looked up at them. Glasses, dull eyes and terrible teeth. Frank had seen the face before. But couldn't put his finger on where. A junkie. Doped up. Eyes that swam beneath his fringe. The junkie grunted. 'Bastard pigs.'

Kampenhaug stooped down. The doped-up face was reflected against a green background in his mirror glasses. Kampenhaug smiled and his hand twitched. The man fell in a heap. Blood trickling from the corner of his mouth. Frank said nothing, spun round and stared at the path and the slope to the river. Not more than a kilometre away from Arvid Johansen's home, probably a lot less. Ten-minute walk. Again he looked at the barely moving water. Tried to imagine someone falling in here. Faced the crowd to locate the woman for whom Kampenhaug was playing tough.

Macho Man's overalls rustled as he stood up. He stretched his legs to allow the material to slip back into place, joined Frank and stood scratching his groin.

'Take a size bigger,' Frank said. 'You're too old to impress women.'

'Quartermaster hasn't got any bigger ones.'

The radio crackled and Macho Man bent down in a macho way. Frank spotted her. Red hair, tired face, green eye make-up. Bare feet in high-heeled shoes. Pointed tits beneath a tight-fitting acrylic roll-neck sweater.

Bernt came back. 'A milcher,' he whispered. 'Finest Norwegian Ayrshire.'

His teeth flashed white under the green sunglasses. Lots of small red marks bedecked his chin and neck.

'You'll have to change the blades in your razor,' Frank replied, but on seeing this sudden change of topic was too much for him, added: 'Ask for her name and address. You can say you'll be back for a statement.'

'Too right,' Kampenhaug whispered. Adjusted his bollocks in his ardour.

Idiot, thought Frank. Left him, stepped over the barrier and slowly ambled up the footpath. Impossible to say whether the dead man had fallen in. The path stretched upwards like an idyll. Nevertheless, he must have fallen in close to here.

Despite the injuries to the old man's face, Frank was convinced it was Johansen. The overshoes, the coat, though they weren't what did it. He just knew. Johansen was dead. Provided that the dead man's fingerprints were readable, Professor Schwenke would be able to compare them with those on file. If not, they would use other medical data and ultimately establish the man's identity. But in reality it was no more than a formality. Gunnarstranda would receive a report saying that Arvid Johansen had drowned. There would be a bit about injuries to the head that could have been caused by a fall or a third party with intent.

He stared back at the bridge. Kampenhaug had clambered over the barrier and was talking to the milkmaid who was running her hand through her red hair and shifting weight from one high heel to the other.

'Hello, Frølich.'

Ivar Bøgerud. The emissary of the tabloid press. Noted that the guy called him by his surname. That was new.

Frank shrugged. 'You'll have to take a risk and talk to the boss himself,' he said, nodding towards Kampenhaug. 'I don't know anything.'

Bøgerud smoked. 'Informed sources', he puffed, 'tell me that the cops have shot an old man taking a dog for a walk.'

'When did you ever start checking a good story?'

'Sunday newspaper, Frølich. Since we're competing with the church we have to bang on the tables with cold facts.'

Ivar Bøgerud's expression was devoid of humour. He had pulled out an old notebook. 'What was the message on the radio?'

'Old man dead in water.'

Frank stared down at Kampenhaug, who had now left the redhead in peace. The man was drifting around with the radio by his face and his sleeves rolled up.

Bøgerud flicked his cigarette in an arc and took notes.

'The man could have fallen in by accident, but so early in the process you can't rule out a criminal act.'

They strolled up the road. Round the school.

'Of course the police are interested in contacting anyone who might have seen or heard anything unusual along the river banks from Beier bridge to Foss in the last few days.'

'The shot?'

Bøgerud had stopped writing.

'Rumours as with every police call-out.'

'There was a dead dog lying there, Frølich!'

'The story's covered under the Press's Code of Ethics. You know, role of the press and all that shit.'

'Was the dog shot by the police?'

'Talk to Kampenhaug.'

Bøgerud nodded. 'Informed sources tell me you've arrested a suspect.'

Frank considered. 'We are in contact with a dog owner who was beside the dead animal when it was found. The man will be questioned as a witness in the usual way.'

'Is it usual for the police to knock witnesses unconscious while they're being questioned?'

Frank sighed. Headed for his car.

'We saw what happened, Frølich!'

Frank opened the car door.

'Was the dog or the owner at any point deemed to be a threat to the police?'

The detective addressed the journalist. 'Ivar,' he began, weary. Changed his mind: 'Bøgerud! This is not my case. I know nothing about the dog or whether it was shot at all or who shot it! The dog is dead. An old man was found floating in the river Akerselva. That's all I know. Talk to Kampenhaug. He's in charge here, and he knows everything that happened. All right?'

'You stood two metres away from the police officer who attacked the dog owner. Have you any comment to make?'

Frank looked Bøgerud in the eyes. Which did not deviate. Lips that tightened. *Am I like that as well?* he wondered, sighed with resignation and got into the car. Closed the door in the journalist's face.

He switched on the ignition. Glanced briefly up at Bøgerud who had a camera in his hand. *My God*, he despaired. The flash went off in his face. *What a shit day! What a truly shit job!*

43

It was early Sunday morning. The industrial areas of Tøyen and Enerhaug lay deserted. Now, without people, the noise of machinery and the sound of metal on metal, the place seemed completely forlorn. Like a film set after the shooting, Frank thought.

They walked arm in arm along Jens Bjelkes gate. Eva-Britt, who had never got over Frankie ending up as a police officer, still came back to how strange this was. Now she had an opportunity to revisit the topic. Twice they had walked up and down the footpath between Beier bridge and Foss, where the old man had been dragged ashore. Eva-Britt hung on Frank's arm, strode out and swung her hips with every step. 'Becoming a cop is the last thing you should have done,' she informed him yet again.

They were on their way back to Eva-Britt's. One of the girls in the collective was looking after Julie while Mummy was on a Sunday walk trying to find slide marks on the slope down to the Akerselva.

He nodded, in another world. Still thinking about their walk. Along the footpath to and fro between the two waterfalls where the old man might have slipped. No one so far had uncovered anything that might explain Johansen's death. Not even they had.

'I would never have believed it,' repeated Eva-Britt, musing aloud.

'Why not?' he said to show he was mentally present.

'Don't know. You're not the type.' She smiled. 'Can't see you beating people up.'

He sighed.

She rolled her eyes when she heard his sigh. 'Now, don't you tell me the cops don't beat people up!'

Frank grunted and threw his arms in the air. 'The job's all right. It's like all jobs, I suppose. You want to be thorough, see results. And for that I definitely have world-class opportunities. The find-the-murderer scenario.'

He fell quiet. Noticed her staring at him. 'The problem is all the night work on poor pay,' he added. 'The only difference from other jobs is in fact the opportunity to fail, to be part of a fiasco. It's immense. The whole time.'

'Are you thinking about the dead girl?'

They had reached the busy road they had to cross. So they stood waiting to dash over when there was a gap in the traffic.

'You meet the world in a different way,' he shouted over the noise of vehicles, pulling her on to the other side. 'It's difficult to grasp that you're still on the same planet as you were before you joined the police. People's madness is in your face. Just the fact that anyone can be so bonkers as to visit a girl and stab her with a bread knife! Just imagine it! A bread knife! And then she falls down dead!'

He paused. Moved aside to let a man in a leather jacket scoot past. Went on: 'To clear up a case like this you have

301

to be totally involved.' He stopped. 'Like Gunnarstranda last night!'

They resumed walking. 'I don't understand it,' he added. Remembered Gunnarstranda with the coffee cup between his hands, the feverish face with the sharp eyes. His tongue going like a clapper regardless of external conditions, circumstantial evidence, assumptions or a hung-over colleague.

'The man's always on form at all times of day or night! Take this case. All along we've thought that a man forced his way into the girl's flat, turned it upside down, got caught, stabbed her and legged it. However, Gunnarstranda realized that there must have been two people. Two perps who may not have known about each other. First, this girl has a visitor who kills her and buggers off. Then someone else comes, and searches the flat. This turkey has broken into her workplace earlier. He does what he has to do around the body, ransacks the entire place, but presumably doesn't find whatever it is he's after. So he breaks in a second time, two nights ago, to do a more thorough search.'

'Why should it be the same person who broke into her workplace and her flat?'

'We don't know. We reckon it is, but we have no way of checking.'

'What about if you're wrong?'

'That's the point. Then everything collapses. The opportunity to fail is immense.'

They walked on in silence.

She stopped and laughed, revealing the gap between her front teeth.

'What is it?'

'I was just thinking about the time you and Dikke used to share a crate of beer at all the parties. There you were, without fail, sitting on the sofa, boozing away and grooving to Pink Floyd and . . .'

She frowned, racked her brain. 'And . . . ?'

Frank glanced at her. 'Van der Graaf Generator!'

'What a name! No one else would have liked them.'

'Van der Graaf were great! Shit-hot!'

'Of course! It's just so odd to think that you joined the police. What's happened to Dikke by the way?'

'He's in clink.'

She became serious. 'What for?'

'Dope.'

He and Dikke had drifted apart. Gradually, slowly but surely. They had met once in two years. One summer evening. Warm air in the streets. Restaurant terraces full to overflowing. Stunning women on the go, taxis with open sun roofs and wild music. People congregating in groups. Dikke was alone in a corner of the square outside the railway station. A portable stereo at his feet. Twitchy head, tapping feet and hands that ran up and down his body without cease. 'I get so nervous if I have to stand in the same place,' he had said, talking to a point somewhere among the stars.

Now he always sat in the same place, cooped up in a prison cell, unless he was strapped down.

He became aware of her silence. Coughed. 'I suppose I was not exactly your dream-boy at that time?'

She didn't answer.

'What I remember best is the night on the Danish ferry.' He laughed and felt her grip on his arm tighten.

'Do you know why I fell in love with you?' she asked, giving him a view of the gap between her teeth again. 'Your woollen socks.'

'Oh?'

'Grey woollen socks and an erect willy.'

She smiled. 'You were completely naked apart from the grey socks which you had half-taken off. You were frantically searching for a condom, knocking things on to the floor.'

He grinned. Stopped. They had passed Gunder's garage. He turned and pointed up to the windows where Brick the solicitor had his premises. 'That solicitor', he pointed, 'is tied up in this mystery we're sweating over, by the way.'

They peered up at the panes where BRICK was written in large letters.

'Gunnarstranda found out the man had his office here.'

'Is he a suspect?'

'No. The solicitor is the business manager of the dead girl's employer. Software Partners.

'And a swindler, I suppose,' he added.

She leaned towards him. 'The solicitor is working on a Sunday,' she said.

'Eh?'

'Yes, I'm sure I saw someone there. Look! The neon tube in the ceiling's on.'

Yes, it was true, they could both see it. There was a light in the window. She squeezed up against him. Bored her chin into his chest and stroked his cheek with a begloved finger.

'If you were a proper cop,' she whispered, 'you would go up there now!'

He smirked. 'With you here? Dame waiting in the street while Dirty Harry straightens his jacket and goes to work?'

She sneaked her gloved hand up under his shirt.

He was a bit nervous with her hands around. With that look in her eyes she was capable of anything.

'I know something nicer we could do,' she whispered to the shirt button. 'Little bonk?'

His eyes twinkled. 'At your place, with the gang of cheer-leaders in the common room?'

'If we go to yours we'll have to take the little one.'

Frank kicked the tyre of a fat BMW parked by the kerb. 'Doesn't matter,' he said. 'This crate must belong to the solicitor by the way. It's expensive enough.'

At that moment a man in a blue coat strode quickly through the gate and over to the car.

'Young solicitor,' whispered Eva-Britt.

They had to move and make room for the man. He fumbled with the alarm system. Soon there was a brief peep as the alarm went off. The man opened the boot lid and threw in a red briefcase. Then a stout elderly lady rushed through the gate. She attracted everyone's attention. Waving a piece of paper in her hand. Face red with exertion. Wearing a woollen jacket and tasselled slippers on her feet, she shuffled out to the parked car.

'Bjerke,' she called. 'Joachim Bjerke!'

44

Gunnarstranda could feel the coffee going down his throat and leaving a thin, unhealthy coating reminiscent of glue over his tongue and the inside of his mouth. It was getting late. He should be on his way home.

The whole of the Sunday had been spent on futile crap. Now it was the evening. Tomorrow was Monday. Things should be starting to happen. The thought of going home to the television failed to attract. He could do some reading, but he knew it would be difficult to concentrate. The pieces of the puzzle were churning round his head. The pieces that refused to fit. There was a piece missing. An important one. His brain was in a high gear, pushing pieces all ways to form a picture that made sense.

In front of him on the desk there was an open newspaper and the autopsy report for Sigurd Klavestad. Lots of mumbo-jumbo in Latin, rigor mortis etc, and other medical jargon. Gunnarstranda was informed that the man had once had jaundice. In addition, his last meal had consisted of bread, milk and red wine, of all things. A sharp object had sliced his carotid artery and damaged the medulla oblongata, the lower half of the brainstem. There was also bruising to the body, caused, it was assumed, by falling down the narrow stairs. Klavestad had died somewhere between three and four o'clock in the morning, before he had been called out.

Gunnarstranda glanced at his watch once more, lit another cigarette and chewed his thumb nail. Then he glowered at the newspaper lying open at the TV pages. He could take the car and go to Hoffsjefveien and collar Engelsviken, or perhaps the maid, give both of them a course on buttoning blouses and see what happens. But the thought of the drive at such a late hour also failed to attract.

The telephone rang.

'Gunnarstranda.'

'S'me,' growled Frølich in a beery bass tone. In the background someone was giggling. The sound reminded him of how tired he was. 'What is it?' he asked wearily.

'I've been for a walk.'

Frølich hiccupped.

'A couple of hours ago, along the banks of the Akerselva.'

Another hiccup.

Gunnarstranda's brow began to crease. He could hear Frølich whispering something, probably telling the lady to let him phone.

'I was looking for some signs of where the old boy fell in the river. Between Foss and the bridge.'

'Oh yes.'

'Nothing!'

Bloody hell. Is that what he'd rung to say?

'Afterwards we went to Eva-Britt's place, the friend I was with at Scarlet, you remember, she lives in a collective with, among others, Gunder who repaired your car.'

'Get to the point. I'm not in a good mood!'

'They live in this house by Gunder's workshop, roughly where you noticed Brick's office. That solicitor.'

'To the point!'

'I saw a young fella coming out. And after him a woman, a secretary. She ran out waving a piece of paper. Shouting his name: Joachim Bjerke.'

Gunnarstranda's brain jerked into action.

'Are you still there?'

'Go on!'

'The woman wanted to give him this bit of paper, but he wouldn't take it. Just jumped into a fat BMW and shot off burning rubber. Could this be the Bjerke you've met?'

'Description?'

'Round thirty-five. One metre eighty, more or less. Slim. Prim features with a straight nose, piercing eyes and long fringe. Layered hair at the back. Made to measure, blue coat. Hollow back. Drives a dark blue BMW 528.'

'That's him,' croaked Gunnarstranda, had to clear his throat to make his voice carry. A deep furrow was dissecting his forehead.

'I just wanted to tell you.'

'Good work, Frølich. You have no idea how damned good! Where are you?'

'Home.'

'OK. I'll ring if there is anything.'

He rang off and sat for a few seconds staring into middle distance. Then got up. Walked slowly like a somnambulant to the hat shelf, to the coat rack. Removed his wallet.

Opened it. Searched. Fingers trembling. He cursed. Wallet crammed with paper, old receipts, stamps and shopping lists. Where the hell was it? There. Red edge. Yellow and red writing. The business card he had been given by Joachim Bjerke, the self-important shit, Reidun Rosendal's neighbour. He read aloud: 'Ludo.'

Stopped. Eyes rose. 'Ludo?'

He read the line underneath: *Finance. Audits . . . Joachim Bjerke . . . Manager.*

Lingered for a moment flicking a corner of the card.

Turned slowly. Made a beeline for the shelf above his desk. Pulled out a box file marked Reidun Rosendal, moistened his index finger and slowly leafed through, sheet by sheet. Reports and appendices. He knew what he wanted. The pile to the left was becoming fatter. At last. Not any old sheet, but greyish photocopy paper folded several times. Stuffed into his wallet the first time he was in the courthouse and had been overcome by hunger after sifting through paper for hours.

A list of Software Partners' legal adversaries for last year. Seven names. But only one name shone up at him. The fourth. Scribbled in blue biro.

A/S Ludo.

Beside a small hand-drawn square. The square that indicated this was the company which had withdrawn its lawsuit against Software Partners.

He studied the list. Could feel himself smiling. The last piece. The picture was beginning to take shape. He sat down and stared out of the window, puzzled. A hazy grey veil shrouded the night sky. Why was Joachim Bjerke in conflict with Software Partners? Why had he kept this quiet from the police? And why had he withdrawn proceedings against Software Partners?'

After a while he fought to lift both legs on to the desk and lit a cigarette. Smoked and considered three questions, without coming to an answer. There was only one thing to do: visit Joachim and ask him. Gunnarstranda looked at his watch. No reason for his conscience to bother him. In a way he had promised them he would be returning.

45

Her face seemed to fill with fear as she opened the door and recognized him.

'Nice to see you again,' said Gunnarstranda.

She didn't reciprocate.

'We often pay people a second visit,' he reassured her in a pleasant voice.

The reassurance did nothing to soothe her nerves. She stood there, her fingers fidgeting with the door handle.

'I'd like to have a few words with your husband.'

She didn't react at once, her eyes roamed. The little boy appeared at ground level. Hanging on to her leg. Nappy on his bottom and dummy in his mouth, wearing light blue pyjamas. Mother in short, pink skirt over thick, dark tights that crackled like electricity as the boy pulled at her leg. She was attractive.

'Isn't he at home?'

She collected herself. Tossed her hair, which was tied up in a thick side plait with a pink ribbon. 'Yes, he is,' she admitted after some hesitation, opened the door wide and let him pass.

The sound of a television could be heard from inside the flat.

He took his time hanging up his coat, let her go ahead and

warn him. The sound of the TV was gone and he heard her manoeuvring the child to a room where the voices became a faint drone. A mother reading to her son.

The detective straightened his jacket and his sparse hair before entering. Joachim Bjerke was on his feet and waiting between the leather sofa and the table.

'You've made no progress, I understand!'

Sarcastic tone, like last time.

'Well?'

The detective didn't answer at once. Caught himself instinctively checking his watch, smiled at his ingrained mannerism. 'We've made some progress.'

He sat down on the sofa unbidden. Leaned back and crossed his legs, relaxed and looked around. Confirmed the flat was as tidy as before, even though three people lived here. Noticed a few property brochures fanned out on the table. Nodded towards them. 'Thinking of moving?'

Bjerke ignored the question, sat down but fortified himself with the same armour.

'Let's get to the point, shall we,' he said coolly.

As arrogant as ever, you horse's asshole, the policeman thought, and adopted his nicest smile.

'This is about the legal disagreement between yourself and Software Partners.'

'What business is that of yours?'

'You knew where Reidun worked, I take it?'

'Indeed.'

'Yet you didn't mention the row you were having with her boss?'

'Why would it occur to me that this wrangle could be of any significance to your investigation? Reidun Rosendal was a low-level employee. The lawsuit was withdrawn anyway.'

Gunnarstranda blinked with his heavy eyelids. 'I can assure you that it has some significance for our investigation,' he declared. 'But it's not the most important matter. The point is that you should have been more co-operative. You should have told us about this relationship whether asked or not.'

'Are you saying I'm not co-operative?'

'You are worse than that. You are working against the investigation.'

Bjerke let the answer sink in; something occurred to him that occasioned a condescending smile. 'You've come here unannounced late on a Sunday night. Are you harassing me?' His smile died and he went on: 'Yes, I instituted legal proceedings against SP.'

SP! Gunnarstranda swallowed the familiarity. Stared across the table and listened to the young upstart say the proceedings had been withdrawn and that therefore the matter was closed.

Bjerke had risen to his feet and gestured.

'So now you have what you wanted. Was there anything else?'

Towering above the detective, he held his hand open in an arrogant gesture of showing him the door.

Gunnarstranda wondered for an instant whether the man was as stupid as he made himself out to be. Leaned back to study the bumptious sod closer. Observed the severe wrinkle in the man's young skin. The pursed lips. Nope. He was not stupid. Just a sack of unusually well fermented shit. This conclusion gave him cause to relish what was to come. 'You might know there has been a burglary in the flat below,' he said.

'In fact, I did. Friday night. I rang and reported it. If you had been doing your job you would have known. You would also have known that I have already been involved in this matter enough as it is.'

'You should not entertain such a poor opinion of us, Bjerke.'

The man sat down again, sighed. 'Do we have to go through the rigmarole once again? May I point out that I wasted two hours last time? Because I reported it. But do you imagine anyone came when I rang? No, you choose to come while people are asleep! Early in the morning, before anyone in the building has got out of bed!'

He heaved a sigh of despair. 'Two brainless clods from the police came. And wrote down every word I said.'

'How did you know there had been a burglary?'

'As I said, I have made a statement.' He made a show of looking at his watch. 'So if the burglary is what's on your mind perhaps we should discuss it more when you've had a chance to brief yourself on the case?'

'You have such a poor opinion of us, Bjerke.'

'Do you know what the time is?'

Gunnarstranda blinked. 'How did you know there had been a burglary?'

315

'Would it be quicker if I told you?'

'How did you know there had been a burglary?'

'I saw the marks.'

'What did you see?'

'I saw that someone had forced the door to the flat.'

'Nothing else?'

'I saw the gate as well, of course! But let's drop this. I can't see the point. As I said, two uniformed policemen have been here and they took a statement. I told them everything. It would have saved the taxpayer a few kroner if you had briefed yourself beforehand.'

The policeman ignored the comment. Ploughed on regardless. 'There are a couple of things about the burglary that strike me as odd. You see, the door to the flat was broken with a small crowbar while the gate lock was smashed with a sledgehammer or a rock.'

'Why is that odd?'

'Because it doesn't seem professional. A bit clumsy.' Gunnarstranda smiled, as if suddenly remembering something. 'Amateur,' he added. 'Our crime scene people think the blow to the gate would not have helped our friend the burglar much.'

He bent forward and explained the forensic officers' theory, that the gate below must have been open when someone smashed the lock with a sledgehammer. The damage to the plaster matched the gate lock case. 'It almost seems as if someone is trying to hoodwink us,' he concluded. 'As if someone wants us to believe the gate was smashed in order to open it.'

'Are you implying that her flat wasn't burgled?'

'The flat door was broken into, you saw that for yourself, but it is far from certain that the same is true for the gate.'

'You don't think the marks on the gate are genuine?'

'There is that possibility.'

'Exactly what are you trying to say?'

'I'm trying to find a connection, that's all. Why did you keep the legal dispute quiet?'

'Because it has nothing to do with you.'

'I have a different view. The only logical explanation for marks simulating a break-in must be that the burglar was someone who could open the gate, one of the residents in this block.'

The detective waited for a moment. 'And then there would not be all too many candidates to choose between.'

'Possibly not,' agreed Bjerke, meeker now.

'At any rate that would entail some poor cop having to make certain investigations.'

'What sort of investigations?'

'Such as establishing clarity concerning the contact there had been between an accountant in upper Grünerløkka and Terje Engelsviken.'

Gunnarstranda was able to confirm to himself that Bjerke was sitting stiffly on the sofa now, concentrating. He rested his forearms on his thighs and bent his upper body forward, slightly dispirited, as though he were sitting on the toilet.

The inspector noted the silence emanating from the child's room. He turned his head. She was standing in the doorway, behind her husband with eyes only for him. Bjerke was motionless. Even when she walked across the floor, sat down, pressed her knees together hard with a sculptured expression on her pale features. The husband ignored her. He maintained his dispirited posture, although the look in his eye had changed character.

Gunnarstranda nodded politely to her. Attractive woman. But the face seemed a façade. Not sure how much you know, he thought. Not sure what it means if you know anything at all. Nevertheless, the detective could not help noticing the effect she was having on the man on the sofa. His haughty face was wan. The armour was gone. All right, all hell is about to break loose, he thought, and he addressed her husband: 'You have consistently underrated us, Bjerke.'

He was silent.

'This evening, a few hours ago, I was considering arresting you.'

The woman gulped.

'Tactically speaking, such an arrest would have appeased my superiors and a number of journalists.'

Gunnarstranda allowed a lull to develop. Bjerke was avoiding his spouse's eyes.

The inspector resumed. 'Sometimes we haul in someone who has been seen at a crime scene. But because we often have to let them go again we always undertake a careful appraisal first.'

Something was happening between husband and wife. It was none of his business. But in his hand he had the best cards and decided to raise the stakes.

He watched. 'Often we don't get the real perpetrator. And

so we cannot influence the confusion he may be feeling when the wrong person has been arrested. As a result it is impossible to observe the mistakes he might make.'

He splayed his palms. 'All that happens is that the newspapers have a victim they can harass. Readers can gorge themselves on spicy sensationalism and satisfy their cravings for the circus on which our times have inculcated a dependence.'

Gunnarstranda's smile was porcelain white, he was thinking it was a good job he was alone, so that no one would attack him for this emotional hogwash later. He stretched out both legs and stuffed his hands in his trouser pockets. 'We are obliged to show consideration.'

He shuddered inside, but continued: 'Even if the real perpetrator were to be arrested afterwards, and convicted and punished, the innocent victim would never be free of suspicion. In two, three, five years people wouldn't remember who the real murderer was anyway. What they do remember, if anything, is the photograph of the person with the jacket over their head. Or the childhood story the newspapers managed to dig up. The story that was supposed to reveal the character of the detainee, to proffer the reader an explanation for the man's brutality.'

He fiddled with a cigarette he had taken from his pocket. Wondered if he had gone too far with this nonsense of his. He tested, by holding his tongue. It was time to show his hand. But first of all Bjerke plus wife needed time to digest the sermon he had just reeled off. Decided to give them two minutes.

'I know who's trying to bluff us here,' he said, showing his hand at last. Met Bjerke's eyes. 'You've carried out three break-ins. You raided A/S Software Partners three weeks ago. And you turned Reidun's flat upside down while she lay dead on the floor. Please note, I am saying she was already dead. But you were so nervous with her lying there you cleared off. Left it to your wife and child to find the body and report it to the police. Then afterwards you had to wait while the storm was at its peak. You had to wait until things calmed down and you were sure the flat wasn't under surveillance. Then you broke in again. To confuse us you decided to demolish the lock on the gate downstairs. Inside the archway with the lock against the wall, that was how you did it. You damaged the plaster on the wall and that was what made us suspicious.'

Bjerke was studying the floor.

'On top of that, you forgot the front door.'

Bjerke smiled, helpless. 'I didn't think of that. It was open.'

The inspector leaned across the table. Twinkled at the woman who was subjecting him to a searching gaze, then concentrated on her husband again.

'Would you be so kind as to tell me everything this time,' he instructed. 'Everything that happened that morning. Everything! Every smallest, tiniest detail!'

46

An hour later he was running down the stairs with no more than a fleeting glance at Reidun Rosendal's flat, then onwards and out. His face was closed and stern as he shot across the street and into the block of flats. Stopped to look at his watch. Past eleven o'clock. That didn't help. He hared up the stairs and was hardly out of breath at the top. Undid the padlock sealing the door to Arvid Johansen's flat and went in. Switched on all the lights. Scoured the room. Opened whole rows of cupboard doors until he found what he was looking for. The binoculars. They were heavy and black. So, quite old. With standard 7x50 magnification. He hung the battered leather strap around his neck, grabbed the faded armchair and dragged it to the window. Deliberated. Johansen had been a big man. Bigger than he was. But how big? He looked around, kicked a pile of porn magazines away from the sofa. Porn magazines, of course. He took off the binoculars, piled up the magazines. Placed the whole heap on the armchair seat and perched on top, removed a few, sat down again. That was better. Raised the binoculars and looked through the window. Dark outside, but the gate was illuminated and the wooden fence was clear enough. Still the wrong angle. He twisted the chair into various positions, sat down, got up, re-adjusted the chair. This was repeated several more times until he was satisfied.

That was how he, Arvid Johansen, had sat. Gunnarstranda searched his pockets for a cigarette. Found one and lit up. He reconstructed the scene. The woman had opened the curtains. And what had happened? Some time had passed. Johansen had probably got excited, seen the two making love, then Sigurd left. What had the old boy done? Given himself a hand job? Smoked? Got up to eat perhaps; the show was over, after all. He had said he went to sleep in the chair later.

Fine, the show's over, what now? Johansen stomps into the kitchen, eats a slice of bread, goes back.

Gunnarstranda stood up, went to the kitchen. Walked back. Looked out.

So, it's a quarter past six. It's daylight out there. Sigurd Klavestad jumps over the fence and hangs around the gate for a while, according to his statement. He is seen by the hippie couple returning home from a party in a taxi. They unlock the gate, but don't lock up after them. So the gate is open. Johansen watches. What does he see? Right, he sees someone coming. Someone he later manages to track down. This person comes in their own car. Gunnarstranda grinned. Smacked his forehead, a habit from his boyhood days. Of course Johansen must have jotted down the car registration number! The registration number of the murderer's car. So obvious, so hit-you-in-the-face obvious. The number and then a telephone call to the vehicle licensing agency!

But where did he write it down? The policeman wheeled round. Crossed the room. Opened a drawer. Here. Pencils. Biros. But no paper. He cast around, thinking. No paper. No pad or notebook. Nothing to write on. Just a pile of porn mags. Of course. Gunnarstranda's fingers quivered. Of course! The porn mags. He smiled. Lifted the pile on to the table. Bent down to the floor, looked for more magazines, crawled around on all fours, peered under the sofa. No. There were only these ones. He sat down, got up again, switched on a wall lamp, sat down again and started slowly leafing through the top magazine.

47

It was morning. The sun was shining from an azure spring sky above Oslo's rush-hour traffic. All the lanes in Bispegata were crammed with fuming commuters, sleepy buses and groaning long vehicles.

Frank Frølich was at the wheel and experiencing butterflies in his stomach. The expectation. Something had happened. What smarty pants call the *breakthrough* in an investigation. They were almost there. It was clear from the way they spoke. The way words were articulated.

The car inched its way forward in the right-hand lane, on its journey west, out of town, under the Traffic Machine, Oslo's spaghetti junction. The queue was barely moving and he was driving with his bumper up the bum of the next car, to stop cheeky buggers nosing their way in. Gunnarstranda had met him half an hour ago, with red-rimmed eyes and a serious face. The boss was a shadow of his former self, as they say. Hadn't even bloody said 'Morning', just dangled a bunch of car keys and led towards the garage with his coat-tails flapping behind him. The old guy's silence was unnerving. The jittery atmosphere had made him feel different, too. His mouth had already gone dry. The silence had been intolerable, so he had started to report back on the conversation with the owner of Scarlet. Afterwards he dropped the bombshell, ventured a theory. Not much to brag about perhaps, but the sequence of events was right. He had gone through the whole story. The restaurant-owner had said that Engelsviken had been at Scarlet at the same time as Reidun. So, the woman's employer, the man for whom she would not be a mattress any longer, this shark, had been there at the same time as her, a short time before she was murdered. Engelsviken, a green-eyed, jilted lover, had stood watching his dream-girl dancing and rubbing her body against an upstart of twenty-five. The MD had had to watch calmly while she was picked up, and he had even made a fuss when the couple went off for further entertainment. Thereafter the man had drunk himself silly and had had so much pent-up aggression inside him that he kicked a glass door to smithereens, causing four thousand kroners' worth of damage, at half past three in the morning, two hours before Reidun Rosendal was last seen alive.

Frank had described in great detail how the man in the silk suit had been carried out of the room and heaved into his wife's car, whatever repercussions that might have meant. He didn't suppose a piss-artist who had just smashed the glass door of one of Oslo's in-places was likely to be very keen to have his own wife collect him. The man had probably made her stop somewhere close by Reidun's flat, then he had staggered out of the car, max two hours before she was laid low with her own bread knife.

Frank thought the whole thing was fairly convincing as he listened to himself babbling away. Granted the theory didn't take much account of the burglaries with which his boss was so fascinated, but there was a good chance they were a dead end, anyway. Nevertheless, he was disappointed at his boss's reaction. Gunnarstranda had paid close, patient attention, but the excitement had not reached his hands. Nor had he lit a cigarette with a triumphant glint in his eyes. Instead he had lowered his head, with three deep creases in his forehead, and had then begun to talk about Reidun's damned neighbour, this Joachim Bjerke, and a company called Ludo. And insisted that it was Bjerke who had committed the burglaries, although he hadn't stolen anything. Just because the guy ran this Ludo company on his own and Engelsviken owed him money.

'Why did this Joachim Bjerke break in then?' asked Frølich after his passenger finally shut up and would not say any more.

'For some letters and a tape.'

Gunnarstranda chewed the inside of his cheek. Eyes in ruminative mode.

'Evidence. Bjerke was Engelsviken's accountant. The accountancy company A/S Ludo was employed by Engelsviken on a contractual basis.'

Frank nodded without saying a word. Let his boss continue with his findings unchecked. 'This is all about Engelsviken's past,' his boss declared, gesticulating, and carried on about angry creditors. Lenders who didn't get either the interest rates, or any instalments, or for that matter payment for goods they had placed with the engineer, who as yet had not gone bankrupt.

'It's about Terje Engelsviken, who was still managing to

bankrupt companies. Every time Engeslviken went bust the lenders never got what they were due in settlement.'

Frank smiled as the car on the right honked its horn. A plump face with a tightly knotted tie and a bushy beard was cursing him roundly from behind the windscreen.

'A/S Bodge 'n' Dodge? As your brother-in-law said?'

'Exactly. Joachim Bjerke told me everything yesterday. The fellow was unstoppable. It was like pulling the plug out of the bath.'

Gunnarstranda described how the air had gone out of the arrogant toad on the sofa, like a puncture.

The inspector had maintained his mask during the confession, and did not let on that he knew all about the barn outside Drammen where warehouse computers and accessories had been sold before and during the bankruptcies. Nor that the profits from the illegal sales were pocketed by Engelsviken. What was news was that Engelsviken's accountant knew how little was left for the creditors when the receiver was brought in. Engelsviken had left them nothing apart from the coffee machine and a photocopier. Of course the administrators were angry. Engelsviken and Co. were reported to the police every time. But then, at the eleventh hour, papers and assurances from A/S Ludo popped up. Joachim Bjerke vouched for the accounts and proved that everything was above board; all the items had been sold a long, long time before. The administrator had therefore to accept that all the equity and assets had leached from the company en route to insolvency.

Gunnarstranda shrugged. 'Of course, the creditors protested,' he sighed. 'They claimed that Engelsviken had transgressed time limits and so on.'

Frank nodded slowly. He knew the answer: case shelved for lack of evidence.

'Each time, the police were faced with a mass of contradictory claims,' the inspector explained. 'Vague evaluations of assets, kilos of paper and dates over which no one ever had a real perspective. The cases shuttled to and fro between the Fraud Squad and Oslo Police Headquarters without anyone delving deep enough in the shit to be able to justify a charge being brought. In the end the cases were placed on the shelf marked "unsolved".'

He closed his eyes for a fraction of a second. 'But it became harder for Engelsviken to gain trust in the business community. Stories started circulating about him. He gained a certain notoriety and had difficulty being taken seriously, black-listed as he was as a bad payer. Engelsviken was a rotten apple long before he hatched the concept of Software Partners. Since the usual creditors could not be milked, he had to find a new target group to bleed dry: computer dealers. The idea was brilliant. To cheat co-owners. The only problem was digging up enough gullible optimists.'

He grinned. 'Investors, I mean, naturally. At any rate people who would invest, people who would risk their money on the emperor's new clothes. And, as you know, the poor co-owners have no rights at all when the company goes belly up. They're owners themselves and are left to face the music.'

Frølich whistled.

'It's what Svennebye said,' the balding officer continued indefatigably. 'Software Partners consists of two groups of employees. Those who are in the know and those who aren't. Those who aren't are the external façade, such as Reidun Rosendal, the babe with the long legs and attractive face who travelled around visiting customers and charming them into ruin.'

Frank Frølich was reminded of the pipe smoker in the fossilized office shop. The old chap would be kissing good-bye to his hard-earned supplementary pension. That much was certain.

'The company didn't have any money,' Gunnarstranda went on. 'Reputable suppliers were no longer giving payment extensions to Engelsviken. Hence the tango with the legal machinery to have goods returned and compensation paid.'

Frank met Gunnarstranda's eyes as he glanced up to see if he was following. 'This in turn hit Bjerke in A/S Ludo,' the inspector went on. 'You see, Bjerke had twenty-five thousand kroner invested in Software Partners. But he didn't get a bean in compensation. That's why he took up proceedings against SP, as he calls them.'

The inspector wagged his forefinger. 'Then Engelsviken's solicitor considered it time to dig up some old evidence. Do you understand what I mean?'

Frank nodded. He had taken his foot off the accelerator. The queue was moving a bit now and he could let the car roll forward in neutral.

'Brick considered the time ripe to remind Bjerke what an accountant risked as a result of forging documents.'

Gunnarstranda gave a wry smile. 'Dear Joachim, this bench-vice is going to squeeze your balls. You can do as I say, or would you prefer a falsetto voice?'

Frank closed the window as they drove into Oslo Tunnel. Bent forward and switched off the fan so as not to inhale exhaust fumes. The queue was still slow-moving and the air not exactly pure forty metres under the ground.

'Bjerke withdrew the lawsuit against Software Partners in an attempt to placate them,' the inspector went on. 'But Brick and Engelsviken had tasted blood. They'd won a couple of cases already, and sensed a chance to extort money out of Bjerke as well. So Brick demanded two hundred thousand from Ludo in compensation.'

Frank whistled again. This time sucking his teeth.

'Bjerke was caught like a nut in a nut-cracker. Software Partners owed him twenty-five thousand in fees, and now there was a risk he might lose his licence or go to prison if he didn't fork out two hundred thou to the same two bastards.'

'That's what I call two cool customers.'

'Yes, Engelsviken and his solicitor!'

Gunnarstranda nodded to himself. 'But now I suppose the game is up. Davestuen and the boys were there before eight this morning. Audit and seizure. Davestuen decided after talking to Svennebye for a few hours and an hour with me last night. So we'll have to hope they can collect enough evidence for a charge. At any rate, the company Software Partners is a con.'

He smiled mirthlessly. 'And will be bankrupt by tomorrow, I presume,' he added.

'What did Bjerke do when he was squeezed for two hundred thousand?'

'The man knew that Engelsviken and Brick were capable of anything. And the evidence against Bjerke was a bloody good hand to have in that situation!'

'It's blackmail, pure and simple.'

'Precisely. Bjerke had threatened them, tempted them, tried to negotiate with them without any success. As he said last night, the way out was a crowbar at night. He had to try to get hold of the evidence and destroy it. That was why he broke into and went through the premises of Software Partners with a fine-tooth comb, but he found nothing.'

Frank looked left and optimistically switched lanes. He felt a need to ask what he perceived as the crucial question.

'Why did Bjerke have it in his head that the evidence was in Reidun's flat? What made him break in?'

'He received a call telling him to go and look there.'

Frank leaned back in the seat. The traffic was at a standstill again. Listened to his boss's dry voice:

'It was the Sunday Reidun was killed. Bjerke was woken up by the telephone ringing early in the morning. There was a crackle on the line and Bjerke knew it was someone with a mobile.'

Gunnarstranda looked across. 'The voice on the phone said four words,' he said, aping Bjerke.

'Reidun has the originals.'

'The sentence was repeated twice,' he said. 'Then the line went dead.'

Gunnarstranda paused.

'Bjerke lay in bed thinking,' he said and hesitated. 'As Bjerke said to me: After all, I hadn't thought of anything else except the bloody papers for months.'

Gunnarstranda continued with the man's story: 'He was surprised. Would a saleswoman in a computer company be trusted with papers? His own neighbour? Could that be right? No, he decided. The telephone call was just another stratagem in Brick and Engelsviken's war against him. So Bjerke stayed in bed thinking. Then he put on his jogging gear and went for his daily run.'

Gunnarstranda interrupted himself: 'Just imagine. The man rushes around the streets with sweat flying off him before anyone else has even got up and had a piss. Every bloody day! Just imagine if this misguided country could make positive use of that energy!'

Gunnarstranda slowly took out a cigarette.

'Not here!'

Frank held his hand over the cigarette lighter. 'We're under the ground and need all the oxygen we can get!'

Gunnarstranda put the cigarette back in his pocket and went on: 'As Bjerke had drawn a blank in the Drammensveien office, he conceded that one of the employees might be looking after the evidence. The girl didn't need to know what it was she had in her safekeeping. So his jog ended up being shorter than usual. He ran back. Rang Reidun's bell, but she didn't open. One look inside and he knew why.'

'Nice guy,' Frank blurted.

'You're right,' Gunnarstranda said in a chill tone. 'He's a cool customer as well. And now he has an extra problem.'

Frank raised his eyebrows.

'His wife. She did not appreciate what she heard him telling me.'

Gunnarstranda turned his head. Looked out of the window. He talked about her fury. The accusations. The husband who would expose his child to such trauma on the staircase. Her husband. The pumped-up toad with the fringe. All the arrogance was gone. Huge sweaty patches under his arms and a squeaky voice: "Mia, you've got to understand me. Mia!" She'll sort that out, though. She deserves better than a bookkeeper. Do you know what he reminds me of?'

'Nope.'

'The kind of prissy oaf who goes in for dancing competitions. Cheesy grin, not a hair out of place, despite falling on his face and rolling over four times. The man just jumps to his feet and dances *Swan Lake* with a Colgate smile on his chops.'

'Those porcelain teeth, you mean?' Frølich grinned. 'What's she like, his wife?'

Gunnarstranda stared out of the window for a moment. 'Great,' he answered at length. 'What the suits call a safe pair of hands.'

'And now?'

'I assured them that he was not under suspicion.'

'How can you be so bloody sure of that?' Frank's tone was sharp.

'Because Bjerke didn't kill her.'

'Who did then?'

'That's what I'm waiting to hear.'

Frank fell silent.

'I'm waiting for a phone call. Then we'll know the answer.'

He looked to the right. Large, red figures on the wall told them how deep they were.

'Which we won't get down here,' he said tersely.

48

'Yes, Davestuen's on the case,' Gunnarstranda mumbled as they drove towards the rental building. Four dark cars parked in a line in front of the entrance to Rent-An-Office. Four cars that were unmistakable. Dark blue, exactly the same model, same shade, consecutive registration numbers. You could smell police from a mile off. There wasn't a lot of room. Frank had to wait and let out a small blue Honda with a ski box on the roof before he manoeuvred the car into the space. 'Did you see that?' he gasped.

'What?'

'Sonja Hager at the wheel with a ski box on the roof.'

Gunnarstranda gave a start. 'Are you sure?'

'Yes, that was her. Strange that Davestuen would let her go.'

Frank waved a 'hi' to the uniformed officer leaning against the first car.

Gunnarstranda had a frown on his face. 'I don't like Davestuen letting her go,' he mumbled, tapping his knuckles against his porcelain teeth.

'Shall we go up?'

Gunnarstranda didn't answer at once. 'I have to think,' he whispered at length. 'And I must have that telephone call.'

Frank reversed the car between two others. They sat looking at a high supporting wall of moulded concrete. The silence was tangible. Gunnarstranda's lighter clicked. Frank could see the inspector's hands shaking as he inhaled.

'Has it ever struck you how little atmosphere constructions like this have?' asked Gunnarstranda, indicating the wall with his cigarette.

'No.'

'People don't think of the big picture any more. In the old days stonemasons were skilled artisans who did more than make gravestones. They even made granite piers for bridges. Dry blocks of granite which are still standing there today!'

Frank hesitated. He could hear how dry and hollow his boss's voice was. The conversation felt affected. 'Until they were knocked down,' he answered.

'But granite has a structure, a colour, a pattern depending on how the blocks interact. There's no structure in concrete, it's a grey surface. Look at that wall!'

Gunnarstranda pointed.

Frank turned to face his boss wondering what the hell he was drivelling on about. 'But no one looks at a wall like that, do they?'

'Indeed they do! It is seen,' the inspector objected. 'The wall is obviously half the landscape. Take note of the dry branches hanging over the wall. *Stephanandra*, a deciduous shrub. The point is that the gardener has chosen that plant because it's bred to hang over walls. But the people who built the buttress didn't give it enough thought. They've just moulded a grey surface which is bound to crack after the first winter falls below minus thirty. Because the ground

336

frost will be so deep that the ice will raise the wall in spring, break it, crack it, because concrete is inflexible. Then the wall will fall to pieces year by year. That could have been avoided if they had considered the whole picture, seen the wall for what it was, part of the landscape. And used granite blocks and made it beautiful, flexible and enduring.'

Frank sent him another annoyed glance. 'Get to the point. Who killed her?'

'It's all about the big picture, as I said. We mustn't make a blunder here and forget to think holistically.'

Frank smacked the steering wheel. 'Yes, right,' he said in desperation, and growled under his breath: 'Holistically.'

'My brain is telling me to focus on the little blue car with the ski box on the roof,' Gunnarstranda continued with the same dry, affected voice. 'I don't like Sonja Hager suddenly driving a car with a ski box on the roof. In fact Sonja Hager drives a silver-grey Mercedes. And I have heard someone mention the ski box contains a double-barrelled rifle. There's something not right here. Sonja Hager's in charge of the keys to the filing cabinet up there. I can't imagine Davestuen would let her go.'

'No one ran after her.'

They both stared at the entrance to the temple where Software Partners had their offices. No activity at all.

'At home in Bergensgata,' Gunnarstranda said, out of the blue. 'Across the street from me, lives a man who for all these years has had a relationship with a widow down in Sagene.'

Frank didn't reply. Just turned and stared at him without

detecting the slightest indication of amusement in his little face.

'The man sees the widow about once a week. His wife kicks up one hell of a fuss every time. At least, so the rumours say.'

Gunnarstranda smiled, exhausted. 'Every time. And when he comes home the wife sheds a few tears, then has a bit of slap and tickle with her old man.'

Slap and tickle, mused Frank, and said politely: 'Really?'

'Sometimes I think about them,' the inspector continued. 'About her putting up with that, I mean. She must know people talk about them.'

He took a deep breath. 'She could have killed the man years ago.'

Frank nodded sympathetically. For a moment he had thought his boss had gone over the edge, but was reassured when the story ended on the usual note, frustration with criminal behaviour.

'Then it suddenly struck me that of course the woman would never wish upon herself the death of her husband!'

Frank jerked. 'Where are you going with this?' he asked, annoyed.

Gunnarstranda looked at him.

'Suppose it were Engelsviken, or his wife, who killed Reidun,' he said, for the sake of argument.

'Yes?'

'Then there's someone we've left out of the big picture.'

'Who?'

'The maid.'

Frank visualized her. The blouse that was buttoned up wrongly and then wasn't. He could feel the sweat breaking out on his back. He could see Sonja's bloodless lips when she was talking about good and bad days.

'Shall I go up?' he asked, nervous now, nodding to the front door.

Gunnarstranda ignored the question. Stubbed out his cigarette. 'By the way, I was in Johansen's flat yesterday,' he informed Frølich.

'When?'

'After talking to herr and fru Bjerke.'

'Why?'

'To find the registration number of the car.'

Frølich was quiet.

'Bjerke was rung up by a mobile phone,' Gunnarstranda reiterated. 'The caller wanted him to make a mess of Reidun's flat and leave fingerprints to lead suspicions away from the real murderer. Bjerke was willing to swear it was a mobile phone. So this caller was in a car. Quite simply, that means the car was parked outside and Johansen saw both the car and the murderer! The old-timer was receiving money from someone who wanted to know who Klavestad was and where he lived. So Johansen sold Klavestad's address for a handful of silver, fifty thousand kroner. The only question was: how could he contact the driver of the car?'

Frølich's spine froze. The only question? What the hell did he mean by saying it was the only question?

'Johansen jotted down the car number and traced the owner. I was up in his flat for one and a half hours. Search-

ing for the number. He had to have it written down somewhere, but where? And do you know what?'

'What?'

Frølich's mouth had gone dry.

'All the time I'd been sitting on a huge pile of porn mags!
Then I had a brainwave. I started flicking through them.
Studied more pussies than I've got plants in my herbarium.
Do you remember by the way that I got ten pools numbers
right that Saturday?'

'Which Saturday?'

'The Saturday Reidun was murdered. That is, she was
murdered on the Sunday morning. But I got ten numbers
right.'

'No, I don't remember. But what the hell's that got to do
with anything?'

'Well, on this woman's tits in the magazine there was a
line of pools numbers. Twelve, as there should be. Ten of
them were mine.'

'So?'

'Beside them there was a car number.'

Frølich nodded.

'That doesn't necessarily mean it was the number of the
murderer's car,' Gunnarstranda pointed out.

'Of course not,' Frank agreed, excited now. Could sense
the sweat on his back.

'But Johansen may have had that magazine in front of
him on the table that very Saturday. Noting down the winning twelve results. He may have done all sorts afterwards.
Perhaps he fell asleep. After all, he had been up the whole

340

night watching Reidun and Sigurd. At any rate there is a limited possibility that the number I found is that of the murderer's car. Of course, it would never stick in court!'

'For Christ's sake, tell me whose it is!'

'I don't know. Fatty from the temping agency was supposed to be finding out for me.'

'Fatty?'

Frank didn't have time to ask any more. They were interrupted. At last the phone had rung. The inspector leaned forward and took notes. Rang off. Showed his colleague without a word.

Frank read: *Mercedes 280, 1990 model. Owner: Sonja Brynhild Hager.*

Frank sighed, already having twisted the key in the ignition.

'Brynhild,' he mumbled, tasting the name on his tongue and revving the engine. Didn't like her name being Brynhild. Recalled her head sticking up behind the wheel of the little Honda with the ski box on the roof.

Gunnarstranda had gone pale. He removed the blue lamp from the glove compartment. 'Drive like the clappers,' he breathed, 'but get this bloody thing working first!'

49

Inspector Gunnarstranda had the microphone in his hand and was speaking into it with unusual intensity. The woman taking the message answered calmly like a tram driver before the doors are closed. Nevertheless, the atmosphere was tense. Her tone of voice was just that bit too polite. No giggles, no witticisms. This was serious.

Frank thought about a maid with a badly buttoned-up blouse.

The inspector put down the microphone.

'That was why the maid was so frightened,' Frank declared and switched off the siren as they approached Hoffsjef Løvenskiolds vei. 'She must have known everything.'

Grim-faced, Gunnarstranda nodded.

'Sonja picked up her sozzled husband outside Scarlet at half past three. The owner said Engelsviken was totally out of it. I suppose the maid must have been woken up when they came home.'

'And Sonja Hager must have listened to so much shit on the way home that it was the last straw,' whispered Gunnarstranda. 'She drove back to town after off-loading her husband. The maid must have heard her come back, perhaps they had a chat, Sonja with blood on her clothes. Bloody hell, how could we have forgotten the maid?'

Frank didn't answer. He was dreading the scene to follow, the boys with the military helmets crawling through the grass and all the drama.

'So, along come Davestuen and his boys today,' he continued. 'She happens to be there. With Bregård. She must have twigged the raid had something to do with us.'

Frank said nothing. So she made a quick exit to finish off the job, he was thinking.

There.

A small blue Honda had skidded to a halt in front of the large garage. Ski box open. Car door left open. Frank parked. Strange that Macho Man Bregård should have such a small car, he thought. Jumped out.

A car radio was blaring out at full volume. 'Fishin' in the Dark!'

He lifted the lid of the ski box. Empty. Bent down and looked inside the vehicle. Open case of cartridges. Eley Grand Prix 12 bore. Half full. As he guessed. A rifle as macho as its owner. Gunnarstranda followed. Frank showed him the half-empty case of cartridges and closed the door. The music was muted. Far away there was the sound of sirens coming closer. Now they would have something to talk about in this suburb, too, he thought. Remembered the maid with the blouse again. Thought about Clint Eastwood. Cigar in his mouth and a Magnum .44. Chewing! *Drop it angel, or I'll make you fly!* No explanations. Dirty Harry never had to explain anything. Certainly not why he walked around with a Magnum in his belt. And Dirty Harry was never suspended from duty. Dirty Harry wouldn't lose his job if he broke the regulations on important missions. Frank opened the car door again and switched off the radio. Silence settled over the ridge. Shit, weren't there any kids living here? He noticed that Gunnarstranda had gone back to the car and sat inside. Busy with the microphone. The sirens were coming closer.

Frank stared up at the house and thought about her. Among the circle of lunatics in this case Sonja Hager was one of the few who had spoken about genuine feelings. For some a vow is serious, she had said. After taking a life.

He looked from the house to the police car and back again. Uncertain. Wondering what was going through her head. If she was afraid. She was definitely under emotional strain. And probably pretty screwed up since she had managed to mobilize so much hatred to protect herself.

Behaviour, rational to a certain degree. She had systematically removed all the witnesses. Possibly in action again now. If the job had not already been done.

Was she in full possession of her faculties? Yes, but still not of a mind to accept her punishment. So actually anything at all could happen, he thought, slowly making his way to the house.

50

He stood staring at the brown front door. The silence lay like a suffocating blanket over the whole area. Soon the sirens would be switched off. Thereafter, only the sound of 4x4 diesel engines snarling their way up the road. Stopped. Doors banging. Silence.

He thought of Reidun. She had opened the door and let Sonja in. Tired, so tired. Had probably told Sonja to go to hell. She would talk about her marriage when she was in a better frame of mind.

Until she lay on the floor with a knife in her chest.

After that Sonja Hager had sliced up Sigurd Klavestad and in all probability despatched Arvid Johansen in the end. She had dealt with them one by one. All those who could have brought her down. The maid must have heard her that night. The last witness. Was she dead already?

The silence roared. Frank remembered Sonja Hager's unbecoming smile that was not a smile. What could it have been? Shock? Because Frølich had told her that Bregård had had a relationship with a woman she had just killed? Or had she just realized the gravity of what she had done? Had she realized that this meeting with the police meant that moves were under way to arrest her, have her charged?

He went up the stairs. Felt the door. It was open. At that

moment he heard running footsteps. He turned. Kampen-haug and two others in full regalia. Who else but Kampen-haug. Mug painted green. Machine guns and helmets. They stopped.

'Frølich!'

Kampenhaug's voice.

Open mouth and moist sheen to the green cheek. Jesus, Kampenhaug standing at the back of the queue. No public to watch him scratching his bollocks here then?

Frank calmly smiled down at them and walked through the unlocked door. Stared across towards Nesodden. The large window in the living room was a picture postcard of Oslo fjord. The islands lay brown in the glittering water.

Kampenhaug's team took up positions in the room. One of them opened the large veranda door and showed himself to the others. Machine gun raised in the air. Helmet, not a balaclava. The scene was like a snapshot of the Olympic Games in Munich.

Frank looked around. Heavy English-style leather furniture. A natural stone fireplace that threatened to capsize the room. Bookcase with metres of red books behind the glass. Oil on unframed canvas and quite a large aquarium with some unusually well grown fringetails that pressed their flat fish mouths against the pleasingly clean glass.

The bubbles from the aquarium were the only sound in the room. The air bubbling up and the tiny taps against the glass as the fish ate something on the inside. Frølich turned to the soldiers. Impressed that they could be so quiet.

The floor creaked as he set off, crossing the room to a partly open door.

'Frølich!'

Kampenhaug again.

Frank stopped, turned and met the man's eyes. Kampenhaug with one hand on the door frame to the veranda. The other on his gun. Silent, breathing through an open mouth. Frølich smiled. What was there to say? Was the woman dangerous? Of course she was. She is desperate and she has nothing to lose. So don't bloody ask me how this is going to end!

Best not to speak. Don't burden this ape with such complicated matters. *Your arms are too hairy for you to be able to understand anything*, he thought calmly, turned and carefully nudged the door open and peeped, before opening it wide.

Engelsviken was on the floor. Naked. Quite a plump man. But the fat was around his stomach and chest. The legs were unusually thin. He was strangely well-endowed in the groin area. The man had been shot in the head and was as dead as a doornail.

She, on the other hand, was alive. Sitting in bed. No badly buttoned blouse this time. No clothes at all. As naked as the sin she had been committing with her employer. Knees hunched up against her body, right in the corner, she had no sense of anything around her; she didn't see him. The intense eyes were directed towards the door. But she was alive. Two pink nipples peered out from behind her knees.

347

Frank stood still in the doorway. Sonja must have caught them in the act.

He raised his arm and indicated to the nearest soldier standing behind him with machine gun at the ready. Frank went into the room. Stepped over the dead man and knelt in front of her squeezed up in a corner of the bed.

Her oriental face was transfixed into a grimace he was unable to read. Two brown eyes stared into the air above a weeping mouth. Looking past him, still at the bloody door; she must have been in shock.

'Where is she?' he asked.

No reaction.

'Everything's going to be all right,' he whispered and stroked her cheek. Her skin was cold. She was like a wax doll, in another world.

'Where is she?' he tried in English.

'Here!'

The moment he heard her voice he became conscious he was sitting with his back to the door. A fraction of a second passed.

He didn't have time to yell. Only time to turn his head and see her. Then to close his eyes to protect himself. An image burned on his retina. Sonja Hager's insane marble eyes. The rifle barrels swung upwards. The mouth open, above the double muzzle; the fingers that fired both barrels at once.

At that moment, or perhaps it was straight afterwards, at any rate the shots echoed and Frølich felt lots of tiny, tiny bits of something or other stinging his face.

51

He pulled the maid down with him in his fall. To the floor.
Rolled around with her. She screamed. Not surprisingly,
after all he weighed ninety kilos. But he didn't hear the
scream. It drowned in the noise of the shots. Armageddon.
He saw only her open mouth and felt the whine transplant
itself into his chest. She lay huddled up against the wall. He
covered her with his body and suddenly experienced an intense pain in his chest.

Silence at last. Perfect silence. He opened his eyes and
looked down at her. She reminded him of Katrine. He had
met Katrine in a crowd of people around a Midsummer Eve
bonfire. They had made love on a small island afterwards.
It was the black hair that did it. The hair and the bare skin
against his clothes. Jesus, his chest hurt. Bloody hell, she
was biting him. 'Let go,' he mumbled, and shook her off.
She looked up. Stopped biting. At last. Stared up at him, her
mouth open wide.

He rolled away from her and round. What a sight! The
wall opposite the door was shot to pieces. And there were
three men in the door with painted faces, staring eyes and
machine guns. The anti-terror unit. This time they had
killed a wall.

'I surrender,' he whispered. 'Without a fight. Write that down, in triplicate.'

He struggled to his knees. Looked down at the two lying side by side in death.

Turned his head slowly to the door where Kampenhaug was brusquely pushed aside by a short man with an almost bald skull. Frølich saw Gunnarstranda's face twitch with irritation, throw him a brief glance, then remove his coat, kneel down by Sonja Hager's dead body and spread the coat as well as he was able over the two.

The butt of the rifle and Engelsviken's skinny legs protruded from under the coat.

Frank cleared his throat.

No one said anything.

Desperate. The word had been furnished with content. He straightened up. Saw rather than heard Gunnarstranda cursing madly under his breath. Turned to the naked woman, took off his jacket and rubbed his chest where she had bitten him. Passed her his winter jacket.

Insane. Those round breasts of hers. Two pink nipples staring at him angrily before they were covered by the zip. The large jacket reached to the middle of her thighs. Five long, pink nails clawed at his arm.

'Shit,' hissed the little bald man from somewhere at the back.

Frølich couldn't be bothered to listen. He took the maid with him to the second room and let a second officer take care of her. Got right out of the house, down into the garden. Drew fresh air into his lungs. Leaned against a tree trunk and watched the activity going on around him. Stood like this until Gunnarstranda ambled up with his hands deep in his coat pockets. A roll-up bobbing up and down in his mouth.

They looked at each other.

Gunnarstranda put the cigarette in his pocket. 'Did it happen fast?'

Frank nodded.

'Don't suppose there was much we could have done to prevent it?'

'No.'

Gunnarstranda looked around. 'Fair bit of paperwork to do now.'

'I suppose there will be.'

Gunnarstranda stepped aside to let medical staff past. 'I reckon we'd better find ourselves an interpreter before we question the young lady who borrowed your jacket.'

Chit-chat, Frank thought. Answered: 'Yes.'

They continued together down the slope. Stopped at the gate.

'Whatever anyone says it must have been hell living with the bugger,' Gunnarstranda sighed.

Frank didn't speak.

'Just look at the façade they projected. The cars, the house, the garden . . .

'And heaps of loneliness,' Gunnarstranda added. 'He had her, but she didn't have anyone.'

They reached the car.

'That night must have been the last straw.'

'Rubbish,' Frank interrupted with heat. 'About a third of all Norwegian marriages come to an end in a perfectly orderly fashion. All she had to do was get a divorce!'

Gunnarstranda sucked in air. Frank could glimpse a hint of amusement behind his eyes. 'You mean she could have saved herself the bother?'

His tone of voice sounded sarcastic while a kind of humorous relief settled over his face. 'Sometimes you never quite get to the bottom of a case, Frølich. Never mind to the bottom of people!'

S'pose not, mused Frank, drained. But nevertheless he still had to articulate his thoughts:

'If Sonja Hager suffered such torment, why didn't she take her fury out on the obvious person closer to home?'

Gunnarstranda gazed up at the house. Opened the car door. 'She did, in the end,' he grinned, and got in.